Happy Day, Sue P.!
Relax, kick-back &
enjoy Rosemary's
Beautiful writing!!

Love,

CHRISTOPHER PARK

A NOVEL

CHRISTOPHER PARK
ROSEMARY CLEMENT

A NOVEL

DELPHINIUM BOOKS

harrison, new york   encino, california

Library of Congress Cataloging-in-Publication Data
Clement, Rosemary, 1939–
Christopher Park : a novel / by
Rosemary Clement.—1st ed.
      p.   cm.
    ISBN 1-883285-00-3: $20.00
1. Women teachers—Oklahoma—Fiction.   I. Title.
         PS3553.L394C47   1993
   813'.54—dc20   93-1486   CIP

First Edition   All rights reserved.
       10 9 8 7 6 5 4 3 2

Published by Delphinium Books, Inc.
           P.O. Box 703
        Harrison, N.Y. 10528

Distributed by Publishers Group West
Printed in the United States of America

Jacket and text design by Milton Charles
Jacket art by Lisa Falkenstern

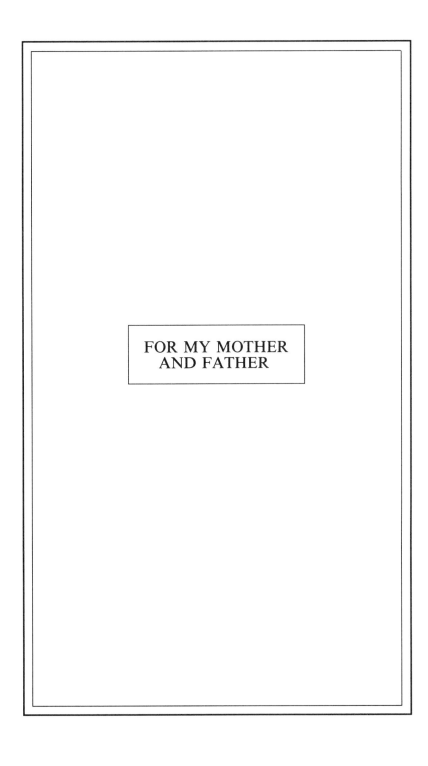

FOR MY MOTHER
AND FATHER

ACKNOWLEDGMENTS

Along the way, while I was writing this novel, my friends who read for me, my teachers—especially H.B., John Gardner, Jimmie O'Neill, and lately, Richard Marek—have been my companions and guides.

CHRISTOPHER PARK

A NOVEL

I

Uno deve sempre amare il suo fato, my people will say. Love your fate.

Mine was inside the opening folds of a letter perched like a sun-bleached gull on the desk in front of my bedroom window. After it arrived from west of the Mississippi, I'd left it open on my desk, which meant my mother had probably lifted it to dust underneath a dozen times since Halloween. I'd have heard if she took a look at the cramped handwriting that filled the page. She respected my privacy. That morning, Thanksgiving in 1960, I opened the window and watched the letter float off the desk and land on a corner of my bed where its wings quivered before it settled. "They aren't going to make this easy," I whispered before I went to help my mother with the turkey.

For dinner, we had only ourselves, my mother, father and me, and the hovering presence of my absent brother, Frank. But, by four o'clock, we collected my Uncle Patsy with his wife, Aunt Ginnie and two of my mother's sisters, Sylvia and Nancy, who left their husbands at home. We sat tight around the kitchen table with coffee, uncut pumpkin pies in the center, and my mother's concession, a wooden bowl filled with the unshelled walnuts she kept for emergency baking. She stood at the sink whipping cream with an eggbeater.

"Why don't you get yourself an electric mixer, Mary?" Aunt Nancy asked.

"I have one," my mother answered briefly, then bent her shoulders into the work.

"Use it, then," Aunt Nancy said.

Uncle Patsy watched me. He assessed things, this uncle. He measured everything: time, affection, the past. He was always looking for a balance. "I see you don't have a date tonight."

"It's Thanksgiving," I said, telling him what he already knew.

"Ah! And you aren't at your books?"

"I finished."

"So, what are they teaching you at that college that the world can't show you?"

My father looked in from the living room. "Didn't cut the pies yet, huh?" He went back to watch television.

"She's there to get her education," my mother said. Her voice throbbed with the rhythm of her work. Wings of whipped cream rose to cover the beater spokes.

My uncle winked. "I know—but why?"

"If she wants to teach, she needs a degree."

"Ah, Claire," my uncle said, "in the end you'll get married and have kids and so what? Can you cook?"

My aunts warmed to this talk. "Her mother says she can't even pick out a good tomato at the store." Aunt Ginnie.

"Or a fresh loaf of bread." Aunt Nancy.

"She can't," my mother said, offering me the beater with clouds of cream, sweet with sugar and vanilla. She passed the back of her hand across her forehead before cutting into the first pie. Her makeup had melted away after hours in this small kitchen near a hot oven. Under the ceiling light, her eyes were liquid as the sea. Shadows beneath the curve of her cheeks deepened; tendrils escaped the mass of auburn hair she swept from her face with tiny combs.

"Listen," Uncle Patsy said, "at the rate she's going, there's a good chance she'll never get married."

Aunt Sylvia: "God forbid!"

Aunt Nancy: "Don't be silly. Of course she will." She brushed hair from my forehead, had a look at my face. "Except, you *do* have funny ideas, honey, you know. Your cousin Jeannie is married and she likes it very much. Did you ask her?"

My uncle answered for me. "When does she ask anyone for an opinion? What kind of man's going to put up with that?"

"Not one like you, that's for sure," his wife answered.

He glanced at her.

He said to my mother, "You know, Mary, about the only thing I haven't heard from your daughter is advice about how to run my store."

"That's only because I'm not interested in business, Uncle Patsy."

"Just you pour us some more coffee, please," my mother told me, then called to my father who'd been watching a football game.

After we finished the pie, we all sat quiet for a moment, pleased with our own company.

Aunt Sylvia, slender, fragile, serene beneath her widow's peak, sipped her coffee and remarked, "I'm surprised you haven't fallen in love, Claire. I fell in love twice before I was eighteen."

"And both of them snakes," her sister Nancy said.

"You were always unusual in that way, Sylvia," my mother said.

"Well, you see, I understand men—it's a kind of gift. They tell me I'm easy to talk to."

"Of course they do! You believe everything they tell you!" Aunt Nancy said. All those burnished curls set atilt around the heart of her face trembled.

Aunt Sylvia smiled faintly in her triumph, then, sympathetic, asked, "Haven't you fallen in love, Claire? Even once? You're already twenty-one."

"No, not yet." Failed at twenty-one. Worry fretted my aunt's forehead.

"Good for her," my father said.

"Remember, there's only so much time for a young girl, dear, and after that . . ." Aunt Sylvia paused, "you could end up alone."

Aunt Nancy said, "A woman can live alone. It's the man who can't."

My uncle waved his hands as though clearing the room of smoke.

"Never you mind!" Aunt Nancy answered him, "A man needs a woman to take care of him."

I announced, "I am certainly not marrying a man so I can take *care* of him. My God! That's a terrible reason to marry."

"Think of a good one," Aunt Ginnie said.

"Love," Aunt Sylvia said.

"Security," Aunt Nancy said.

"Children," Uncle Patsy said.

"Leave it alone," my mother said.

"What will become of you?" Aunt Sylvia asked me.

"I'm going to work. I'm going to be a teacher."

"What? You can't do two things at once like everyone else in the world?" Uncle Patsy. "She'll never make any money, Mary."

"She doesn't care about money," my mother answered.

"Where will she go, Mary?" Aunt Nancy bypassed me.

"It's a mystery to me," she answered. "I haven't seen anything in the mail yet."

Now, I thought, now, I should say something.

But, my father spoke up after he put his plate in the sink. "What's the matter with your own town? There's a brand new high school a mile away. Don't they need English teachers?" He waited for an answer.

"Nothing's the matter with it, exactly."

"All right then, I'll find you a little car and you can be a teacher right around the corner."

"It's not that simple."

"Oh no?" my mother said.

"Uh-oh. Look at her face," Uncle Patsy said.

It was my father who took care of one thing at a time. "Why isn't it that simple?"

"Because I'm thinking about an out-of-town school."

"Not Cleveland, I hope," Aunt Nancy said. "It's dangerous in the city."

"Cleveland's not exactly out-of-town," I said.

"Are you only thinking about this? Or did you *do* something about it?" my mother asked.

"I wrote a letter."

"And?"

"I have an answer."

"I see."

She did.

"So where is this school?" her brother asked for her.

Softly. "Oklahoma."

My father heard. "Oklahoma?"

"We don't know anyone in Oklahoma," Aunt Sylvia said.

"It's a little school, a little Catholic school. It'll have to close unless a teacher comes."

"And that would be you?" my mother asked.

"What's the matter with the children right under your nose? Don't they need a teacher?" my father asked.

"Are they Indians?" Aunt Sylvia. "Will you be on one of those reservations where they drink and catch tuberculosis?"

Aunt Ginnie shivered. "Is there indoor plumbing?"

"What a thing to spring on us," my mother said.

"Wait, wait a minute," I said. "Let me get the letter the priest sent."

"What priest?" my father asked.

"The one I'll work for. Father Foley."

"My goodness! Is she going to be a nun, too?" Aunt Nancy wasn't helping me.

I hurried to get the letter, but I really needed a lawyer. They were quiet, waiting when I returned. My father read the letter slowly, carefully until my mother snatched it from him, skimmed it and passed it around.

"He doesn't say how much he'll pay," Uncle Patsy remarked.

"I'm a volunteer."

"She's a volunteer," my mother said.

"So," my uncle said, "you're like your Aunt Sylvia here—you fall for a good story, too."

Aunt Sylvia, weary with my mother's mistakes, sighed. "And Mary, why did you send her to school all these years, and buy her pretty clothes and wash and iron them and cook supper for her and let her play all summer? So she could leave you and go to work for nothing? Poor Mary. You aren't fortunate in your children."

My mother looked as though she were falling for that. "I'll only be gone a year," I told her.

A lot can happen in a year.

Look what happened to Frank after a year.

Then the talk slumped under the burden of exonerating my brother who left home to become a doctor and forgot to come back. My father went back to the living room while my mother and her family patiently opened the drawer where Frank's virtues were kept neatly folded, as fresh, as snowy as my father's handkerchieves. The day dwindled with judgments examining his indifference angle by angle, in profile, in depth, and ended, as usual, with celebrations of his mind and prophecies of his homecoming. He didn't come home, though. He was a heartache that crimped my mother's mouth, a shame that forced my father from the company in his own kitchen, and, as usual, the defendant sitting next to me in court.

After my aunts and uncle left, after the polite splash and rattle of dishes done, after my father shook out the tablecloth, but before he could sweep me up with the crumbs, I left the kitchen. It was too small for the silence that ballooned between my mother and me.

The lamp was lit in my bedroom. It glowed beside the old mahogany bed. My mother had crocheted the ivory spread, Queen Anne's lace. My father had built the oversize bookcase where I read titles from school: philosophy, linguistics, history—nothing I could use tonight. The carved wooden crucifix hanging high above the bed against a wallpaper strewn with rosebuds was from the Abruzzi, my mother told me, the cross her grandmother guarded in steerage on her way to America.

I sat at my desk, opened the notebook I wrote in some nights to make sense of what the day brought. The present cannot hold, always, what we drop into the moment. Father Foley's letter, returned as though for repair, was in front of me. After I dated the page, I listened to their hushed voices on the other side of the wall. They were sitting on the sofa talking things over.

I opened the window a crack. November chill and the excitement of darkness broke into my room and found a place to settle in me.

In the spring, I graduated from the school for girls. We escaped, finally, that college where nuns taught lessons for the unlearned, remedials for the unredeemed. We escaped to discover a still moment to wonder in: what would we *do?* My friend, Peggy, who was in love, told me she might marry at Christmas. She set a tension in me because I wanted to be like her. I wanted protection from this strange desire that coaxed me to leave home.

If I confided to Peggy that sometimes I had these glimpses in midsummer, sitting in a rough lake, my legs loose in the push of waves speeding sand over stone, braced for the undertow that sucked hollows from beneath my thighs, that I was lost in its rhythms, and then I'd hear its music, was the music until the sun, it seemed, catapulted motes of light into my very pores, she would laugh, then scold and remind me of my real life. She would point to Steve who walked into my life right after Thanksgiving. And when I remembered nights alone with him or imagined our future together, I knew there was more girl than mystic in me.

There was a surprise party for me in Uncle Patsy's basement.

Steve was another surprise.

He was my Aunt Sylvia's idea.

Aunt Sylvia believed she'd been a queen in a previous life, maybe in Egypt, and had committed some ancient wrong there. She was confident that she was put in this life to suffer and make reparation. So, she was in a corner, suffering the festivities, remembering her kingdom, maybe. I kissed her cheek. She held my eyes.

"Look," she nodded at Steve. "Look at him. He's handsome, yes?"

I nodded. He was. Perfect in as unimpeachable a way as Henry Fonda.

"He's in love with you. He told me."

"You *asked?*"

"Of course I did. I'm your *aunt.* He can take care of you."

She was right. He could. He and his father already "took care" of a large chunk of Cleveland business.

"You need that, Claire, you need someone to take care of you."

Why did she *say* that? As though it were good for anyone over ten. Take care of me! It meant I was helpless. "I don't need anyone to take care of me!" Strident, hasty, the words broke into my aunt's reverie. I hurt her, so she had to scold:

"Where did you get that dress?"

"Jeanne picked it out for me," I told her.

Jeanne's mother, Aunt Nancy, moved in. "Look how it fits her," she said. "Beautiful."

"It's too tight," Aunt Sylvia said.

"What do you know?" Aunt Nancy answered. "It fits her just right. They call that a sweater dress. Not every girl can wear a dress like that."

"Looks like she's waving a flag to me," Aunt Sylvia said.

Jeanne showed up just in time to push me away before the tears ran down Aunt Sylvia's long, Sienese face. Even though we expected her to cry when she was upset, it was hard to watch and wrong to mention.

Jeanne said, "They know a lot about making these parties, but not so much about fashion, our family. Come on."

I saw the back of my dad's fringed head over the knot of kids at the stairway. "They all look a little worried when they wish me luck," I told her.

"Well, it took you a long time to start," she said.

"Start what?"

"Your life."

We shared a stuffed artichoke.

"You're ignoring Steve," she said. "Go talk to him."

Steve. At that moment he was charming my uncles. Two weeks before, on the way home from the Cleveland Play House, Steve had stopped and parked the car. "It's true," he'd said. "So, there's no going back, no denying it. I love you, Claire. Why not tell you? Why not make plans?" he asked himself. He laughed, he kissed me. "We're young, just beginning. We have the world ahead of us. You're beautiful and I love you. I love you."

I thought about answering, but couldn't find the question.

"God, this is a wonderful night," he whispered. He breathed, touched my cheek. "We'll never forget tonight." While he held me, he described our life together beside the lake with ducks and swans, behind the private park his family owned. (Did I really have to go to Oklahoma? Ah well, he'd wait.)

At my back door, under a mason jar porch light, deep in the scent of grape hyacinth blooming in the bed beside the steps, Steve kissed and kissed and kissed me.

I turned in bed, punched my pillow. Love, I thought, does not happen like this. You have to feel something, something that drops you to your knees. Equilibrium ought to be upset.

"I don't know what to say to him," I told Jeanne.

"He's crazy about you."

"That's what he tells everyone."

"I thought you liked him."

"I did."

"He thinks you're going to *marry* him."

"I know."

"So, how did he get that idea?"

"He talks to himself."

Jeanne's baby, asleep in his bassinet beside us, woke, hummed, screwed up his mouth and slept again. She passed her hand over his body. "Anyway," she said, "they bought you suitcases, one in each size. They think you're planning a long trip, I guess."

"They gave you a vacuum cleaner and a set of dishes," I reminded her.

"Yeah, we're each prepared for our fates." She looked across the room at her husband. "But, mine is sealed," she said.

Jeanne and I were born half a year apart in the big house our parents shared. Frank had been living there surreptitiously for seven years. No one introduced us. I'd notice him at suppertime sitting at the table with Jeanne and me and thought he was the paperboy, that when he delivered the newspaper my mother would invite him in to eat. Frank didn't like intrusions, so Jeanne and I could go for days and miss him entirely. Our families didn't break up housekeeping until I was four and Aunt Nancy's new baby needed space.

The first morning I woke in the tiny new house, I saw Frank lurking in the hallway. I think he was as surprised as I was because he forgot to cuff me. Every day after that first one, I reported to my mother and father that someone had made a terrible mistake: Frank belonged with Aunt Nancy, Jeanne with me. I was patient, but nothing happened, except Frank stayed to menace me. I gave up the daily reports and tried fasting. They explained carefully that Jeanne was my cousin, not my sister, and now she lived across a four lane highway I was forbidden to cross. I added silence to the fasting. They took me to a doctor. In the end, I ate, but I didn't give up. The heart holds first things.

Jeanne and I cleared dishes. Then they presented me with the luggage. White. Uncle Patsy pressed a fifty-dollar bill into my palm and whispered, "Don't tell your mother." Aunt Nancy clucked her tongue and reminded me I'd already given my mother enough heartache, so I better write every week. Jeanne's father, blushing with drink, made a speech about freedom and education. Aunt Sylvia smiled remotely and told me to be good and not lose my heart to a charlatan. Then my father spoke into a pocket of silence: "My daughter is the first girl in this family to graduate from college."

Steve held me until nearly dawn.

A month later, settled into the coach car of the Nickle Plate, I watched the city flee through a square of glass. Behind me, out of its shadow, I left my family like a wall against invasion.

II

Three rivers meet in Christopher Park, but only one finally empties into the sea. The rivers, skinny creeks in summer, flush their beds in spring, leave behind sticky black dirt and follow the vagaries of land swell and dip to their confluence. I saw it in July from the window of the Santa Fe Texas Chief when the rivers dwindled and the treeless fields spread into squares of melted chocolate. I wanted to see gold. I looked for its flash from the train window. I expected to see it dance pale and bright in sun-soaked fields, but I arrived after the wheat harvest.

No one was awake in my car when I stepped over the feet of the man next to me and walked up the aisle to the triangle lavatory to wash and dress before dawn. I bumped my elbows and knees changing clothes, leaned on the aluminum sink and drew an eyebrow to my ear when the train swerved. In the end, I looked demure in a gray dress with a white collar and cuffs, my hair pulled back, held with a clasp. A few people snorted and shifted when the train slowed and stopped at the depot. I was swallowing dry when the man next to me opened his eyes and said, "Good luck, little lady."

Ponca City. Eighteen hundred miles from home. The one-room station baked in early sunlight. I wrestled with my suitcases long enough to be soaking wet and embarrassed because I was the only moving thing in sight. Two men were sitting on a bench in front of the station, hats slouched over their eyes, grinning while they measured my progress. Finally, one of them walked my way.

"You the missionary going over to St. Thomas?"

"The 'teacher,' I said.

"Miss DeStefano?"

"Claire."

"Uh-huh. Claire. Well, you sure dress different, you talk different, and you're movin' entirely too fast for this time of day. This oughtta be interestin'. I'm T.J. Cobb. Gonna have my girl, Paula, in your class this year."

We drove south on a perfectly straight road with sectioned fields on either side. If I'd been farsighted enough, I could have seen Christopher Park forty miles ahead. The fields stopped abruptly at the edge of town where a privet hedge had been planted to divide the last farm field from the city property. Landlocked, the town was an island, a sea of land surrounded a cluster of buildings and houses set on a dozen wayward streets running east and west of us.

Pickups were double-parked with motors running on both sides of Main Street.

"Farmers," T.J. said. "Come to town on a Saturday and don't know how the hell to park when they do."

He turned up a sidestreet, Seventh, and parked in front of a small frame cottage across the street from the church and rectory. "Here we are, Claire DeStefano. This is it, your place. We been workin' to set it to rights the last few weeks. Just some finishing touches left."

I didn't know I'd have a house of my own.

"Father's outta town, sodality conference. He's the keynote speaker. Very important," he said and winked before he hauled my trunk and suitcases inside. "He'll be back in the mornin'."

My luggage filled what space was left in an alcove off the kitchen where a single bed was set against the wall with a window facing the church and a small dresser and mirror on the opposite wall. "The bedroom," T.J said. "Just *about* room for one."

The kitchen was a card table, sink and drainboard and in a corner a stove with its oven door opened as though its tongue were out. I closed it and it fell open again. "Needs to be shimmed up front," T.J. said. "Bathroom's right here." He pointed to a door flush with the wall across from the sink. The living room was full with a sofa, chair and a dining room table shoved against one wall. "Work table," T.J. said. "I don't think you'll be entertainin' here. No room. That's it. Whatta ya think?"

"It's fine," I said. I wasn't going to tell him that this was the first place where I'd live on my own, that it could have been half its size and I'd have loved it. But I was tempted. T.J. seemed okay.

He shook his head on the way out. "Don't know, don't know," he said. "I don't think you're what Father had in mind."

After he left, I stood under the shower in the little bathroom and changed into shorts. I unpacked, hung my clothes on a row of hooks next to the dresser and put snapshots of my family in the dresser mirror. Then there was nothing to do.

I looked for signs of life. Across the street I watched a frail woman in Father's backyard strain to pin two white sheets and pillow slips on a clothesline a bit too high for her. The wind whipped her until she went inside. The wind began, it seemed, above in the treetops, but it sounded like the sea. In a constant rush, it tunneled through channels between houses and trees, scoured my scalp, made needles of my hair.

I tied a scarf around my head like an Apache warrior before I jogged to the field in the center of the square block that was St. Thomas's church, rectory, convent, school; the buildings set out like hotels at the four corners of a Monopoly board. Father's house was ringed with trees, a shady pocket of a corner. The church, built of the same red brick, stood on the opposite corner. The spire was pure white and climbed to three brass bells the sun polished and pigeons used. The church and rectory faced Main Street a few streets up.

On the other side of the field, twin buildings, convent and school, white frame, flat-roofed, like military barracks, squatted under the July sun looking at the backside of town. That yard was clean of trees and bushes. The sparse grasses, burned yellow, were as tough as cactus spine. I looked back at my little house, across the street from all this, sitting behind a few old pecan trees with trunks thick enough to hide behind.

I thought I ought to say hello, to introduce myself to the

woman who was probably Father's housekeeper. The scent of petunias engulfed me by the time I reached the back door. The massed flowers blooming against old brick were vivid as candy drops, fragile as butterflies. I could see her working at the stove when I knocked at the screen door.

"What?" she said.

"Good morning," I said.

She gave me a sidelong glance, her way of saying hello.

I introduced myself on the other side of the door. "Are you Father's housekeeper?"

"Josephine," she said.

"It's nice to meet you, Josephine. I just got here," I began, my hand on the door handle.

"Father is gone. He said, come in the morning for breakfast. Ten o'clock." She opened a drawer, selected a wooden spoon.

"All right, thank you. Want me to check on the sheets? Take them down when they're dry?"

She stopped stirring to look at me. "I take care of my sheets."

I let go of the door handle, mumbled good-bye before I backed down the steps. Guardian of the gates. She didn't waste a word.

I walked through town in the midday sun under the great shallow bowl of sky outlining the curve of earth in the distance until the heat baked in cement and pressing down from the sun sent me back to the shade of the pecan trees in my yard where I watched a pale dumpling of a man paint shut the only window in my bedroom. My mother joined me long enough to whisper, "And what kind of priest is it who asks you to travel two thousand miles and then turns up missing?"

Alone at sunset, I spread my hands against a west window so the sun's glancing beams fired red into the scallops between my fingers. I paced, smoked cigarettes. I felt strong and ready, but with empty hands. I was full with something about to break out. I wondered who I would tell. When.

I woke to see morning sun break sky from field. I dressed, waited for the decency of day, for morning to hurry to ten when I'd been told Father would, in fact, meet me.

When I knocked at the kitchen door this time, Father Foley

appeared. He filled the doorway. "Claire!" He tasted my name. "Here you are! Here you are! I got my miracle! Thought you'd be fat. You met Josephine?" I nodded. She blinked. "Come on, let me show you around."

We walked in a circle through a great arch between the kitchen and dining room into his study lined in books, across a center hall to a sort of Victorian parlor where he nodded at the door that led to Josephine's room with the kitchen on the other side. I wondered how much he weighed, three hundred, three hundred and fifty pounds? And Josephine big as a thimble. "Four bedrooms upstairs besides my suite," he was saying.

"It's enormous, Father, and beautiful."

"Folks built it and furnished it when they thought they'd find oil here. Never did."

"If it's empty except for you and Josephine, why did you fix up the house across the street for me?"

His chin dipped. "You aren't in the East anymore. Folks around here are still searching for the babies we priests and nuns bury in the basement. You live across the street and the population can relax. Let's go have breakfast."

He lifted his arm like an eagle spreading a wing. I arranged myself beneath it, and we walked into the dining room that way. It was regal; the carpets, laces, crystal reminded me of an opera house. The table was elegant, set for two. Light from chandelier prisms danced on my plate two places down from the head of the table where Father lowered himself carefully into his captain's chair. He guarded the swell of his stomach from harm at the table's edge. A white box, like a cake, sat between us.

Josephine brought us iced tea and stationed herself in the archway to watch and listen.

She nodded while Father told me he was not always a priest, no, not even a Catholic. He was born and bred Baptist like most of the folks in town, including his mother, who never understood and lived forty miles away. (These days, he and his mother corresponded almost entirely by mail.) "Total immersion," he said.

While Josephine kept herself in plain view and I longed for a cigarette, he sipped iced tea and told me his conversion to the Faith occurred mid-air over France on his first paratroop jump. A two-hundred-and-fifty-pound man hurtling to earth is a serious man. He promised God his whole life if God would only let him keep it. And, didn't he land true and upright? (Josephine nodded, yes.) Like the Word? (And kept on nodding.) Like the Promise? (Oh, yes.)

He pointed to a framed photograph on the facing wall. From a distance it seemed a parade of finger cigars topped with white ash and pearls of smoke. A shot of the seminarians' papal visit. Father Foley smiling high and wide next to Pope John in repose. "A hint of things to come," Father told me.

A sharp report from the kitchen cued him. "Couldn't make it without Josephine," he said. "There are only two things a person rightly needs in any day—a good bed to sleep in and good food to eat. Am I right?"

"Well . . ."

"Question like that doesn't require an answer, Claire."

I looked up and caught Josephine's glance. Something fled her face like a discovered rabbit. Then she went glassy and blank as the plate she carried.

Father handed me the cake box. It was filled with stacks of three-by-five cards bound with rubberbands and dense with the tracery of his hand, like the careful footwork of a hummingbird. These were his personal records of the fallen-aways, some lost as long as thirty years. "You'll be leadin' them home," he said. He spread his hand-drawn map of the farmlands surrounding the town. "No place for hiding," he said. He told me my report of the return of these souls would just naturally become a book. (Wasn't it fortunate that I was an English teacher?) And this book would be the first of its kind, a book the bishop would have to notice.

I would write that book.

I would do that after I taught school in the morning and before I taught adult classes at night. But first, I had to visit these folks on the cards. The first Catholic census.

While he went on and on, I thought, this is where I came in.

With my father, with Frank, with Steve. Am I fated to run into men who make speeches to themselves? My stomach responded to that question.

Just then, Josephine entered with a tray of basted eggs and crisped bacon. She returned with a plate of sliced melon and good strong coffee. Then she took her post in the archway to observe Father while he ate and drank. I broke a yolk with a point of toast, stared at the yellow pool crawling toward salmon melon. I didn't mean to watch as long as I did. I thought I'd better say something if I couldn't eat. These people liked gratitude.

"The eggs are perfect," I said. "I've never learned how to baste eggs."

"You could do the eggs if you practice," Josephine said. "I cook for rich people, fancy food, and you can bet if they don't like it, they say, 'Josephine, you go!' " She looked at my plate so no one made any mistake about what was going on there.

"When you do the dishes," she went on, "put the big plates up." She pointed. "The silver in this drawer. No spots, please. Father is fussy. Now, I go rest. My arthritis . . ."

Her hand rippled down her thigh to show us.

"I stand in this kitchen a long time to make breakfast," she told Father.

"I can always find another missionary for this misbegotten town," he said, "but a cook like Josephine comes once. She's a pure gift of God."

She left satisfied. I ended up with the box and the dishes.

Father leaned back, snapped forward, rubbed the nape of his neck. "Doilies!" he said. "My mother tats 'em, starches 'em, and Josephine pins 'em on every last chair in my rectory."

I lit a cigarette.

"I wouldn't do that in public. Isn't seemly for a woman."

I could have told him I had my misgivings about a man who lived a half hour from his mother and didn't visit her. Instead, I drew deep.

He stood. There was nothing left to eat or sip. He tapped the cake box. I was dismissed.

I turned on the cold water tap in my kitchen, wet down my wrists, neck, finally pushed my head under the faucet. In the airless alcove that was my bedroom, I pushed dripping hair off my face, examined myself in the mirror. The snapshots of my family smiled back.

I told them, "He wants a mute, nonsmoking missionary who'll write his book and do his dishes."

I wanted my mail.

III

I met Charlie Pepper that first week outside the post office. Charlie and I seemed to understand one another right away, and so far, we'd only discussed my teeth and catfish.

"Seen you walkin' around town, little lady," he said. "Don't know where you're from or what you're doin' here, but this ain't no kind of town to start out in. Folks mostly end up here."

Charlie didn't talk about himself, but he didn't need to tell me a couple of things. He lived alone and he drank alone.

"You've been took good care of," he said. "Know how I kin tell? Your teeth. All straight and white up front and silver fillin's in the back."

One morning, he brought an orange crate that he'd cut down to make a miniature box of lath with a hinged top, and then he'd lined it with plastic. "Catfish," he said. "For you. Fresh caught. You dust you some cornmeal on these, then you pop 'em into a greased skillet and in five minutes, you got yourself a feast. But they got to be et right off and they got to come from a free runnin' river."

It was Charlie who got me to open the cake box that had sat on my table like a threat for a week. "I'll begin the census Monday morning," I'd promised Father, remembering that when the bells for seven o'clock Mass broke into my dream. I buttoned my trench coat over my pajamas, ran across the street and got to my pew in the third row just in time for his entrance. I ducked out as soon as he left the altar before he could invite me to another one of Josephine's breakfasts or give me any more instructions. I risked a walk to the post office dressed that way because I wanted to read my mail before I started out on the streets to meet strangers. Charlie was lighting up an Old Gold on the sidewalk after I picked up my letters.

"Get you a lotta mail, don't ya?" he said.

"My mom, my friends. It's my first time away from home."

"First weeks is the hardest. Have a smoke?" He lit my cigarette right there on Main. I kept forgetting Father's rules.

"Let's go get us a cup of coffee at the grill," Charlie said, and with the delicacy of an elegant man, added, "Won't be no one there you know 'bout now."

"Won't be so much time to miss folks after school starts," he said when he brought coffee and toast to our booth. "You'll be fine, just fine."

He walked me to the turn-off at Seventh afterwards, and I thought, maybe Charlie's right, maybe I'll be fine, just fine. I dropped my coat in the doorway, actually opened the cakebox, slipped the rubberbands off the cards and dumped them in the middle of the table.

"Pick a card, any card," the magician says. With my eyes closed, I reached into the pile and picked Myra Russel who lived on Tenth Street just as Helen, the operator, rang. The bell screamed in some strange code. Helen had no sense of rhythm.

"Where are you?" Father demanded.

"I'm here. You called *me.*"

"Where've you *been?* I've been tryin' a half hour!"

"I was outside."

"I need you for a faculty meeting. Sister Camille's here. She's waiting."

"I'm not dressed, Father."

"Yes you are. I saw you at Mass."

"I need a few minutes."

"Be quick!"

His receiver was down. Helen and I took longer, then I scrambled.

At the rectory, Josephine's voice drifted from Father's study. I nearly walked in, but I heard her again: "I don't know nothing about her, Sister, and I don't think poor Father does, either. He trusts too much."

A pause until she spoke again to her friend on the other end of the line. "I can tell you this, Sister, she hangs out her clothes in the after*noon*—after mine are washed and dried and folded. *And* she hangs her underclothes on a priest's clothesline! In broad daylight! What do people think?"

The pause.

"Hah! She can't cook, but she can eat!"

Silence.

"I don't think she's doin' nothing. I only see her when I put food on the table. She's used to being served. She learned *that* somewhere."

I called her name.

There were muffled sounds from the office like someone gathering things from a dropped purse. She stood in the doorway, short legs planted, arms crossed high on her chest. Her arthritis wasn't bothering her this morning.

"Father called me," I told her.

"A long time ago."

"Is he here?"

"School meetings are at the school."

"Thank you."

"You going dressed like that?"

I'd washed my face, combed my hair. I looked down to see what offended her. My shorts. I crossed my arms high on my chest and wished for my Apache headdress. "That's right. Like this."

Who is tougher than a righteous old woman?

I tucked in my chin, stepped outside to see Father marching toward me across the field. He walked like an ungirdled matron. My father would shake his head at Father's dewlaps and chins. My mother would probably offer him something to eat: "He has to have *some*thing. He can't have children." He punched the ground so hard his heels squirted puffs of dust. I met him underneath the mimosas. He looked funny, like someone who'd swallowed wrong.

"Hi," I said.

"You're late," he answered.

"I only took a few minutes."

"Too late. Sister left. It's nearly lunchtime."

"I just finished breakfast."

"This time of day?"

"I'll go to the convent right now," I said.

"Not without me, you won't."

He looked at me. I looked at him. Nothing in a man disappoints me as much as a pursed mouth.

"There will be no faculty meeting without me," he said.

Apparently things hadn't gone so well between them. He was probably upset because nuns aren't susceptible to priests the way other women are. But, I was used to nuns. I'd met them every morning for sixteen years right after sweet dreams and oatmeal. Behind oak desks, standing at blackboards, floating up and down corridors with complexions like fresh peaches framed in snowy linen.

His exit lines came from his stoop, from that rosebud mouth. He was furious. "She's the reason you're here, don't you know? And when I need you, where are you? She lost me every last Indian youngster for good and all, whippin' on 'em. Nearly got herself brought up on charges last year with that temper. Took the pointer to the Hanford twins. Sent one boy to the hospital. Good thing the mother drinks 'cause that's about the *only* reason I could keep her from prosecutin'."

"You did what?"

He was slow returning from that jumble, but he heard me. Camille pricked him from behind, and I was in his face. He gave me a second to recant. I gave it back. He crimped his lips, hooded his eyes. He sighed the sigh of a worried man. Who wants to trouble a worried man? He said, "Most things are simple, simpler than you think. Obedience is the key."

While I was forming words, the screen door slammed.

I squinted at the convent, shimmering in the heat, to make a mirage happen. It seemed a bunchy tree, that rose as high as the low slung window, was planted next to it, everything bent in heat waves. A knob unfurled, another. Suddenly, it was a cross. A rip of wind lifted a veil, scooped skirts from the base. It was a nun. Sister Camille. The white linen framing her face was radiant with sunlight.

I lifted my hand to wave. She gave me her back before she went inside.

Charlie's box was sitting on my back step when I got home. Inside, the fillets were wrapped in newsprint and bedded in ice. They were milky pink, matched like pearls, sweet with the scent of fresh water. After I put them in the refrigerator, I felt like I was leaving a note for a friend when I set the little box back out on the step.

I looked out my front window, afterwards, unwilling yet to think things over. The rectory and convent were occupied, the residents about to enjoy the comfort of good food prepared for them. "Prepare ye the way." For them?

I locked the doors, latched the hook and eye on the bathroom door and soaked in a bubble bath, powdered dry. After I washed my hair, I rinsed it in lemon juice because my mother told me it made highlights. Then, because my mind still couldn't get around the events of the morning, I took my letters out back, sat on the step and smoked furiously while I read and my hair dried in the sun.

Well Claire,

has it become increasingly clear to you just how useless English literature is in the real world? At Empire Junior High, we need day care and a clinic to take care of pregnant fourteen-year-old mothers. Cleveland schools this deep in the city are a joke. Another little secret they kept from us in Methods and Measurements.

I continue to meet my paramour daily in the teacher's lounge which doubles as the boiler room, which gives you some idea how far I've fallen since our Scotch-and-soda days in Harvey's Backroom. Are there any men *in that burg?*

Write!
Peggy

Dear Claire,

We hope you are well and that the work there is to your liking.

You will find enclosed the ditto masters of maps of Africa and America that you requested. We trust these will prove useful for your eighth graders. Do let us know if we can be of more help.

What an exciting adventure you have embarked upon. Godspeed!

Affectionately,
Sr. Thomas Ann, O.S.U.

Claire dear,

We have cleaned and aired your room. Papa turned the mattress yesterday and I put fresh sheets on the bed this morning. Tonight, your Uncle Patsy and Aunt Ginnie are coming here for supper. We're having macaroni with spareribs in the sauce. You know how you love spareribs. I wonder what you're eating . . .

Love,
Mama

I patted Charlie's box before I went inside to look at their pictures. My mother's face reminded me I'd left her. My father looked ready, ready to begin everything. He made me feel tired.

And me, there in the mirror, I was their New World Experiment.

I knew what to do.

Inside Camille's classroom, the geopolitical map of Africa, a chunk of fresh pineapple, was pulled down until the Cape of Good Hope nearly touched the chalk tray. Before I broke it in half, her pointer lay like an arrow beneath the bright triangle of the dark continent.

IV

Myra Russel opened the door a quarter.

"Yes?"

I introduced myself. Her face changed from inquiry to doubt.

"I've come to visit," I finished.

"Are you wondering if it's convenient?" she asked. Her voice rasped like a zipper.

"Have I come at a bad time?"

"No. The time's all right. I have time."

She opened the door wide. Thick white hair pulled back and looped high in a topknot framed the oval of a face as dusky and weathered as a walnut. She wore a high lace collar clasped at the throat with a cluster of seed pearls. The rest of her dress was a mass of tiny flowers on starched cotton fortified with tucks that plumped her narrow breast like a robin's.

"I believe we ought to sit whilst we visit." She pointed to a chair covered at the head and arms with lace, like Father's. The furniture rode a quiet procession of plumed flowers woven into the faded carpet. Once seated, she waited for me to make a sound in that dim, hushed room. Beginnings are important.

"Your living room is cool," I offered.

"I keep out the midday sun," she declined.

I was startled by the sidle and roll of an old cat who brushed my leg and journeyed to her feet to nestle. The breeze from a fan riffled its topaz coat.

"My cat," Myra said.

"I'm a teacher at St. Thomas," I began.

"A teacher? My! You young women amaze me. Barely a child

and you already know something to teach."

"I work for Father Foley and—"

"Foley? Don't believe I know him. Last one I knew was Father Taylor. 'Bout fifteen years back." Remembering now. "We was friends. We both sorely needed one then. That was when my Dave died."

"I'm sorry."

"So am I."

The cat lapped itself over Myra's shoe.

"The truth is, I can't place him," Myra said.

I thought she had trouble remembering things. "Your Dave?" I reminded softly.

"Shoot no! This new priest at your church, but now that I think on it, maybe I have seen him. Portly man, isn't he? Does *he* drink, too?"

"Well no. I mean, maybe . . . I don't know."

"Father Taylor drank. Too much. Gets to a man, livin' alone. Gets to a woman, too." She stroked her cat. "Did Father Foley send you here?"

"In a way—not exactly . . ." She left me out there. "I volunteered to visit," I said.

"Did you now?" Her smile sent wrinkles racing into new networks.

I pushed on. "Father misses you at Mass on Sundays."

"Misses my envelope, does he?"

"No, not your envelope."

"What's he after then? My soul?"

"He's concerned. He wonders why you stopped coming."

"Do *you* wonder?" Myra asked, suddenly serious. She stood. "I'm going to pour us a glass of sunshine tea. Unless you want beer. Think I do."

"I'd like tea, thank you."

I'd lost my place in this conversation. She returned with the cat following. After she handed me a glass, she held out a slender hand. Myra wore a ring.

"Pretty, isn't it? Sapphires and diamonds. Eastern Star." Her voice was as tart as her tea. "How is it?" she asked.

"The tea? It's fine."

"Too bitter? Too strong?"

"Just fine."

"Is everything this easy for you?"

I didn't answer. I drank. I wanted to leave, but I knew I had to finish that whole glass of strong, bitter tea, first.

"I'm off sweets," Myra said. "And, I was off beer, too," she added, giving me a significant look. "For about as long as I've been off the church." She was thoughtful. " 'Bout the time I reclaimed myself."

I breathed the sweet scent from a bowl of cut roses on the table beside me and felt my sense of mission drift like the petal from one of the blooms. "Yes, Mrs. Russel, now I *do* wonder about you," I told her.

"You bring up serious subjects in the middle of the day—to a stranger," she commented and drank. "You stir up things that'll weigh on me the whole night."

"I didn't mean to do that."

"Then you didn't think, did you?"

I met her eyes.

"Don't do it anymore, child."

Even with her tone softened, the grating edge of her voice bit. "There are reasons to talk to a person," she said. "They ought to be your own."

"You're the first," I said.

"First what?"

"Fallen-away."

"Oh my, really? Well now, I got to admit, it fits."

"You're the first one I've met. Beginnings are important. They're like forecasts."

"Is that right? Then maybe you ought to retire," she said kindly. "And maybe I ought to put some sugar in that tea."

This time the glass was filled with sweet, cold tea that rinsed my throat.

"I had reason to quit the church," she said. "I was alone. Never had been. I married Dave when I was just sixteen. Had to do that, too. Got so neither one of us could get through a day without that we had to be next to one another. After he passed on—bad times, bad times. I told Father Taylor how it was. He figured it was hopeless, too. We drank to that. Pretty often. He told me I had to wait for eternity same as him."

"Didn't you believe him?"

"I'm a country woman. Lived on Hawk Road. Reason it was named that *is* the name, them hawks worryin' my hens. That plain. I worked in the dirt, planted gardens, cared for animals. So I could never get ahold of that 'heaven' he spoke of 'less I was drunk. And I didn't care for bein' senseless with drink the whole time I was waitin'."

"But you left Hawk Road."

"Didn't choose to. Had to. Too much for me."

"So you were a stranger in town."

"Like you."

"No, I can leave," I said. "It was different for you."

"This time you're right, young lady. What I did, I quit being a stranger. I took up the offer of the Eastern Star ladies."

"Do they have what you want?"

"What I need. Companions."

"Is what they believe a comfort to you?"

"Doesn't much matter to me what they believe. Can't think it matters to God at all. What does matter is I have friends and reasons to see them."

I had a few companions of my own after I left Myra, the whole crowd from Ohio I kept with me, and they whispered, "Just what in the world do you think you're doing?"

"I'd better try once more," I answered them, "or I might never do it again."

I knocked on the unlatched door of a cabin set on a starved lawn. I knocked again, this time on the doorpost.

"Oooooo Ooooooooo . . . you are callin', you are callin' me."

"Shall I come in?" I asked.

"Only come, only come," the voice said.

I took a few steps into the dark room. I made out the shape of a picnic table ahead just as I felt his hands clamp my ankles.

I tipped against the wall, balanced myself and saw him lying on his back on the floor.

"Let go!"

He hung on.

"Oh my angel," he crooned to himself. His eyes were shut as hard as his grip. "My angel of the sweet Lord."

"I am *not* an angel of the Lord," I said. I bent to undo his fingers, but he was serious and I was off balance.

"Let me go!"

"I must wrestle with my angel," he sang. "I have my angel in my arms."

"You do not. Let me *go!*"

"I called for you in prayer. I called and called."

"Why are you on the floor? Get up. Look at me."

"And the sweet Jesus, He sent you."

I crouched to meet him halfway. Halfway I smelled the whiskey. Close to his ear I asked, "What does your sweet Jesus want you to do?"

"I got to wrestle with my angel. Got to get free of my burden. Got to keep my angel close. And then I will be washed clean of my sin and sweet Jesus will call me home."

"Listen to me," I whispered. "You don't have to do anything. Sweet Jesus wants you right now. He loves you now. You are in His hand."

Suddenly, his eyes flew open. He was defenseless with those eyes bloodshot and open. He couldn't bear to see. He shut them and clung to me.

"If you save this sinner, if you save this sinner, sweet Jesus will banner you in gold and silver. And you will be joyful for all time."

"Who are you?" I asked.

"I am Daniel in the lion's den. And my angel is savin' me from death. I am Noah and she is keepin' me from the flood. I am Jonah and she will deliver me . . ."

His arms fell slack, his face relaxed, his mouth opened, but by habit or command, his eyes were locked shut. He passed out.

I couldn't move him to his cot, so I put a pillow underneath his head. There was nothing else to do. I could have left a note, but he wouldn't open his eyes to this world, not even to read a message from his angel. I rinsed a cloth and covered his forehead. The heat would dry it out, but maybe in his sleep he'd feel the hand of someone who kept watch.

V

The trouble with Sunday mornings was the post office was closed, but I went anyway. The restlessness had something to do with waking hours before Mass. I walked uptown past houses as still as folded moths. Main Street began at the edge of the fields with the granary tower, white with a painted red heart in its center. Then the eye dropped to the line of storefronts strung like knots on twine, built in fits and starts according to need. First, the Santa Fe depot with a siding that shunted open cars for loading grain, a bank to finance that, a market, dry goods, hardware, The Church of Christ, grill, post office, drugstore, Bijou.

The sun blaring into Annie's Christopher Grill made illuminated script of the Donald Duck orange juice cans stacked in the window. The Church of Christ's twin bells boomed, a baritone and contralto. Cottonwoods whispered at counterpoint. The street was empty except for a doberman crossing Main a block away, close enough to make me nervous. He trotted past the newspaper office which was a secret behind venetian blinds. I'd never seen them open, or movement or light behind them. But, every Thursday, I picked up a copy of *The Eagle* at Annie's. It was the editor's feature, "Weekly Dog Bites," that put me on guard when I saw a stray.

"I could have been a Billy Graham," Father'd told me, "but I love the robes, the ritual . . ."

At just ten, he entered an altar bathed in morning sun diffused, rosy and cubed, through stained glass portholes on either side. The light that sank into the white silk chasuble he wore sparked from the silver underweave. It fell in deep folds to his knees where it met the French lace of his alb.

"Bless yourselves with me," he intoned in his Sunday voice. "Let us ask our Lord Jesus Christ to bless the work of the children and their teachers this school year." He turned, a draped pillar, and said, almost conversationally, "I will go into the altar of God, to God the joy of my youth."

I watched from my assigned place, third row, aisle. Across from me, Sister Camille, who had managed to avoid me for days, read from a gold-leaved prayer book. Sister Bernard, her companion, frowned at squirming children, both nuns in the pew behind Josephine saying her rosary.

It was all very safe and familiar except for the jangle of English. I'd tell people I missed the Latin of three thousand Masses because it was elegant and fitting, that the echoes of plainchant reminded me of monks singing for centuries in stone choirs. But, the truth was I really missed the dream hour when I made up my own life. The dream would have lasted until the bells rang for Communion if English hadn't interrupted. The Epistle, first, Saint Paul's letters to strangers with strange names, Colossians, Ephesians, Thessalonians. Anyway, I'd resume the dream right after the sermon, as soon as the priest politely turned his back, mumbling to himself, to leave us alone with ancient rhythms, both stopping just short of glory until the bells chimed like birds, warning that Jesus was coming. And then, Communion. Communion was feeling as though I were the sheath of grass that rolled from my bedroom window to embrace the whole earth and love it. I knew Jesus was real because with the host melting on my tongue, I even loved Frank.

"Go, the Mass is ended," Father said. "Bless yourselves with me." He lifted his arm, palm front, fingers together, thumb extended and described a slow, precise line, forehead to thigh, shoulder to shoulder. His cross was signed on us. He held his shining arms aloft, descended the altar steps like a bride after vows and swept up the center aisle. The redheaded altar boy, dreamy, exited a little late.

I didn't leave right away. Across the aisle, Josephine was still saying her rosary. Probably all fifteen decades. Probably every Sunday. Crystal beads floated rainbows between us. I watched her lips moving so slightly, they seemed to tremble. I felt at peace in the soft light of the quiet church. It made me companion to Myra Russel, the old man who wrestled with his angel, Charlie Pepper sobering up somewhere. Even Josephine. But, when I crossed the aisle and she saw me, she jerked her hands closer to her breast. The beads clattered against the oak pew. I saw a tiny ear half covered with a lace mantilla.

Camille was nowhere in sight when I got to the Church steps, but the farmer and his wife, the Ridgeways, who'd tithed a side of beef in my name, were waiting for me. They'd brought it shrouded in plastic, white with clouded ice. The farmer and his son, Jerry, had tipped and angled it until, finally, they eased it into the freezer chest in the church basement. "Ought to feed a little thing like our missionary for the *en*tire year," the farmer'd remarked. After they left, I touched an edge of iced plastic and locked the freezer. It was safe from me.

This morning, they smiled their expectant smiles, and I called to mind good things I'd eaten at my mother's table: sirloin tips with a little wine, swiss steak with celery and carrots, short ribs and new potatoes, round steak with garlic and onions. The farmer and his wife left smiling, left me dizzy with hunger, and the side of beef, chaste in white, lying intact below us.

I brushed a zooming bee from my hair, but it wasn't a bee; it was Father, sotto voce, "The school—the faculty meeting—one half hour—*be on time.*"

I was carrying my books, wearing a skirt and early, but not early enough.

They were waiting. Sister Camille sat at her desk, a woman with a leonine head even allowing for the bulk of her headdress. Her mouth sagged into a frown on either side. I was buttoned with a mole at one corner. Salt and pepper brows were a thicket above eyes deepset in shadow. Both hands were palm downward, fingers splayed on the polished oak.

"Sister Camille," I said.

"*Marie* Camille," she answered. "Take a seat in front."

I sat in one of the children's desks, put my books underneath. Did she expect me to call her *Marie* Camille?

"You will take notes, please."

"Yes, Sister."

"How will you accomplish that without paper and pencil?"

"Here," Father said. He grabbed an unopened ream of paper from a shelf and gave me his pen while she watched.

"You will make three copies. I receive one; Father, one; and the third copy will be filed in the school office."

"The school office?"

"The room next door, Claire," Father said.

"The room with pails and mops?"

"The school office," Camille said.

Father paled under his ruddy tan. His nose was pinched. "We can be brief, I think," he said. "I've made the year's assignments. Sister, you can see your duties are considerably lighter since Claire will be assisting you."

He sounded like a master of ceremonies giving me a cue, so I looked up and smiled.

"Is she a teacher?" Camille asked.

"Of course she's a teacher," Father said. Red streaks, like fingermarks, rose on his neck. "I'm satisfied with her credentials and so is the bishop."

"I did not ask if she has a paper that *says* she's a teacher."

Father said, "I said I'm satisfied. No need to concern yourself."

"The children are my concern," she said. "The children are my work in this life. It is unsound to divide them between us."

I read and reread the date, the only mark I'd made on the sheet in front of me.

Outside, two girls walked by slowly so they could look in our windows. One of them leaned against a tree to shake something from her shoe. I'd seen them together at Mass. They seemed suspended on a shelf of land beyond my reach.

When I looked back, Camille was rocking slightly, forward, back, tick-tock, tick-tock. She lifted her thick hands, milky and blue veined, like new marble, crossed them at her breast and clasped her shoulders beneath the gimp. Her head tipped a little as if to accommodate a weight. Her lids drooped. When she spoke, her voice followed the sway of her body, and then, I heard the rhythm of plainchant.

"Next door, my fellow sister, Bernard, is preparing lunch. The new breed. She doesn't wake until a noise signals. Once, when the alarm didn't sound, Bernard slept through breakfast. Something inside the brain, as common to the spirit as the habit to the body should click, should say: Awake! Then you wake. You don't argue or decide if it is time. Because that click is the Voice of God. Inner, irresistible. Bernard is young in religion. Bernard probably sat down to decide if she would enter the convent, and it is likely that one day she will sit down again to decide if she should leave. Bernard is like this one in front of me."

My scalp pricked.

"Sister!" Father called, a warning that frightened me, not her.

"She is a sign of disrespect to me, this new one."

"Do you hear me, Sister?" he repeated. But she didn't.

" 'I went out from the house of my infancy, I forgot my father.' "

That voice did not begin in this place where the eye was scalded by a bald sun and burnt sky. She spoke from within a deep wood where icons were her companions, where fallen leaves, ancient in a forest bed, defined the geography.

Father strode to her desk. The floor trembled but she rocked on and on.

" 'And what shall I receive as a reward for this?' " I thought she was asking me. She smiled, looked refreshed. " 'And the King shall greatly desire thy beauty—' "

Father slapped the top of the desk.

She lifted her heavy head, dropped her hands to grip the arms of her chair. Her fingers looked as trapped in the slats as her wild eyes behind her face. When she focused, it was on me.

"You are to submit daily lesson plans."

"Yes, Sister."

"Specific, detailed."

I nodded.

"Write that down."

I wrote.

"I do not want misunderstandings later."

I wrote some more.

"A girl with no history believes 'new' is better."

Something warm began to rush through me.

"You are no exception."

It reached my throat.

"That, too?" I said. "Shall I write that, too, Sister?"

Father whispered, "Enough! This meeting is closed."

They left without good-byes, and might as well have crossed a churning river for the distance they put between me and them.

Charlie Pepper had warned me, "This here's a tight-assed ole town, but polite. These here boys'll smile at ya while they're drawin' a knife." Only, he'd meant strangers, not my priest and his nun. I crumpled the "minutes."

Outside, the two girls I'd seen split up. The stocky girl walked toward town, the tall, slender one toward me. Her hair was a cap of burnt-gold curls. With the light behind her, she looked as though she were bringing me the sun. But, after she walked inside, she didn't bother with amenities.

"I'm Paula. My dad brought you into town. I'll be in your class. My mother volunteered me to help clean the room."

"Hello, Paula." She nodded. "Your friend didn't want to help?"

"Can you blame her?"

I said, "I guess I owe your mother a favor."

"Why? I'm the one who's going to work."

She'd had enough talk. So had I. I came from a long line of women who scrubbed and polished their way to peace of mind.

Paula emptied and dusted the shelves while I washed the windows. Then she scrubbed the blackboards with soapy water and rinsed them until they came clear while I waxed the desks. She brushed the corners and ceiling with a broom while I wet mopped the floor. We worked like a pair of silent exorcists.

I straightened to stretch and look things over. My skirt was limp and waterspotted. Paula's cheeks were stung with color.

"Don't work so fast," I said. "Your face is red."

"It always is. I look like I'm blushing forever."

A row of books, long as a loaf of bread, were marshaled between brass bookends on Camille's desk. I reached for one. The tip of a red felt bookmark drooped from it. "Sister Marie Camille" was written in Spencerian script across the cover. I put it back.

"Finished?" Paula asked.

"Almost. Help me pin up these pictures and we'll call it a day."

"Where?"

I pointed to the blank corkboard facing us on the back wall. She hesitated. "Are you allowed?"

It was the first time she sounded thirteen.

"Sure," I said. "Why wouldn't I be?"

"She puts up stuff every year, that's why."

"Sister Camille?"

"Yeah, posters with the parts of speech and some proverbs. A new one a month until she forgets."

"This year we'll start with my pictures," I said.

"I'll pin them up," she said. "I'm about a foot taller than you. Who's this?"

"Charles Dickens and that's Ralph Waldo Emerson—"

"What a silly name . . . Waldo . . ."

"And this is John Steinbeck, and you just put up Herman Melville—"

"A Waldo *and* a Herman?"

"Herman is one of my favorites."

"I have a feeling all these guys are." She grinned.

"Chaucer, James Joyce, and that's—"

"Thank you very much, Miss DeStefano, but even *I* know who Shakespeare is."

She knew my name. I wondered what else.

"Who's she? She's the only woman."

"Put her in the center, Paula. She's a poet. Emily Dickinson."

"She's beautiful," Paula said as though she found something she lost.

The effect was wonderful. Paula had arranged a double frame

of portraits with Emily in the middle. Chaucer was in profile opposite and looked as though he might be inviting her for coffee, and she, with an enigmatic smile, might have been weighing the invitation. "It's perfect," I said and thought this was the one moment that was perfect this Sunday. "We're finished."

"Wait," she said. "Let's be sure so I don't have to come back. This place gives me the creeps when it's empty. Know what it was? A prison barracks for Nazis. They actually brought it here from out of town, and the convent, too. You'd think they'd have burned it or something."

She was tall, long-legged and graceful when she didn't notice herself. She wore a man's white shirt and cutoffs, but her face was like a cameo. She was ivory and rose, her eyes carnelian. She ran her hand through her hair and it jumped back like sprung coils. She took a last look around and stopped at Emily's portrait.

"So, what's she important for?"

"Same thing as Columbus. She discovered a new world that was always there."

"What was wrong with her old one?" That curious tone, again, the dare embedded in it.

"She didn't belong in it," I said.

"Yeah? You have her poems?"

I handed her my book. She pulled a pair of glasses from her shirt pocket and began to page through, stopped, read. When she asked if she could take the book home, I nodded, and that seemed to settle something for her.

"We didn't think she was coming back this year," she said.

"Sister?"

"Yeah, she's so old she could've died or something over the summer. Do you know about her?"

"She's famous."

"It's *in*famous, isn't it?"

What could I say. I felt tied by guy wires. "This is a small town, Paula. People gossip. And I just got here a month ago."

She let it go. "Gemma, my friend, she says this ain't no town at all. It's an accident."

"Does she?"

"She's from Texas, though. They're weird in Texas, but Gemma's okay. I told her you were taking over for Sister, but she said I was crazy. Guess she's right. She tried to get in public school 'cause Sister hates her, but her father wouldn't let her."

She stopped at the doorway with the book under her arm and asked me, "So why did *you* come?"

As recently as a month ago, I could have answered.

I went back to the little house to wait for Sunday to end. It took a long time. I answered Steve's letter: yes, he could set a date, yes, I'd be home for Christmas, yes, I missed him, and even this, yes, I loved him.

I answered my mother, Jeanne and Peggy with the same kind of pretty fiction. I didn't have language, yet, for what was really happening. I let my mother in a little. I used "difficult" when I mentioned Camille. My mother had insight.

I sat on the back porch and stared at the empty sky. My lungs were boiling in smoke. I was taking drags like my father, the first, then doubled to take in enough to feel it fire down. The phone did not ring. Click beetles crawled, and great shelled insects crashed into the door screen, but I held my ground, hidden in the backyard. The wind ebbed to a cool breeze, blackbirds cracked the silence, vespers rang, and then, sudden as a flashfire, sunset drenched treetops in coral and washed the sky in rose-gold that seeped into wood, stone. It was a moment the men at Stonehenge might have fingered bedrock and wondered.

VI

The night before the first day of school, I sat at the great table that took up most of the living room, an atlas in front of me, an open blank notebook beside it. I was tracing the Nile for the first time since I was thirteen when Helen pressed the phone alarm. I ran. I was a little too quick. She pressed a long signal that streaked into my ear. Maybe Helen could see.

I heard my mother. "Did your package come?" she asked. She'd sent long-sleeved white blouses trimmed with lace, soft wool skirts and a crimson blazer to cheer me up. She also sent brownies and twenty dollars.

"It came, Mama, thanks."

"Are you eating your supper? You should be eating now, it's suppertime."

"I'll eat as soon as I finish these lesson plans."

"You should eat at regular hours. Do you have something decent for supper?"

"Sure."

She was worried that I might be working too hard. "Young people need to have fun," she said. "And try to *look* nice. Wear some *lip*stick, for heaven's sake. Children examine their teachers and decide things about them right away. I've been reading about this."

"What have you been reading?"

"My librarian finds articles for me. I read them. Now that both my children have left home, what else do I have to do? Incidentally, I have not heard from your brother in over a month."

"That's normal for my brother."

"And there *you* are, two thousand miles away. Living in rooms I've never seen. I do not understand my children," she said. I hoped Helen was listening in on someone else.

"What you don't understand, Mama, is the climate."

"I know, I know the clothes are too warm for now, but who knows when a cold snap will strike? And just how is that nun treating you?"

"I keep out of her way."

"She'll find you when she wants to. And when she does, you hold your ground, hear me?" Her voice was as bright as the blazer. I was beginning to feel more confident. "And, another thing, you can at least eat an orange before you leave the house in the morning."

"I—"

"Don't tell me any stories. I know what I know. If you won't fix yourself a decent breakfast, you can peel an orange. Now, say hello to your father."

Hello was pretty much all I said to my dad on the phone because he was hard of hearing. He held forth in his muscled baritone about his delphiniums surprising him with September blooms, about the Browns beating the Giants in a hapless game that they lost as far as grit and precision were concerned. I imagined him in this part of the country. He could have been a whistling cowboy. I saw him riding a plains horse, which was lean and hard like him. Alone at night, before sleep, he'd watch while a scarlet bloom broke from a burned cactus and purpled in moonlight. One day, he saw this woman, my mother, whose eyes just drove into him, so he broke stride, reined in . . .

In the background, my mother was saying, "Give me back that phone." On the line, she said, "I have decided to send you the letter that your brother's wife wrote to me. I am very upset by it."

Beside her, my father said, "Why bother her with that?" I agreed.

"Never you mind," she answered. "I am very interested in hearing your opinion, Claire."

"I've already told you my opinion, Mama. She doesn't like you. Maybe she doesn't like Frank, either."

"I'd just love to know what you *do* take seriously," she said.

I was in the kitchen the morning Frank surprised us with a visit, home from medical school, and then amazed her with the news. He was going to marry a girl named Susan. He showed us a picture. I was just about to ask what a beautiful girl like her wanted with him when I saw my mother's face. It rode the wind. A cigarette drooped from carved lips for just a second before she took it with languid fingers. Her face said, what happened? What now? Frank disappeared for a while. He walked back in with milk (not one of us drank milk), oranges, coffee, sausages, eggs. Food! He brought food to my mother's kitchen. He walked like a woman, small fussy steps. He folded the grocery bag in thirds, creased and recreased the edges until it was a sheet of brown notepaper.

"In the meantime," my mother was saying, "you get a good night's sleep."

The next morning I walked from Mass to the school yard, shoulders back, chin high, heart beating. Behind me, tires whined, cinders spit, from a car that was braked too fast. It was Paula and her mother who leaned across the seat to kiss her daughter and wave to me before her wheels squirted gravel on the way out.

"Hi," Paula said. She was blushing. "My mother says to tell you, 'Good luck, Claire,' a direct quote. She sent you this, says you're gonna need it."

Her mother had sent me a magnum of wine, which I pushed back into the bag before the children trailing behind me could see it. All three of the church bells pealed, sending pigeons scattering from the belfry windows, just as I got to the door of my room.

My students sauntered in.

The altar boy, his mouth pinched up into a grin, all topped with a wedge of red hair, said, "I'm *probably* gonna be a priest, so Father is real interested in me."

"She doesn't care. You have to do homework like everyone else, Mike," Paula told him. "That's Mike," she said to me.

The short, stocky girl I'd seen with Paula hung back in the doorway, one hand on her hip, hiking up a short skirt. Gemma.

"Harry can't read," a dark girl confided. "What will Harry do?"

I looked over her head to find where the anonymous whispers started:

"How old is she?"

"I don't know, maybe forty."

"How many showed up?"

"Where's S'ter?"

"Maybe she died."

"Nah, didn't you see her in Church?"

"I slept."

"How many came back?"

"An even dozen, lost two."

"The twins."

The girl walked in from the doorway, paused at my desk. "I'm Gemma," she said before she joined Paula.

I said, "Find a seat, please."

I heard, "Find a seat, please," in falsetto.

I said, "Stand for prayer, please."

And heard, "What does she think we've been doing for the last hour?"

"Harry, too?" the dark girl asked.

"Of course."

"But Harry's not Catholic. He's here 'cause he can't read or figure."

"Harry?" I said.

He stepped forward, a pale, blue-eyed boy, with fine blond hair wet combed into a pompadour, a dimple poking his square chin.

"Yes, ma'am," he answered. "I belong to the First Church of Christ over on Main."

"Do you *want* to say a prayer with us, Harry?"

"Sure do. I know a couple of yours by heart."

We recited the Lord's Prayer out of respect for Harry, and afterwards, as I'd hoped, they sat without thinking.

I smiled. "Good morning—"

The redhead beat a tattoo on his desk.

I began anyway. "My name is Miss DeStefano. I'm your new teacher."

"Your name's not English," someone said.

Should I ask them to raise their hands, I wondered. But, we'd just met, after all. I pushed on. "I'll have you for English, history, geography, spelling and religion. And, after lunch, Sister Camille will take you for science and math."

"Harry, you're dead!"

"Don't whisper," I said, but had no name for the face, so I scrapped my opening speech, that the night before brought tears to my eyes, and faced my real work, to name and place these children. I told them they could talk quietly for a moment, and they scattered like the pigeons. I explained the difference between talking and moving, and told them the seating began with the front seats. They moved forward and I breathed. Introductions were over.

"All right," I said after I scribbled names attached to desks on a sheet of paper, "I want all of you to bring your library cards to school tomorrow. We're using the library to find the books those people on the bulletin board wrote."

"What library cards?" Mike asked the girl next to him.

"Address your questions to me," I told him. In five minutes, the altar boy had me talking like a nun.

Harry said, "I never did go to the library, ma'am."

"That's all right, Harry. The librarian is expecting you this afternoon. She'll help you sign up."

"Can she make us do that?" someone asked.

"Yes," I answered. "She can."

After Paula passed out the geography books, I said, "We'll begin with the Nile. For tomorrow, I want you to know the countries that border it."

"Homework? On the first day?"

"On paper?"

"In ink?"

"Can we use pencil?"

"May we use pencil," I said. "And don't whisper. Ask me. I'm right here and you know my name."

And from somewhere, "How should we head the paper?"

I looked over their heads and met Emily Dickinson's unflinching gaze. "No papers," I answered. "Be ready to recite the names when I call on you." How long could it take to hear twelve of them?

"Maybe you oughtta roll up that map in front, ma'am," Harry said soberly. "See? I kin see the words right here from my seat."

"Thank you, Harry."

Mike muttered something murderous to Harry and that's how things were when Camille walked in. The children stood.

She didn't acknowledge us until I'd moved aside after she labored her way to the front. In place, behind her desk, she fingered the rope of beads hanging from her leather girdle while she looked at my sloppy seating chart.

"Where did you leave your manners this summer?" she looked up to ask.

"Good morning, Sister," they chanted.

She glanced at them, took in the pictures on the bulletin board, the open windows. The children shifted from one foot to the other.

"Good morning," she said, finally. "You may be seated."

Window shades slapped. I tied one down. She lifted a hand. "Let it be," she said.

We were so quiet that the wind, sweeping through treetops and whistling into the classroom was the only sound we heard. We couldn't take our eyes off her.

"This year," she said, "I will take your tuition payments, as usual. Due this Friday. A word to the wise."

The wind ripped a cloudbank. Sunlight broke into the room, profiled the children in a still life.

"Need I remind you there will be no exceptions to prompt, full payment?" she went on.

Then slowly, as though with regret, she said, "You have met your new teacher. She represents me. When you disobey her or fail to do work, you will answer to me. To *me.*"

Paula shifted in her seat. Gemma stared out the window.

"Is all of this understood?"

"Yes, Sister," they answered as one.

"I see you have begun with geography."

She went to the map, colored in patches, gold, periwinkle, green, like a field of wildflowers. Her brow was pleated, lids drooped, but when she lifted her head to make me her audience, some pinpoint of steely light behind her eyes, probed like a finger behind mine. The children watched as though they were at a magic show. When she lifted her arm, I saw the new pointer. She raised it slowly, pushed the rubber tip against Africa, and traced the path of the Nile, a wayward line of watered blue that washed down the map.

VII

The glory days didn't last. Father began challenging me in the confessional. "And, these are my sins: I failed in charity, maybe five or six times."

"Against who?" he asked.

"Not exactly *against.*"

"Lack of charity is active apathy," he said.

"Apathy can't be active."

He waited.

"Sister Camille," I said.

"Aware of the effects of that, are you?"

"Well . . ."

"Dissension in the world."

"Mmmm."

"What?" he demanded.

I held out.

"Began with Adam and Eve, didn't it? Began with 'I' at the front of every sentence. Chaos, pain, punishment. Caused the very crucifixion of Jesus Christ!"

"I've only *avoided* her, Father."

"Would Jesus? You thinkin' that over?"

Silence.

"You thinkin'?"

"Yes, Father."

"Proof of that'd be not repeatin' it here."

"Yes, Father."

"For your penance, you seek her out. Show her some Christian love. And, a rosary."

A rosary!

"Now, make a good Act of Contrition."

". . . firmly resolve with the help of Thy grace . . ."

I learned geography and history a page ahead of the children, and they read library books in school for the first time. Except for Harry Lee and Gemma. He couldn't, she wouldn't.

Saturdays, Harry Lee came for reading lessons.

"What do you see, Harry?"

"Um . . . I dunno. Sorry, ma'am."

" 'It'."

"Oh, 'it.' "

"That's right. Short 'i' and a 't.' Remember?"

"Sure do, ma'am."

"Okay, let's put the 'f' in front of 'it.' "

"Ffa—it."

"Together, Harry Lee. Put them together."

"Fffff—it. Uh, faaaa—it."

"There's no 'ah' after the 'f.' Listen, now. Watch my mouth: fffit—fit."

"Fit!"

"Good. Now, what do you see?"

"An 's' and 'it.' "

"Can you read it for me?"

"Sssssss—saaaaa—it."

"Together, can you?"

He looks up. "No, ma'am! Not 'til you say it first."

He doesn't see. I can't make him see.

I worked out the knife-edged pain between my shoulders after those sessions.

Gemma refused everything, homework, classwork, appointments to see me after school. Paula said, "Let her be. She's got problems at home, you know." I didn't know, but I wanted to ask. Paula blanched. "No! Don't *say* anything!" What could I say? I didn't know what we were talking about.

People of all ages came to my Saturday night class on sin. It was Father's idea. "Don't forget Onan's sin," he reminded. And with his eyes fixed on me, "Don't forget to tell 'em it was disobedience in the Garden, cause of all human woe. Tell 'em that's why Moses missed the Promised Land."

Just before class one night, Kay, Paula's mother, called to invite me to play pinochle with them afterwards. "I dug up a partner for you," she said. "Our local editor."

I loved to play pinochle. My father taught me, and my father is an intrepid teacher. Once, while my mother was in the hospital, he taught me to wash the bathroom sink: "You forgot the faucets . . . the sink has a *side,* Claire . . . Take a look at the drain . . . Should there be scum in the soapdish?" We sat through Algebra I and II the same way at the kitchen table after supper, hours that ended with me in tears, Frank smirking, my mother's "Leave her alone! Maybe she can't do it."

"Sure she can," my father'd say. "She has a brain." And then, somehow I'd do something right.

"Good," he'd say. "Now, do you know *why* you did that?"

"No! It doesn't matter as long as it's right."

"Yes, it does. Think about it."

"I don't have time. I have two more problems and it's after ten."

"Think, Claire, think. Until you can explain it."

I suffered, I sweated, I ate my mother's carrot sticks while my father watched with the patience of a man prepared to wait until the Colorado broke Hoover Dam. And, somehow, I'd do it and go to bed.

But, pinochle, that was another thing because I was the elect. Papa needed me because my mother and Frank refused to be his partners. Frank said it was like volunteering to go before a firing squad. My dad and I began the way of the sink and algebra, the Socratic method:

"Why did you play that king?"

"Because I thought it was good."

"No, the ten was still out."

"How was I supposed to know?"

"You know because you memorize every trick, Claire."

There it was, the principle. So, while Frank grinned and my

mother said that would take all the fun out of the game, I did it. I locked myself inside an egg where there were only aces, tens, kings, queens and jacks, forming endless red and black patterns on the white oilcloth, registered each one and played like a machine. We won and won. My mother and her son complained. My dad and I were a study in modest victory.

With the game ahead of me, I could hardly wait to finish answering the last question about the sixth commandment from an eighty-year-old farm woman who wanted to know how she could be *sure* if she gave full consent of the will. I ran across the street and had just changed into comfortable clothes when Jerry Ridgeway, who'd been at class (and hadn't asked about the side of beef in the freezer), knocked and invited me for coffee because he needed to talk to me. I told him about the game at T.J.'s and Kay's. "That's okay, it won't take long," he said. "I'll drive you over . . . I'll teach you the bootleg turn on the way."

He told me he had a sort of problem, needed a little advice. "I just sort of discovered it last year, y'know?" he said. "Belt up, Miss DeStefano—and boy, I love it. I unzip every chance I get, every night, right now—I mean if I weren't with you, ma'am. See, I'm pretty sure it ain't no sin 'cause it's just the natural thing, but sometimes like tonight, you make it sound like it kinda could be."

He was racing up Seventh Street in his father's pickup while he talked. I was clutching the seat beneath my knees.

"I mean I *know* it's a sin if, like, the girl's *drunk* or something."

He pressed the accelerator.

"Hey," he said, "I don't *do* that. Even if she *asks* me to."

We reached the corner of Seventh and Main. He downshifted, slammed on the brakes and we skidded a wide turn. Lights appeared in windows just as the smell of burnt rubber hit my nostrils.

"That great?" he asked. "You never know, you might be able to use that someday for a quick getaway. So, whattya think?"

I thought about Sunday last when I saw him whispering something in Gemma's ear after Mass.

"What about the girls?" I asked.

"I love them."

"All of them?"

"Sure do. Every one's different, every one's pretty. Like a big bouquet of flowers."

"What about afterwards?"

He was puzzled. We cruised at forty miles an hour.

"Afterwards," I said. "What happens to the girls?"

"Afterwards? Same as me, I reckon. Go on to the next one. I don't bother none that ain't ready and willing."

Could he think Gemma was? I told him, "Girls aren't 'ready' the way boys are."

"You'd be surprised," he said.

I was. Sitting in a pickup looking at this beautiful boy with a smile like Steve's, a smile that glowed in the dark to make everything all right, I could think of nothing to say. He braked the truck in front of Paula's house, leaned across to open my door and said, "Thanks a lot. I'm real glad I got this straightened out. I feel a lot better now."

Good for you, I thought. Kay hugged me, T.J. kissed the top of my head and poured me a glass of wine. I was thinking of a way to get Paula aside and grill her about Jerry and Gemma when the doorbell rang.

"Hi, Uncle Leo," Paula said.

And then, Leo Fennery walked into the kitchen.

"Hel-*lo* there," he said to me.

He kept his eyes on me long enough to flood me with regret, regret for ignoring Sister Valeria, the most secular and beautiful nun I'd known, who tried to teach me the arts of makeup and fashion, for wearing these clothes, jeans with pale moons on each knee, a tee shirt that was pink once, for not reading all of the *Time* magazine (including "Business" and "Science") that Frank subscribed to for me so I wouldn't go native in the heartland, for shortcutting Kant and Kierkegaard, for not trying to love Dryden and Milton more, for the genetic trick that made my feet flat and my hands too big.

"Hello," I answered, a stunning reply. I couldn't have told you what he looked like just then, only that the top of my head reached the top of his shoulders, and I saw his eyes, crystal blue with olive floaters, see me.

It was one of those moments that freeze. The way lightning flashes a midnight scene just before the wind and rain slap you. We were still like that in a half circle around the table in that second just before. Then we were sitting and whatever it was I thought I ought to remember was gone.

Leo is my partner. I hold six spades with a double king and queen, but I stop bidding when Leo starts. He makes hearts trump. I have one heart, a nine. For a second, only that, I count the twelve meld we'd have if I'd taken the bid. ("No one knows your hand but you, Claire. Take it as far as you think you can. Even if it means outbidding me." My father.)

But, there's no backtracking in this kitchen, not now.

Leo says that ever since he walked from Palermo to Siena in World War II—"Wait," he says to me. "Do you remember that one?"

"Sure," I answer. I remember: Step on a crack / And you break Hitler's back.

"Anyway," he says, "Ever since then I've been looking for an Italian woman with ten thousand years of those miraculous genes racing in her blood." I feel my blood race and play a nine on his ace.

He says he loves everything Italian: Mediterranean coral, lamb with rosemary, the feel of words like *mortadella* and *Pinocchio* rolling off the tongue and clicking at the back of the throat. He's grinning at me and pulling in tricks with a single move. He slips the cards together with his little finger, caps them with his thumb and sweeps them home. I forget to trump while I watch.

Leo says he thinks Italians should be sprinkled like salt and pepper all across America to plant gardens the way my father probably does and spice up kitchens the way my mother can. When he mentions them, I play a king on Kay's trump.

Leo's looking at that and grinning again, which melts the hard planes of his face. He shakes his head, and chestnut hair, thick and fine, falls aslant over his forehead. He says, "Some reason I don't understand why you're giving the enemy my points, Claire?"

My name sounds lush.

T.J. says *he* doesn't understand why I didn't take the damned bid in the first place what with all those spades he's been watching fall out of my hand.

Kay understands. She says it's time for coffee. T.J. pours bourbon into his instead of cream and some straight for Leo.

"Tell me all about home, Claire," Leo says. "Tell me everything."

I start talking and can't seem to stop. Every time I tell them a story about my family, Leo laughs and gestures for more, but all the while I wonder if he really believes the poetic version of my people. My Uncle Patsy told me something else, about priests who sold young girls to soldiers and pocketed the money, about the mothers who closed their eyes and prayed to their saints while their husbands drank the American coffee their daughters earned. If he knows, he keeps it to himself.

When I stop to catch my breath, Kay says, "They must be wonderful. Look at you. You're positively glowing!"

"Incandescent," Leo says. "I'll see the lady home."

VIII

Father insisted that I come to Sunday dinner the next day. He said Josephine complained that I was ignoring her, and he didn't want any trouble. After I'd had two helpings of her meatloaf filled with hard-boiled eggs that appeared in the center like small suns, after I undid the first button of my jeans, cleared the table and filled the dishpan, she tapped my shoulder instead of making a quick exit to her bedroom. Neat in faded blue, arthritis making tender bulbs of her wrists and ankles, she stood in slippered feet and spoke.

"I have to think about Christmas." She was furious. Still, it was the first friendly remark she'd made since I'd overheard her talking to Camille.

"Yes?" I said.

"Already, it's the end of the month. Pretty soon it's November. A month they need to sit and soak."

I washed a glass.

"What?" she asked. "Shouldn't there be one for Thanksgiving? Or two, even? How much more work to make four instead of two?"

"Four of what, Josephine?"

She looked at me as though I were something burning on her stove. "Fruitcakes!"

I rinsed a fork, tines held upside down under the water flow as she'd instructed. "How nice," I remarked to the fork. "You're going to make fruitcakes."

"No I'm not! I can't!"

A mystery. "But why not, Josephine?"

"I need the *brandy!*" She thrust one tiny foot forward.

"Why not get some brandy?"

"Whynotgetsomebrandy? Whynotgetsomebrandy?" she muttered. "I *can't* get the brandy. I'm Father's *housekeeper.*"

"I see." I rubbed at scraps of crisped potatoes crusting the side of a glass baking dish. She yanked the cloth from my hand and plunged steel wool into my palm.

"Use that," she said.

I tried another path. "I didn't know you needed brandy."

She threw up her hands although it must have cost her some pain. "I talk about fruitcake here, what do you mean, do I *need* the brandy?" Hands on hips, "Yes, yes and yes! And good brandy. I make *good* fruitcake."

She was honing in on me like a hornet on clover, so I gave her another target. "Maybe Father will get you the brandy."

"Ah, he can't get it. He's the *priest.*"

So, I finally understood. *I* could get it. I was only the missionary.

"Then, would you like me to buy it for you, Josephine?"

Her taut little body relaxed. The tedium of silly talk done, she took a piece of paper from her apron pocket. "Two bottles. This kind I write down, and don't get any cheap kind. Then you taste whiskey, not fruit. And *you* tell Father." Exhausted, she shuffled to her room, ending the tidy circuit of her days, dining room to kitchen to bedroom.

I'd have to borrow Father's car, his long, sleek, air-conditioned Chrysler. That concerned him. And even though the liquor store was out of town, he worried someone would recognize it parked there. "They carried the last three priests out of this town raving drunk," he told me again. I had to promise to park at a distance and not make a public spectacle of myself while I was there. "You have a way of gettin' yourself noticed, Claire."

He wrote out directions and made a shopping list of his own, "in case I have to entertain some priests over the holidays, maybe even the bishop. Might show him a rough draft of that census book by then." He counted out the money, and smiled when I took it. "Listen here, go early," he said. "Take the mornin' off.

Take the *day* off. Get your hair done. You been lookin' a little ragged since school started. I'll teach those children of yours. By God, I've got a few things to tell those children."

In the morning, I bathed in bubbles. I missed Mass while I dressed in blue. I tied on a cream sash with streamers that sailed out when I walked. I brushed my hair, sprayed on jasmine, skipped stockings. I was thinking of Leo.

The wind lifted my hair, the pigeons bleated while I walked to that licorice Chrysler. I stopped, first, at the post office, parked on the diagonal in front, praying no one would shear Father's taillights. I took a look up the street at Leo's office, the gray, shingled warehouse that was *The Eagle.* The doors were closed, the blinds shut.

Fred Bullitt, the postmaster, dipped behind his counter and rose with my letters fanned like a poker hand. I took them with just time for a good morning to him and left before he could ask me any questions. I watched myself pass in front of the mirrored post outside Fred's door, and decided to read my mail in Father's car with the air conditioner on. A letter from Frank, no, from Susan with a strange, dark sentence about my mother and a check. Maybe she thought she was hiring a spy, Frank's wife. A short note from Peggy, who'd succumbed, she admitted and would marry her Lou in December and I better be there.

And a postcard in an unstamped envelope. A lithograph rendering of an old book, Indian pipes clustered at their roots, rising to open cups. The title read: *Poems* by Emily Dickinson. I turned it over:

> *Faith is a fine invention*
> *When Gentlemen can* see—
> *But,* Microscopes *are prudent*
> *In an emergency.*

And beneath Leo wrote, "Is this woman proper company for you to keep? I think we better discuss this, don't you?"

His hand had pressed into the thin pasteboard. My fingertips felt the message on the flowers as pale as moon growth climbing a scalloped border. I felt as open as the cups above.

How could he know me this way?

". . . I think we better discuss this . . ."

Out of the car. On the sidewalk seeing myself again in the mirrored post, past the pale brick of Crawford's Pharmacy, the scarlet Bijou, between the auto shop and pyramid of tires stacked at the curb.

I walk into the office of *The Eagle* on floorboards dark with packed dirt, spongy with age.

"Hel-*lo,*" Leo says and startles me. He's out of his chair. I push my hair behind my ears. Jasmine surrounds me like an aura.

"Got your hair stuck behind your ears like you mean business," Leo says. "Like pulling back the curtains."

His arm's around my waist when he escorts me to meet Billy, whose lamp casts a lemon pool of light on his littered desk, the floor around it filled with twisted, curled papers like hair in a beauty shop.

Billy smiles when he looks up and tells me he plans to do a story on me.

"Don't say no," Leo says. "Were you planning to say no?"

I have no plan. For over a month I've done nothing without a plan: lesson plans for school, my class on sin, the convert class, the subtler one to avoid Father and Camille, the programmed speech to save me and the fallen-aways on the census. But, this morning, even though I'm trying to keep an eye on the girl in the blue dress, she's just out of my reach. I have no idea what she'll do or say next.

"Come with me, Leo. I'm on a holiday."

"Where we going?"

I tell him. He ushers me to the door, but Billy says, "Where are you going, Leo? We've got to get this stuff to the printers by ten."

"I'm on the clock, Billy Boy," Leo says and picks up a camera. "On my way to a breaking story. You take care of it." And we're out of that dim sleeve of a room. Suddenly, both of us are reflected in Fred's post.

"Look at us," Leo says. "You look spectacular. That's from the Latin—*spectaculum*—means worthy of special notice. Means you catch the eye. This will be a front page picture."

He thought we should duck Father's car behind his office and take his. He drove a bottle green sedan with a body as rounded and dimpled as a girl's. It whistled.

"How old is this car?" I asked and ran my hand over the felt upholstery.

"Made it the year you were reaching puberty, I'd guess," he said.

"Too old for air conditioning," I said and rolled down my window. The wind slashed in, then swelled to lift my damp hair from my face and neck. Leo looked me over and whistled, shifted to high and we sped up the empty highway.

The liquor store, twenty odd miles out of Christopher Park, was one of a line of low slung buildings of raw, red brick strung out like the cars of a toy train. They squatted unprotected beneath the dry, relentless sun, as though all of them were together in their defiance. Not a single tree to shade the shimmering asphalt or baking brick. We passed a sandwich shop whose window was spiked with dusty snake plants. A gathering of crows swooped to feed on the crumbs at the apron in front.

I handed Leo my list inside the liquor store and let him find the bottles. Father would be taking my class about now, probably talking about purity, the presence of God in man's body, which wasn't his body at all, but a temple of the Holy Spirit, Who wasn't merely a spirit, but a dove and a tongue of fire as well, and the bird and the flame somehow guarded the temple. But, not against surprise attack.

A man, who'd been watching from a window like a projectionist's in the back wall, walked up to Leo and they began to chat. He managed to keep an eye on me while he toted up the price and Leo packed a carton with the bottles.

"Do you know everyone in town and out of town?" I asked when we were back inside his car.

"I have to know everyone. It's my business. But, I don't know much about you, kiddo. This is my best time of day. Let me scoop Billy. I'll do the story on you right now."

"But, there's no story."

"Ah, there's always a story, Claire. Cigarette?"

"I'm trying to stop."

"There's not much here to distract us after harvest, just football. A feature on the new girl in town would be just the thing." He winked and turned on the radio. "Always do it to music when you can." Country blues argued with morning sun. He lit a cigarette. "So, you're running errands for the priest."

"Father Foley."

"Do you get along with him?"

I didn't hesitate. "Sure."

"And the nun?"

"Sister Camille."

"Troubling woman. Lives an unnatural life, though, so it shouldn't be a surprise."

"Is this an interview?"

"Is that an answer?" But, he turned to me and smiled. "Nah, this isn't an interview. This is a holiday. Auspicious."

"You aren't from Christopher Park, Leo. I can hear it."

"I'm a Kansas farm boy. I lost the accent in the army."

"What brought you here?"

"Ten years ago, I was hot on the trail of a lady. The trail ended here. So did I."

The song ended, too.

"More rabbit than fox," he said in appraisal. "So, no story, huh? How about the picture?"

"I guess so."

"An affirmative! I'll shoot you at a local site. The granary. Seen it yet?"

"Not up close."

"No kidding? A ride up the grain elevator's as good as anything at Coney Island." He glanced over at me. "You're all dressed up like a teacher. Can we do it now?"

"Sure we can," I said and wondered what else I could do for Leo today.

IX

The silo thrust up from the scorched grass like a tower that cast a shadow deep as night. Leo opened his arms to it. "Huh? It's something, right? Wait 'til you see the view from the top."

I followed him on the balls of my feet because my heels sank into the pitted gravel yard. We headed for a man who sat in front of a weathered shack in a spot of shade cast by a thin old tree. Leo introduced me to Tom, who like everyone else I met, looked me over before he said hello and lifted himself from the straight-backed kitchen chair he'd set outside. His face was pale and flat, like a pen-and-ink sketch without perspective. His voice was the same, as though he were conserving his energy for something else.

The elevator car dangled from cables and pulleys like a locket. At amusement parks, they strap you into rides like that and pull up a steel pushbar that locks in front of you so you can grab it, hang on, feel your nails meet the heel of your hand. When I reached behind myself for a bar or strap, my fingers felt steel mesh so fine I could only push my fingertips through and I did that in secret because Tom and Leo, standing on either side of me, were gesturing with free hands while they talked across me.

Suddenly, a hummmmmm, and the car jerked, swayed. It rose. I closed my eyes. I felt drunk. Behind my lids, I saw red suns that seemed to plunge to the pit of my stomach. I opened my eyes and looked up to see the sky tip and jiggle on its way to meet me.

An overhead spark, a shudder, stop. Tom got off and walked out on a rusty catwalk suspended over the silo's open mouth.

"Tell her to come and see," he shouted. The wind flung his words into his face.

Leo offered his arm. I clamped his wrist.

"What? Are you all right?" he shouted.

I stood on tiptoe to talk in his ear the way you have to at a stadium when the crowd is cheering, but I was heavy, underwater. My heel sank between the elevator floorboards. I fell and grabbed the edge. I saw a sea of sparkling grain in front of me. It was amber, green, gold, washing down rim from rim, rolling and spinning into streams that met and spun slow, slower to find the center that eddied but never filled.

The wind shrieked, the car rocked, the grain spun. Tom was a clothespin on an empty line. Leo's sleeve fluttered into my eye. I blinked. My fingers were loosened, hands held my shoulders, a rush of cooler air hit me just before the thud that signaled bottom. I crawled out onto cinders that bit my knees.

A shadow fell over me, an obelisk, it seemed. Leo. He helped me up, put my hands beneath his on the top of his shoulders and walked me back to the car. We looked like a couple rehearsing the box step.

I leaned against the hot car, swimming back to myself. Leo opened my door. I sat with my legs outside, feet on the hard ground. The upholstered seat was like an arm around me. Leo felt my forehead, my pulse. He lit me a cigarette that tasted like ashes. Then he knelt and wiped my knees with his handkerchief.

"I've been watching you mornings on your way to the post office," he said. "Turn that corner at Seventh like a colonel, pivot on the ball of your foot and take it neat and square. Those khaki shorts could be military issue for all they show—except a pretty smile behind these knees." He tipped up my chin.

I breathed and felt as though I ought to hold on because I was losing something I needed.

"Vertigo," he said.

Equilibrium was upset. That, too.

"Take your time," he said. "And then, let me buy you a drink."

I took a deep breath.

"Think it over," he said.

I thought. I thought of Harvey's on Saturday nights, warm lights, Alma playing jazz piano, Scotch mists, Steve's eyes making promises, promises for later. Only, Leo was in Steve's place. Yes, I'd like a drink.

"I'm better," I told Leo.

"You don't look better."

After he shut my door, he stuck his head inside my window, winked. "We'll see. There's time. It's a few miles out of town."

Everything is, I thought.

"Do you feel up to a ride?" he asked.

"A ride sounds wonderful." Just then, I saw myself drowning in that sea of wheat. My stomach contracted, but I was calm when the car picked up speed on the straightaway.

"We'll go to Cals. I don't think your priest'll get wind of that."

"He isn't *my* priest, and his name is Foley. Get wind of what?"

"Of you showing up in a roadhouse with me in the middle of the afternoon."

"Why shouldn't I? I'm not a nun."

"No, indeed."

He put his cigarettes between us and after I lit one, remarked he was happy I'd given up smoking. He was going seventy miles an hour, making a beautiful breeze inside.

"What time should you be home?" he asked.

"I don't have hours, Leo."

"Your best guess."

"Before dark will be just fine."

Leo laughed and then I laughed. And the bottle green sedan skimmed the highway.

Cals blinked in orange neon over the blind frame door of a cement block building that rose barely higher than the tree weeds surrounding it. The shaded windows, nearly meeting the eaves, looked like postage stamps stuck on it. We turned into a cracked asphalt drive that surrounded the bar like a moat. The music from inside wasn't Alma's jazz. This was the thwang of guitars, the whine and moan of country heartache.

A couple left Cals just then, arms looped at their waists, her head settled into the crook beneath his chin, bobbing with his strides. They walked past us. I heard the man, "What the hell, we'll go to your place and what we'll do is fuck away the afternoon." The girl lifted her head to smile up at him. I watched their retreating backsides, swaying like the tops of cottonwoods in a rhythm of their own.

Leo laughed. "Don't consider a life of crime, Claire. You don't have the face for it. Come on, let me get you that drink, and we'll put some color back in those cheeks."

The sun went dark after the door slammed shut behind us. The juke box glowed in soft rose and cool blue near the door. Leo guided me without talking because the music was loud and shut out casual conversation like the blank windows the day. He said in my ear, "I'll order," and pointed to a door with a sign: CALS LADIES. Cal didn't bother with the apostrophe.

Cals ladies liked pink, mirrors trimmed in eyelet, pictures of beribboned kittens and frosty air. I lifted my skirt to have a look at my scraped knees and saw myself do it from three angles.

Leo stood at the bar in the square room thronged with people, some sitting at small tables and booths, couples dancing, their arms locked at neck and waist, the rest leaning against the bar. Leo was rubbing the neck and shoulders of a pretty waitress while she waited for pitchers of beer. He laughed at something she said while she arranged them on her tray. I wanted to see him do it again, but not because of something *she* said. He gestured to her, his hand indicating that he, too, believed that some indifferent fate arranged things in this world.

I crossed the room—too fast. The waitress noticed.

Leo said, "You look like you're escaping. Are you all right?" I nodded. "This is Louise. Louise, Claire."

Louise and I exchanged dangerous smiles.

Leo offered me his hand. If he were asking me to dance, I'd have fit perfectly in his arms. He guided me to a table against the wall; his hand at the small of my back was warm in the icy air.

There was a lull between songs. In the quiet, Leo told me he only kept bourbon here, Wild Turkey. He wondered if I'd like it.

The odds were good. I drank iced Scotch that tasted like tar and didn't mind. Drinking was something to do after and before.

Louise brought the drinks. She didn't stoop to serve, but bent from the knees and smiled the moment into Leo's eyes. I couldn't blame her.

We touched glasses, but neither of us drank. Instead, he stood. "Dance with me, Claire." He walked me to the juke box and punched in a song. When he held out his arms, I walked into them, felt them close around my waist. I put my arms around his neck like Cals other ladies. We moved so slowly while Patsy Cline sang about sweet dreams.

Leo said, "I'm sober, Claire."

"Of course you are."

He pushed me from him a little so I could see his face.

"Not necessarily," he said.

Neither of us spoke or moved for a moment. He pulled me back. I could hear his heart beat.

"Have you noticed something?" he asked. "Have you noticed anything about us? For instance, how long ago we met?"

A day.

"And I'll have you back inside that tight little house before dark."

Dark.

"Only, Claire, that isn't what we want to do at all, is it?"

I looked up into eyes brimful. I wanted to tell him secrets.

That was Monday. People will insist that the earth revolved around the sun only once that day.

X

Leo seemed to be everywhere I was after that day at the granary. He called at odd moments. Once, I heard the phone while I was hugging my pecan tree and scraped my arms running from a dead start. I forgot Helen could listen. I forgot to answer letters. I forgot to open some of them. I asked the children to write reports on Chad and the Dred Scott Decision and learned while they read aloud. I seemed to see everyone but him through a telescope.

After school for the next few weeks, instead of going out on the census, I'd run home and change and meet Leo at *The Eagle*. I was sort of hiding, I guess. Anyway, we'd drive all sorts of places. It didn't matter. One day, Billy was at the office on his day off, working on a novel. Leo threw up his hands and whispered, "Let's go shopping and get this kid a pair of cowboy boots. Maybe they'll give him ideas." At the shop, he said, "And how about a pair for you?" Mine were the color of pecans, glove soft and carved in leaves at the top.

I wore them when he took me to Ponca City to meet his friend, Joey McWilliams, who ran a dairy farm with his brothers. Big, warm, dappled cows surrounded me like walls.

Leo thought I ought to milk one.

"I think not," I said.

They grinned and pushed me into the barn. I sat on the stool, stiffened and leaned away from the cow.

"Just go sure and steady," Joey said.

I tried, but my fingers sort of stuttered.

Joey knelt beside me and covered my hands with his. "Squeeze and pull, squeeze and pull." Twin streams of milk hit the pail, and I didn't notice when he left me on my own. Before I finished, she let me rest my forehead against her side.

Afterwards, Joey's mother gave us apple pie and milk. "Oh," Leo said, "Look at this, *look* at this, deep dish apple pie."

"Do you get lonesome on the farm?" I asked Joey. We looked out his kitchen window at the lean sweep of land, the barn, the pens.

"Nope."

"What do you do?"

"Pretty much what needs to be done. Fills most of the day. Go to town sometimes, play a little ball. I even read books, ma'am."

They were grinning again.

Joey said, "The way you do it, Claire, is you have to love them." He meant his cows. "And then, you begin to think like one of them."

Leo said, "It wouldn't hurt to marry a wife."

Joey's mother said she told him the same thing every day.

We could have been in my mother's kitchen.

They walked me through goat-burr, trumpet lilies, blue sage and yellow grasses knee-high, up to a bare shank of hill called Schoolmarm's Nipple. "No offense, ma'am," Joey said. On the way back, they swung me over cattle guards—one-two-three over—and their arms held.

When Leo and I were on our way to Oklahoma City to see *La Dolce Vita* on a stolen Saturday, I said, "Stop Leo. Show me how to work the gear shift. It looks like fun."

"I don't know," he said.

"Look, the highway's empty."

"Think of it as an 'H,'" he said, taking me from first to third and reverse.

I did it a few times. "I've got that," I told him.

"You sure, now?"

"Yes, I'm sure."

He showed me the footwork for the clutch and accelerator. I pumped and released, pumped and released. "Do you know how to make a bootleg turn?" I asked.

"Just work the pedals," he said.

"Enough. I've got it."

"No . . . I think you should—"

"Leo, how hard can it be? I *know* how to drive."

"Go ahead, then."

I turned the key and the motor whistled and hummed. The car lurched and stalled. "That was second. Go to first," Leo said.

I flooded it. While we waited, Leo lit a cigarette and looked out his window. When it started again, I put it in first, and almost got us back onto the highway before it stalled and rolled backwards.

"I've had this car for, oh, almost seven years. I've built up a certain respect for it," Leo said.

"Give me a chance!" The third time, I heard a terrible grinding. Leo closed his eyes. "It's fine, fine," he murmured. "Let me ask you something. Have you ever played basketball?"

"No."

"Baseball?"

"Well . . ."

"Do you swim?"

"No."

"Uh huh," he said. "That might explain it."

"Explain what?"

"You seem to fall apart when your hands and feet have to do something at the same time." He tapped his forehead. "First, you have to believe it's possible up here."

I handed him his keys. "You sound like my brother. You drive."

Later, after the movie, I was amazed. "Those people," I said.

"A little lost," Leo answered.

But how did they get that way, I wondered.

Helen rang late on a Sunday night.

"Hel-*lo* there," he said. "What're you doin'?"

"I'm writing lesson plans." Every Monday, Camille collected and locked them inside a red notebook, like evidence.

"If you're writing, Claire, make it worthwhile, like Billy. Write a novel."

"I'm on the Ivory Coast."

"No plot."

"And after that, I begin the Civil War."

"No mystery."

"I have to be prepared, Leo."

"Come have supper with me."

"It's too late for supper."

"Then we could have a drink."

"Oh Leo, you always want to drink." Where had that come from?

"I'm always looking for salvation, kiddo."

"Who do you think's going to save you?"

"Aphrodite would do."

I heard myself say, "Be serious. I have to get back to work." I sounded as though I meant it. "I'm beginning a new section in the morning. Beginnings are important."

"And we've had ours?" A cold note.

Both of us paused.

Then Leo said, "Take the night off, Claire. Keep me company."

He was in front of the house in ten minutes.

"Have you eaten?" he asked.

"No."

"Have you ever been to Adele's?"

"I've never even heard of Adele's."

"Tonight, you're going to have a Kansas rib eye there."

He was moving me all over the map.

Adele and Leo knew one another. She seated us in the parlor of the old estate she'd made an inn in a little place called Runsons Flat. We were alone in the room with soft lights and piped in Bach. Adele waited for our order.

"I keep one of everything here, Claire, so have what you want."

I wanted a Scotch mist.

"There's a direct ratio between drinking and trouble. Noticed that in your work?" he asked me. "Of course not. How old are you?"

"Twenty-two."

He settled back in his chair. "Too young?"

"You?"

"Thirty-six."

"Too old?"

I loved to watch that smile happen. Adele brought the drinks and Leo made the toast: "To beginnings."

We touched glasses, mine a globe filled with shaved ice and amber Scotch, his a short, frosted glass with no ice.

"Whatever are you doing in my town, Claire? What did you come here to do to me?"

I found a cigarette that he lit, and our hands touched. I left my free hand on the table and he covered it with his. Adele returned with another drink for Leo and news of dinner. We were closer than I thought. I could touch his toes underneath the table. Knee to knee, palm to palm, our glasses an opal and topaz in a wash of soft light. Bach became Mozart, Mozart, Chopin. We made promises while neither of us knew we were making them.

Adele served the steaks herself. They sizzled over most of a platter; a baked potato burst into bloom. A salad, hearts of romaine and cherry tomatoes rested on iced glass. She and Leo watched me begin. The only problem with that supper was that I needed both hands to eat it.

It was nearly midnight when Leo pulled off the road a little ways from town. We got out of the car and held one another at the edge of a wheatfield. I couldn't tell where I ended and he began. He hands moved up and down my back in rhythm with his telling me he loved me. Peahens screamed to one another from a dark corner where the town emptied. The moon, a blood orange, lit the purple fields. Crickets as big as my thumbs climbed the runningboard. I told him I loved him, too, and felt myself drift like a nightshadow over the cool, flat land.

XI

In the night, I dreamed of rivers flowing to the sea. I moved in these dreams like the rivers, stopping for no one, reflecting light, peaceful in wide passage. Mornings I'd wake to watch the sun top the bell tower, blink, remember Leo. Everything I dreamed was possible. I'd lie there and watch the sun flood the belfry. I don't know. Maybe I didn't wake. Maybe that would explain what happened at Adele's.

Anyway, I took care of whatever came my way.

When I read the letter Susan wrote to my mother, a dark, tortured piece, I felt sorry for both of them. I wrote to my mother about forgiveness and love. But, Frank was another matter. The enormity of his dopiness amazed me. It was a word I learned hanging around his doorway while he painted his model planes with dope. He was as stuck to us, Mama, Papa and me, like it or not, as that tissue paper to balsa wood skeletons. And he was about as durable as one of his bombers. Tissue bombers. No flight. No bombs. I wrote him a letter and let him in on this.

When the Baptist boy, one of three in my convert class, said he didn't want to hear another word about Baptism until he examined the confessional, I unlocked the church and showed him. He was looking for the two-way drawer where money was exchanged for absolution. He was disappointed when he didn't find it, but he liked the gadget that made the little red light go on outside when a penitent knelt and tripped the switch. I didn't think we had much of a future together, but I didn't mind.

Every day, after school, I pulled cards from the cake box. I met a couple who served me sliced bananas and told me they'd joined the Radio Church of the Air, and I told them that was just fine. Then a timid woman, old, drunk, a rusty braid to her waist, named Melanie Bright. She wanted me to hold her in my arms and look at the dolls she made for her granddaughter in Louisiana. I did both and made her tea. Mr. Cortes, an old, Spanish gentleman who called a cab every Saturday to go to confession because he missed Mass three times and still didn't feel forgiven. Those three weeks were the last his wife lived with cancer. I forgave him.

And later, at the end of the day, I didn't mind washing dishes for Josephine, who was calmer now that her fruitcakes were soaking in brandy inside sealed tins. She packed leftovers for me while I worked. It was good to do something with my hands because it was at just about dusk that the excitement overtook me. I didn't mind the days because they were the beginning of the nights when I'd meet Leo. I didn't mind meeting him after dark in his office. I wanted privacy. I wanted to kiss Leo in the dark.

One morning, I woke but there was no sun. Glowering clouds encrusted the belfry. But, I didn't mind. It was Friday, and Leo and I were having a late supper at Adele's. At school, the low lying clouds framed Gemma who sat next to the windows. Anything was possible. I stopped her after class.

"I was thinking, Gemma, we could plan a Halloween dance."

"Where?"

"In the church basement."

"When?"

"The Saturday before Halloween?"

"Who'd come?"

"I don't know. That's why I thought you'd like to help me plan it."

She took a step back, shot me one of those withering looks only children can, and I felt ancient.

"Plan it? I wouldn't even *come* to it."

Not yet.

You could smell the rain by noon, so I chose a card close to home. I met a wiry man, sizzling like a pepper in hot oil. His name was Pete. After I told him who I was, he was seized with anger. His body was agitated. He stood, paced, gestured, talked and talked.

"Whose business is it? Whose? If I worship like my mama said I ought? Ain't no one's I know of, I'll tell ya. She—my mama—she upped and died and left me here."

I cleared my throat.

"I ain't finished yet!" he said. "She give me sin to begin with. Sin for a start in life, know what I'm tellin' ya?"

"Yes, I do," I said. "That's Original Sin—"

He pushed off the wall and bent his face to mine. "Ain't no such a thing! Somebody made it up, somebody felt like he had to say what the beginning was like, even the beginning of God! So, he calls this here sin *original,* and next thing, he says I done it, too. That right?"

"Only, it's not that simple," I started.

"Yes it is! And then the whole story is God made us so he could take revenge."

He let that stay a moment.

"What do you think, Missy? Did God make us to get even? Does he want a footrace with cripples?"

It was as though he'd found the screw that for centuries held sacred dogma intact, and given it a sharp twist to the left.

"Uh-oh, look at you," he said. "Don't get upset now. Remember who you answer to. That'd be Jesus, honey, and what you are, well, same as me, just another one of His sweet children. Now, ain't *that* exactly right?"

I smiled. I couldn't help it. He laughed like a man who smokes too much, "A-heh, a heh, a heh-heh-heh." It cleared his throat and relaxed his restless body. He took my hand and led me to a table in back where he served me a root beer he fished from under a cake of ice in a galvanized tub. Before I left, Pete patted my hand while he confided that he didn't like upholstery, automatic shifts, didn't like much that took a man away from first things, didn't even like to use glasses for the soda pop we drank together.

I started home in a drizzle, but on a whim stopped at the grocery store. Lily Smith, who couldn't have been thirty, but who'd already dyed her hair an unforgiving black, waited behind the counter. You had to face people to do anything in Christopher Park—make a phone call, buy liquor, pick up mail—and most of them expected an explanation. So, when I told Lily I needed Crisco, tart apples, flour, her expression asked what for? But, what she said was, "They aren't going to bury me in this town."

By the time I was back inside the little house, the sky was charcoal, lightning put bones in it. The wind came up, spun dust into little skipping piles, flung rain against my windows. It was cozy. I turned on the radio, half-listened while I began mixing my first piecrust. How hard could it be? Tonight, after supper, Leo and I were having deep dish apple pie in this kitchen, only he didn't know it yet. I hummed, sang. I understood the lyric of every love song. I began one of my phantom conversations with Leo in which I was intuitive and everything I said was full of flashing wit. When I was with him, I listened mostly, and sometimes watched his lips move but never heard a word. Well, some words, "eyes, lips, beautiful." I ran to the bathroom to see if thinking about being beautiful made me beautiful. I couldn't tell.

I was working on my second piecrust when I saw Charlie Pepper at my back door.

"Charlie! Did you fish in the rain?"

"Rain don't bother the fish none, honey."

"Come inside and dry off."

He wasn't sure.

"Got any beer?" he asked.

I only had Paula's wine.

He took a look at what I was doing at the counter. I told him I was aiming for a deep dish pie with tart apples and cinnamon and butter, but so far, I couldn't get the dough to hold. "Uh-huh," he said. "Guess I'll stay." He had beer in his truck, and he brought it in, iced in a pail.

"Let's eat together, today, Charlie," I said after he dried off.

"Okay. I'll cook up the fish."

He fried catfish and drank from a can while I cleaned up the mess I made and daydreamed out loud.

"You're in love, honey," he said over the spitting fish. "Have a beer."

I thought over what I'd just said. I hadn't mentioned Leo. I never mentioned Leo. I'd talked about school and Pete and apple pies.

"I thought it was gonna hit you broadside when it came," he said. He put the fillets on plates I handed him. "Eat your lunch."

I took a bite so he'd understand I was calm. Then, I began, "I'm not in love, Charlie. In the first place—"

"Dead giveaway," he said. "All that stuff that starts off with 'in the first place.' It's worse 'n I thought."

"You know, Charlie, I'm a missionary here." The things that we say to one another, I thought.

"Uh-huh, and I figure he'll want to get ya in bed before the mess I see comin'. I expect you'll wanna clear up the mess first."

"I can't do that. I've never done that."

"I know. Have a beer like I tole ya."

I drank some beer while Charlie did the dishes.

"See if I got it right, honey," he said. "You're standin' upright, like the polestar's pullin' you up, gravity down and your heart's hangin' on a cable rockin' east to west. You think no one but you knows 'cause you're standin' so still. You're dead center, but you ain't dead by a long shot. You could feel the color on a butterfly's wing. And sober, honey, stone cold sober."

He turned to look at me. His face was pinched. "Happened to me once."

I watched his skinny back, his knobby elbows jutting out and wondered who she was and where she was, this woman who taught Charlie to see with his fingertips.

By nine, I'd stopped wondering. I tidied up, put things in their proper places, Father, Camille, my family, Charlie, Gemma, safe inside a balloon tied to my wrist, floating out of sight.

I dressed for Leo while thunder cracked and rain rang against the glass. I heard the little whistling car, and as soon as I was inside, I was home.

I don't remember what we said on the way. I remember that I couldn't stop touching him, his shoulder, his arm, his wrist.

That his profile was sculpted in a lightning flash. That I caught my breath when his hand brushed my leg when he reached for the lighter. I remember Adele smiling us into the dining room, sipping Scotch, eating bread Leo buttered. That when we finished, his eyes found some new place in me that broke open when he asked, "Claire?"

And I answered, "Yes."

I remember walking up the stairs to one of the rooms at Adele's and a fillip of panic. My clothes felt like adhesive tape, my knees almost went. My body, the thing I brought last, was going to speak for me. I remember Leo closing the door. And my hurry to him, my head buried in his shoulder, so he would keep his arms around me and stop the panic. Maybe he knew, because it stopped and something else, something else began. And this time, it wasn't a dream of rivers.

XII

I didn't leave Adele's. I walked downstairs inside the circle of Leo's arm, sat close to him on the ride back to the little house, unlocked the door, washed my face, went to bed, but, I mean, I didn't really leave Adele's. Not then.

The next morning, I woke chilled from the howling wind that blasted through window cracks. I took the cherry blazer from the closet. It was time.

Dreamy, I watched butter melt on my toast remembering last January when deep in snow, facing another icy blow from the lake, I stood on the beach and pressed the hard black buds the old willow flung on limbs caught in crosswinds. The January thaw. Beneath, seeds like those were, even then, pushing up through mute earth. Out on the frozen lake, dark waters swirled under crusts of blind ice. Like me, melting and budding. I dreamed my family in for breakfast.

First, I kiss Aunt Sylvia. "Look at me," I say. "I fell in love. See? There's nothing wrong with me."

She touches my cheek, pleased. My mother picks up a dishrag and wipes everything within reach. Uncle Patsy shakes his head. My dad won't come into the kitchen. Jeannie holds her baby in her lap while she drinks coffee and feeds him pieces of buttered toast dipped in it.

"Tell us about him," Aunt Nancy says.

"He's handsome."

"And?"

"He loves me."

"Why wouldn't he?" my mother wants to know.

"He's brilliant," I go on.

"But tell us about him," Aunt Nancy insists.

"He makes me laugh."

"Then he'll make you cry," my mother says.

Jeannie laughs. "Does he make your knees go weak?"

I hit her.

"Okay, just had to check," she says. "Just checking."

My mother's mouth is crimped. She lights a cigarette to do something with her hands. She asks, "And what does all this mean?"

"I love him, Mama."

My father hears that. In the other room, he crosses his legs and turns the page of his newspaper.

"What do you plan to do about it?" my mother asks.

"The usual things, I guess."

She's silent, examining the live ash at the end of her cigarette.

"Mama," I tell her, "I think this is the reason you took such good care of me. Why you braided my hair every morning so it wouldn't fall into my eyes while I was learning to read and write. Why you insisted I eat my greens every night, go to bed early, wear boots when it snowed. This is what it was for."

Leo appeared at my back door. I knew he would. I saw him before he knocked. His face looked bright, almost as though it were lit from within, in the gray morning.

"Claire," he said, all the world of the night before in my name when he spoke it.

He held grocery bags in both arms. "I brought you fruit," he said.

"Fruit?"

"Girls fresh from their mother's kitchens do not, as a rule, think of buying fruit." He put the bags on the counter just before he kissed me. "They believe their mothers produce it."

He held a pyramid of pale green grapes under the faucet while the water lapped them in a waterfall. Plums swam like birds in the palms of his hands. He looked around. "I understand this kitchen," he said. "I live alone, too. You use the same plate and fork and leave them on the drainboard for the next time."

"This isn't like my mother's kitchen," I told him. "Hers is always full of people, food. There's always something to eat in the refrigerator." I looked up. "I don't know how to cook," I said.

"How did you escape?"

"It's a very small kitchen."

He wiped toast crumbs from the drainboard. "I wonder, Claire, do you know why men fall in love with women?"

I shook my head.

"Not for their domestic talents, kiddo. Can you think of anyone more ungrateful than a man who loves a beautiful woman and then complains about how she keeps house?"

"Well no, Leo. Not when you put it that way."

He took me in his arms and I felt like a plum in the palm of his hand. I watched a handful of hair fall across his forehead when he let me go to finish unpacking fruit. From the largest bag, he produced a honeydew. I had no idea where he'd found plums and melon this time of year, but it was a day when miracles were ordinary events. "Feel the weight of this," he said, offering it to me. It happened when our fingertips touched, these currents running between us. "This melon is ripe," he said.

"Then let's eat some."

The halved honeydew shone like a great pearl washed in sea water.

"This is its moment," he said while he looked at me. We smiled at one another like conspirators.

And then, he was leaving.

"Tonight?" he asked, making all the daylight hours an adventure.

"Yes, tonight."

The day ran liquid. Not much, not enough before the world intruded. Before that, all the angels on the head of a pin were dancing for me. Before that, there were miracles everywhere.

I went to the school to meet Harry Lee. He walked in pouting.

"Do I have to?" he asked. "See, Miss DeStefano, I try and try, but see? I can't."

"Yes you can, Harry Lee. We only have to find the secret lock that opens the door."

"No kidding? You think I got a secret lock?"

"I do."

"Do you think you can find it?"

"Sure I can. And the key that'll open it."

"So, what do I do while you're lookin'?"

"Trust me."

He slumped back in defeat. "I *been* doin' that! It don't go nowheres. I still can't figger and I can't read."

"You will."

"Will what?"

"Read and write. Add and subtract."

"Oh sure!"

"That's right, it's sure."

He gave up. "Okay, which one you gonna start with today?"

"It's six of one, half dozen of another. You pick."

"What?"

"Reading or math. Which one?"

"No, I mean, what's that you said? That six, half-dozen thing?"

"That? That's only an expression."

There was something going on behind his eyes. "What's it mean?"

"You tell *me,* Harry Lee. Oh, listen, I just made a little rhyme for you." But, he wasn't about to be distracted, so I repeated it for him. "Now, you say it, Harry."

He sang it like a nursery rhyme. "I can't tell what it means, though," he said.

There were egg cartons, that Bernard used to start seedlings, on the bookcase. I gave one to Harry Lee. "Count the egg pockets for me," I said.

"The holes?"

"The holes."

He looked down, poked his finger into each of the pockets, looked up, shrugged, slouched. "Twelve," he said.

"That's right, Harry. Now, tell me about one-half."

He pulled back after he returned the egg carton, crossed his arms on his chest and lifted and thrust his square chin.

"All right, Harry," I said. "Don't get worried. Don't get upset. Hasn't anyone talked to you about one-half before?"

"Sure. S'ter did."

"Tell me, tell me all about one-half."

He tilted his head. "You can cut a pie in half."

"Or a doughnut?"

"Yeah."

"Or a mountain?"

"I guess so."

"Absolutely right," I said. "Now, how many eggs in the carton?"

"None. It's empty."

"How many eggs *were* in the carton?"

He was impatient. "I tole you—twelve!"

"When you go to the store to buy eggs for your mother, what does she say? Does she say, 'Harry Lee, go buy me twelve eggs?' "

"No . . ." He slowed down to catch at the corner of the word he was chasing. He leaned forward, shoved his fist under his chin and pushed back and forth. I sat still, but barely.

He said, "A *dozen* eggs. 'Go buy me a *dozen* eggs, Harry Lee.' That's what she says."

I caught his eyes. "The expression, Harry, say it again."

This time he heard himself. "The box, the box," he said suddenly. "Give me back the box." He put the heel of his hand in the center and counted the pockets on either side, and looked up. He wiped the smooth curve of his pompadour. "Half of twelve eggs, I mean, half of a *dozen* eggs is six eggs, ma'am."

"Yes, indeed. But, where do we go from here? We have a question left to answer," I said.

"I can answer. Six of one, half a dozen of another means it's the same on both sides, like the eggs, like the pie. Even. Like a tie game. It means one thing's the exact same as the other thing."

He opened out a beautiful smile that I returned.

"That's just what it means," I said.

He bounded across the field as beautiful as any deer. I'd have to tell Leo.

I wore the blazer that night. "Now that's *red,*" Leo remarked. We drove to a Ponca City hotel that was carpeted in red with crimson tapestry on the walls.

Afterwards, when we were quiet together, Leo kissed my ear, told me it was as perfect as a shell, lifted the hair from the back of my neck and asked if I knew what a pretty place that was, and when I closed my eyes, he kissed my lids. "Beautiful," he murmured. "Well, almost."

"What about the woman, Leo? The one you came here to find?"

"Oh, you remembered that, did you? Part of the past, the deep, dead past."

"What do you mean, 'almost?' "

He smiled, kissed the inside of my arm, told me my nose missed being perfect by a fraction, but who'd notice? After all, a man could feast on my eyes for a long time, fall in, if he were invited, and overlook the nose completely if I smiled. Then he put a finger over my mouth. "But you already know that, don't you, Claire?"

I knew enough.

And then he sighed. "It's time, Claire, it's time to leave."

It leapt from my mouth. I didn't hear myself think it. "How can you leave me, Leo?"

A stop. His eyes didn't narrow. He didn't jerk away. But, I felt the rush of air from his retreat. And his answer, like the space between us, nothing. Silence is an answer, too, if you listen.

In the hallway, the red carpet is rusty under greasy lamp globes that hang over endless blind doors. An icy wedge presses in my stomach. I walk as gingerly as Camille. A false move and everything will drop. We're on different continents in the parking lot, Leo and I. Rain sputters. Inside the car, the sad smell of damp wool and faded jasmine.

Asphalt and field edge swim past in the after light of the car, pitch behind and before. I'm building a dam in the dark to hold back everything that's breaking loose. I'm working very hard. I open my door, am out of the car before there are last words I can't bear to hear.

He doesn't follow.

My mother's blazer didn't keep me warm. Nothing did. I wrapped myself in blankets, looked at myself look out the bedroom window. Like a stone. No thought followed another. Somebody else was in my head, talking at me. It was me, prattling. "I don't need a man in my life. I never want to marry. I know how it goes. He says, 'I love you. Marry me. Now, put your hands up and don't move!' " And then, fifty years of conversation that's white noise.

Broken sleep, broken dreams.

I wake sitting up. Church bells are ringing. At Mass, I approach the altar rail because everyone is watching me. "The Body of Christ," Father says while the choir sings. I open my mouth, feel the wafer melting as soon as it touches my tongue. The beginning of sacrilege. I drop my face into my hands and I tell Him, I tell Him, "How can it be a sin? I love him. I won't confess it! I'll take my chances." And the cold wedge returns. The jingle of Sunday talk and flutey laughter is like a wreath spinning round my ears.

And home. Sitting on the bed again. I was afraid to move. I couldn't move or get warm enough. And then, in spite of myself, memory percolated, burst in scattered images, the mystery of my own heart partly in each.

The boys in parked cars with condoms in their glove compartments. "No." So simple.

Much later, the New York lawyer, cool and sexy, who invites me to his bed, and for a second, a flicker of desire urges me, but I say no. His paternal smile. "Are you that celebrated myth, then? The twenty-year-old virgin?"

And Steve, after nights of Scotch, warm jazz, dancing close. "But, I love you, Claire. What's the harm?"

No. Roots of that "no" planted as deep as an oak. What would my father think? What would happen to me afterwards? Until Leo.

But, even then, all that afternoon while I sat on the bed with the shade drawn and the door locked, I was kidding myself. I was waiting, waiting for him to call. He'd call. Of course he would. He'd find a way to make us both laugh. He'd tell me to stop playing Medea, to remember that things between us weren't as dramatic as that. He'd tease, remind me my people grew up on a diet of opera and wine, which made them passionate and romantic, but, after all, Claire, he'd say, you have to give us ordinary men a second to hesitate. And pretty soon, I'd hear the Chevrolet whistling outside my door.

But, he didn't call.

And I hadn't learned to wait.

I knew his number, looked it up in the phone book the night of the pinochle game at Kay's because I wanted to see his name in print.

"Number, please," Helen said in her operator voice.

"Four-three-seven, please," I said in my teacher voice. My heart was like a wild bird beating its way out of a trap.

"One moment, please."

Three rings, five, seven. No answer. I put the receiver into its cradle very carefully, and just as carefully brushed my hair, buttoned my trench coat, opened and closed my door.

Annie's Grill served breakfast all day on Sundays. Most of the booths were empty except for the one where Leo sat with his back to me. Louise, pretty Louise Hanford, his waitress at Cals, faced him. Her face was an oval framed in a sweep of honey blond hair that tumbled in loose waves to her shoulders. Leo poured a shot of whiskey from a half-full pint bottle into her coffee, some into his own. She lifted the cup with both hands, tapered fingers, nails pink almonds. She closed her eyes while she listened to the hum of Leo's story and Patsy Cline singing about walking after midnight. Leo was drunk. It slowed him down. Lighting a cigarette took half a second too long. Louise offered her hand and he took it, laced his fingers with hers. She saw me standing in the doorway just then. Leo turned. He looked confused when he saw me, as though I were a pinochle hand that, maybe, had a chance, but needed consideration.

Outside it was cold and still, quite still. Someone came out of the Grill saying, "Patsy, she says it all, don't she?" I don't remember walking home.

The house was like a bull ring. I dumped the fruit he brought me first, slammed the refrigerator door, slammed a cupboard door so hard it bounced open, kicked it shut and the phone rang. I picked it up, held it away from my ear, and heard my mother asking why I took so long to answer. After all, it was Sunday night and where *else* would I be, but home? And she'd heard on the news there was a cold front where I was, and was I keeping warm? And so quietly, just after good-byes, "Is something *wrong,* Claire?" And then, that was over.

"Helen," I whispered. "Can you *see* me, too? Watch, then. I'm ignoring the atlas, the geography book. I've skirted the great table. I'm leaning against the one chair in the living room, staring out the window. I'm dreaming, Helen, of a man, his smile. Wondering why I let him do this to me."

The street was quiet, the air still. Across the way, Josephine switched on the porchlight at the back door of the rectory. She came outside and shook the small rug she kept in front of the sink, then placed it carefully over the porch railing to air until morning. Her work finished, she walked inside and the lights went off in the kitchen.

Across the field, Camille's bulky form was framed in the screen door of the convent. She raised her arm, held her hand to her forehead for a moment. She wondered something, too. Then she pushed shut the storm door and the convent went dark.

Three women, like rivers, none tributary to the other.

The hunter's moon spilled light on the red brick of the church, backlighted the fading maple that wore its leaves like old bronze medals.

How simple it is to watch the night.

I turned on the radio to find the strong Cleveland station that sometimes broke into the local one late Sunday nights so the music would keep me company. But, tonight, it put distance between me and home. Between me and my mother and father whose trouble I hardly felt, who were more real in their photographs than in their hurried telephone voices since I met Leo. But, it was the sound of my mother's voice tonight that reminded me I was alone with a carefully guarded secret bounded inside the walls of a house maybe sixty paces square.

Within a few miles of that radio station, Peggy was probably having drinks with Lou. Maybe they invited Steve, and Alma was playing something sad at the piano bar, and maybe Steve missed me beside him. I was only as alone as I chose to be, after all. There was not only the one voice in my life. I could call Steve, hear his clipped voice, listen to a little pretty flattery. The idea captured me like a hunch. Steve's number was in my book, the book in my hand, my hand on the receiver. I'd tell him—what? Whatever it was, it was nothing Helen would hear.

Out on the highway, the blue rivets outlining the public phone flashed in passing headlights, the phone set low for the disabled, for me. And a girl nearby, hair whipped to a sheet in the rising wind, shoulders squared like Camille's, short skirt skinning thighs above thick muscled calves, hands stuffed into pockets of a man's windbreaker, the pouch of wind trapped within it the only curve of her against low, empty fields. Gemma. Gemma at midnight.

"What are you doing here?" I ask. So could she. Hiding. Hiding from Helen, hiding from home.

She's angry. For a second she lowers her head like a ram ready to butt. Then she looks up. In dead moonlight, Slavic cheekbones flare, her eyes shifting. "Go away," she tells me.

"It's all right," I say. "Come back with me."

She watches headlights approach.

"Something's wrong, Gemma. You should be home."

"I should be *home?*" she hisses. "I just left *home.*" Home is a four letter word. I smell whiskey and chocolate. She says, "Jerry's coming for me. He won't stop if he sees you. At least I like it when Jerry does it."

At home, bourbon sweet with coca-cola in her milk glass, and her mother and father, who are not her real mother or father but people who "took her in," this mother at her kitchen table overlaid with papers, sitting on a chair twice covered in limp sheets, sitting in a room where bugs scuttle behind unemptied garbage bags and rows of soda pop are set straight as soldiers on a cherry parade, at home with this father in his den, she drinking her "nice little drink" for a while, his hand reaching her thigh, his hand pulling away her underpants, then his fat finger probing and rubbing and, somehow, even while she hears the rasp of paper, the sorting of grocery coupons a room away, she feels a wave of pleasure, feels it before she looks up to see the egg that should be his head, stares at the saliva gathered in the pouch of his lower lip, ready to drop into her moisture. So, the wave of pleasure is nausea, but she must hold it in until he falls back and his lids close after his last spasm. It's something they all seem to understand without speaking. She leaves while he sleeps, mouth open, his saliva a snail's track down the globe of his cheek, spreading dark on the pink pillow beneath him. Now, the mother is stacking typed sheets in separate piles, tomorrow's agenda for the Ladies' Guild meeting, and pretty soon she'll arrange her plastic bowls with airtight lids to start a potato salad for tomorrow's refreshments. "Sweet dreams, Gemma, sweet dreams."

Gemma trembles while she washes, changes clothes, leaves from the side door. Who notices her exit? Her run up First Street, her man's stride two miles to the highway where she calls Jerry from the phone for the disabled? And later, she'll feel another wave of pleasure, but this time look up to see Jerry whose eyes belong to a sweet face, and she'll be all right, for this time.

"Don't you ever tell!" she says.

I promise her I won't.

"Swear!" she insists.

I swear.

"You have to go now," she says. "I told you, he won't stop if he sees you."

Nothing I argue matters to her.

At home I opened the wine Kay sent with Paula. It changed the pace. It tasted good. I'd never before drunk for taste, only to seem to be in good taste. My grandfather drank to stop time in the end. He was a rogue who charmed me and insulted his son. "No, no, no," he said one Sunday morning during the ritual visit

I made with my dad. "The broom! The broom!" I was making headway with the broom in the dusty room he presided over in his wheelchair. "The hand! The hand is the tool. Everything else imitates the hand. Put down that broom?" What did he want? He nodded, yes, when I used a damp rag to collect the dust. "Stay close, Clara. Use the hand, always, when you can."

I couldn't feel the wine's pinpoint needles breaking against my tongue anymore. My fingertips were sort of numb after the next glass. I could stop time, too. It was easy to believe that sooner or later I'd put down the broom and use my hands. Easy to float Gemma and Leo, like toy boats on a pond, bobbing farther and farther from me kneeling at the edge.

XIII

The sun thinned in November. The rain drizzled pock holes into dusty furrows of winter wheat that the wind beat into dust. Grain was stored in the keep of the granary and silos. The open fields were whittled to pale, broken straw, the rimy stubble of an old man's whiskers. Withered flowers melded into rusty soil. Annie's Grill served meals to a few regulars whose pickups were strange, bright ornaments on wet asphalt.

Main Street was quiet in the afternoons after school when I followed Gemma and looked for Leo. A week after the red hotel and Leo was nowhere I was. Once, when I walked slow past the shuttered office where he was supposed to be, Billy walked out. He told me Leo was "a little under the weather these days." Gemma kept herself in a crowd until she turned down her own street where I couldn't be seen with her.

But, one day, when the clouds settled low on Main Street, she was careless. She said good-bye to Paula outside the drug store with a half mile between her and her street. I caught up with her near the granary. "Gemma!" I called. "Wait a minute."

Hearing her name called on an empty street surprised her, so when she turned, her books pulled up, an open bag of chips nested between them and her chin, her hair curling around her face in the mist, for a second she looked innocent, like any girl on her way home from school. For a second. "What do you want, spying on me every day?" she said.

I had to run a little to keep up with her. "I'm not spying. I want to help you."

"Did I ask?"

"Gemma, there are laws against this, laws that protect you."

She stopped so abruptly, I nearly bumped into her. "That's right outta some book you read, right?" She forced an ugly, hacking laugh.

"But it's true. And if you give me permission to tell Father—"

"Him? Tell *him?* He's the one who—" She shook her head in disbelief.

I didn't have time to think what that meant now. "Then we could talk to, I don't know, a social worker from somewhere, Ponca City or—"

"Wanna know how many of them I've been through?"

"The police. I'll go myself."

"The police? In *this* town? Jesus!"

Somehow, we'd reversed positions and she was in charge. "You tell me then, Gemma. What do you want me to do? What?"

She cocked her head as though this were what she'd been waiting to hear. "Okay, I will. And it's the last time. If you tell anyone, *anyone,* I'm gettin' outta this town and damn quick, too. I don't need any more trouble!"

It was her exit line, I guess, because she turned to walk into the blue fog gathered at the end of Main. But, I couldn't leave it that way. "You can't keep running away," I said to her back.

"Oh no? Who says? That's what I do. Didn't anyone tell ya? I do it pretty good, too." Her voice trailed behind her. "Want that on your conscience?" I watched the back of her legs flashing, step after deliberate step, until the fog blurred her outline and she was just a stick shadow in the gloom. Going home.

While I stood there, Charlie Pepper appeared out of the fog. "What you doin' out here in the rain, honey?" he asked. I let him take my arm and walk me to the grill. "Don't you know you're supposed to come in outta the rain?" He picked a booth and ordered coffee for us. "When a storm's brewin' and the wind's up like this," he said, "reminds me of the bad times." He began to tell me about the days the dust storms hit out east where he'd farmed stingy land. I could hear the howl of the wind scooping earth and ripping crops from it while he told it. "It was a fierce act of God. He musta been mad at the whole lot of us," he said as though the men who broke virgin sod had nothing to do with it. He sounded like children who believe nothing begins until they notice it. He sounded like me.

Suddenly, I knew what to do for Gemma.

I left Charlie and ran most of the way to Father's big, well-appointed house that could be the answer. I stopped to catch my breath for a moment near Josephine's drooping petunias on yellow stems, while I looked up at the windows on the second floor where there were four big, empty bedrooms. All I needed to do was flatter Father and then throw myself at his mercy.

When no one answered my knock, I walked past Josephine's door on tiptoe, knocked at Father's study door and opened it when he didn't answer. Three walls of books greeted me. For the first time, I climbed the stairs to the second-floor landing with six doors, all shining with fresh varnish, all closed. He opened the second door.

He couldn't read, fall asleep, do anything while his vacant stomach rumbled, he told me before I could say hello. For over a week, Josephine had followed his orders. She reminded him of his fresh resolution to diet. (Always a trouble when you told a woman a fleeting thought. Never did meet one with any imagination.) So earlier, he'd found her standing over the kitchen sink. She was locked in her own embrace watching the rain spit at the window. He'd told her that he needed a good lunch, to bring him a small sandwich, maybe two would be better, the chicken they had the night before with lettuce and mayonnaise and sliced tomato and a dish of her good potato salad would be fine, just fine. She'd served him a sliced apple with a small cut of swiss cheese on a bone china plate. And then, she'd grumbled about her arthritis. He told her to offer it up. (How many times did he need to repeat that? Arthritis was the birthright of the old. Why such surprise?) She poured fresh coffee, shoved the bottle of artificial sweetener next to his cup and sighed. He'd told her to go take herself a nap before supper. Now, he had to content himself with potato chips (his tin three quarters empty), chocolate bars and a bottle of R.C. Cola. What did I think I was doing getting soaking wet in this weather. And what did I want now?

I wondered if I would always find him in the wrong mood. But, carefully, I thought, go carefully. "I came to talk to you, Father," I told him. "I need your advice."

"Do you? I notice you aren't looking for it in Confession. Missed two Saturdays I count."

"Saturdays are so busy, Father. You know, Harry Lee's lessons and your census—"

"Now that's right, the census," he said. "Hang on." He pushed up from his overstuffed arm chair to get a slip of paper next to his phone, which sat primly on one of his mother's starched doilies. He dropped it in my lap before he settled back in his chair. "Hugo Thode," he said. "Called here a little bit ago. Tell you the truth, I didn't know he ever was Catholic. What it is, he saw your picture in the paper and says he wants a visit from you."

"Father," I interrupted. A mistake.

"See the map I drew there? He lives out a ways."

"Yes," I said. "I see it."

"Hugo Thode owns maybe a quarter section of this town outright. Go this afternoon."

"I will."

"And report here right after."

"Yes, Father."

"Now, what is it you're all worked up about?"

If I'd kept playing with my handkerchief while I played out my fantasy, if I hadn't looked up, I might have told him. I don't know. It would have been sweet relief to get rid of Henry Brodenwort's dirty secret, give it to a priest who could become Gemma's good father with the power I didn't have to keep her safe. And it was so simple. He could do it here, right here in one of the empty rooms next to us, give her sanctuary in this oversized, empty rectory.

But, I did look up, past his impassive body settled in like a Buddha draped in black, to his restless hands scrubbing the arms of his chair, and above his collar and chins, his pursed mouth twitching a little, his eyes blinking, all in readiness for a little rich gossip to pass the time between a disappointing lunch and meager supper on a rainy afternoon.

A window shade slapped up on cottonwoods reeling in the wind, and what Gemma said broke loose: "Tell him? Tell Father? He's the one who—" It was Father who placed her in that house with the Brodenworts. It was Father who called them pillars of the church, who praised Ellen for playing the organ Sundays and Henry for tithing enough to keep the school afloat. Gemma understood the politics of her life.

"What you are," Pete had said, "is just another of His sweet children." I looked up at Father's, "Well?" Him, too, and Henry Brodenwort, both God's sweet children whom I was called to love. I put the slip of paper he'd given me in my pocket. And was careful with my voice, calm, calm. "It doesn't matter, Father. I can take care of it."

"Now that you're here, let me in on it."

I waved my hand. "Not that important."

"Important enough to interrupt my day."

"I'm sorry."

"Now that you have, let me be the judge." He folded his hands.

"I don't think so."

"You don't think so?" The pink rose on his cheeks the way it had with Camille's arrogance. "It isn't your job to think." And then he went on about Eve in the Garden, holy high priests and his sacred duties as pastor. And I agreed with everything so I could get out of that room. But, he needed a sign, proof that I understood my place in that hierarchy. "Don't waste anymore of the afternoon. Get over to Hugo Thode's soon's you clean up. And don't be forgettin' I'm waitin' to hear about it."

"Yes, Father."

Hugo Thode lived on an estate with outbuildings that dotted his land like rabbits on a lark. He and I sat against walls covered in plum damask. A dark old servant, his skin shrunk against bone, served iced fruit juice with lemon slices, an island drink, Hugo said. Hugo's face, hairless and smooth as candle wax, was dateless. He might be fifty or seventy. He wore a yellow panama hat with a wide brim that drooped in the center between eyes countersunk in its shadow. His nose blossomed like a strawberry in the middle of the field. His mouth, plump and pink, pouted over his chin that began on a true line with his forehead, then sloped and narrowed to finally hook up like a finger pointing at his nose. His face was like an argument. I sank into purple silk to listen.

He held the arms of his chair like a child about to begin a roller coaster ride. While he examined me, he rubbed his pale hands. He looked excited, solicitous.

Wild things surrounded me. A scowling tribal mask in ebony, a candlestick carved in ivory, footstool of zebra, wall hanging of ocelot, cock of woven rush, a fingered hand of coral. He noticed my feet didn't quite reach the floor. He sent for the footstool. The old man stooped to set it beneath me. I ought to have helped him up.

I looked up to see Hugo staring at my legs with his searching eyes. My chair was marooned at the edge of an emerald and jet Persian carpet, Hugo's on another ten feet away. He rubbed his chin and wondered aloud how long it had been since he'd had such a nice surprise, an intelligent young lady with some time on her hands.

"I'm just back, you know," he said. "From Johannesburg, little lady. Beautiful! South Africa is the most beautiful place in the world. You trust me, it is. I've been back twice. Of course, there's trouble now. See what the trouble is, is you can't mix the white culture with the black. I wish I could report you could, little lady, but it won't work. Be a bloodbath. A real bloodbath there. Cannibalism. Still doin' that, you know. This nun, they caught her and pulled the flesh from her thighs and ate it whilst she watched, and then they killed her. Animism. Crazy. Animism. They believe everything's alive, like this chair or that glass you're holdin'. Crazy. You can't reason with crazy people. They don't understand. But, you, now you can go ahead and visit, a young, healthy girl like you, 'cause it's safe if you stay in the city."

His roller coaster climbed the first hill. I accepted the second glass of the island drink, tasted the rum this time, this time saw the Indian in the old man.

Hugo cleared his throat, took a drink and waited for the audience to settle down. "Now, myself," he said, "I'm goin' to Russia. Not Moscow. Minsk. There's this woman in Minsk, just an ordinary housewife, and doesn't she see one of the buggers out in the danged field? But there's more. She sees this creature walkin' out the ship, and this creature's a little devil, a red color, pointed ears, a tail and all, only real small, maybe four feet, which doesn't surprise me at all. I have known Bible scholars will confirm this—the forces in outer space are demonic. De—mon—ic!"

A derailed car. I lit a cigarette. The old Indian slipped me a jade ashtray. Hugo told me I had just such a pretty tan for this time of year and the biggest blue eyes he ever saw. The Indian waited for a signal. Hugo lifted his glass and I nodded toward mine.

"I travel all over the world," he told me. "Of course, I been hampered. Mother and Father needed care, don't you know? And there's all this land, investments, tenants and all. Now, Mother died two years ago, so I began my travels. Mostly it's been fine, except there's one thing I'll never forgive Mother for. Infuriates me to this day! She's sittin' out in the kitchen like she does every night, starin' out the window by the table and it's after midnight. Says to me later, she's afraid she'll miss it herself if she gets up to call me. I'm in bed, of course. So the darned thing comes flying by and doesn't she see it? Lights flashing at angles to one another, hovering there in the sky so she could see the shape of the danged thing shootin' light out into the night and then the thing just vanishes. Just slips into the night and disappears. But, that's how they do. And I never saw it. But, I checked it out, you got to be careful 'cause people will call you crazy if you aren't. Looked it up, and there it was in the *Enquirer,* spotted in Australia and Ireland on the same night. Do you get that paper? Tells you the bottom truth on just about everything."

I thought if Hugo's hat were the lid to his head, and I opened it, I'd see a handful of crystal marbles, shooters, his mother locked in one, the devil in another, God, women, money, all secret from one another, all rolling around and bumping into one another behind that waxy forehead.

I slipped through town in the Chrysler, delivered Hugo's check to Father at his table next to a smiling Josephine who'd just put a platter of steaks on the table. He laughed aloud, wondered aloud how it happened, decided this generous gift was the result of his laying the groundwork over the years, of showing Hugo Thode the respect the rest of the church declined to show him. And allowed, as he put the check in his safe, that for once I got it right because I must have shown him that same respect that we, as Christians, owed one another in the name of Jesus. What I showed Hugo were young brown legs, the shape of small breasts beneath starched cotton and big blue eyes that didn't waver, maybe because they were dazed with rum.

My letters from home were on the atlas open to the map of the world, the continents like dolphins poised to dive into seas of banked blue silk. I picked Mama's. It was full of news about Frank and Susan shadowed with anxious phrases that should have reeled me in: "I need your help, Claire. Your father wants to go there and have it out with them. What should I *do?*" But, I didn't care, didn't care what they did, didn't care about that mysterious enclave my mother and her son formed.

I found a rag and filled the pail. In a little while, the floors were shining, the rooms dusted. The tiny house was perfectly clean except for the ghosts. Leo peeked in, smiled, opened the door a crack and disappeared. Charlie had tried to warn me, I should have listened.

He does call, of course, very late, his voice is foggy with bourbon. "Hel-*lo* there. What're you doin'?"

"Where are you, Leo?" I sit on the floor where I'm safe.

"Hangin' on, kiddo."

I can see us at the red hotel the last time we were together.

"Are you all right?" he's asking.

"No, I'm not all right."

A rumble deep in his throat. "Good. If you were, I'd come right over and beat you up."

That night, at the red hotel, I woke in the dark. Undressed, in bed with a man. I mean, that's how it came to me in the dark. His arm was across my shoulders. I watched him sleep, and suddenly needed him to prove he wasn't a stranger. I moved, he woke.

I began to talk before he could kiss me.

"It's dark. Should we have a little light?" he'd said. He reached for the lamp.

"Never mind," I'd answered because I remembered I was undressed. And talking, talking. "Sometimes, Leo, I don't know what I'm doing in this town, except in school. I didn't plan to come here. I wanted to go to Doctor Dooley in Laos, but he only needed doctors and nurses, so I'm here instead, with, you know, Father and Camille."

"You can't tell," he'd said. "There may be a pair like them in Southeast Asia."

"The thing is, Leo, I have to go back home. And my family—"

"Claire," he'd said, and took me to himself, "do I have to hear the part about how your mother, with no money at all, bought you the dance dress you saw in the window, and how your father didn't finish school and learned how to read blueprints by firelight? Because if that's it, Claire, let it rest for now."

"I don't feel guilty," I'd said.

"That's good." He held my face in his hands.

"Leo?"

"Claire, think," he'd said. "Think before you ask. Is this question important? Do you need an answer now?"

"Leo," I say to his voice on the phone. "Why don't you just come over?"

"Ah well . . ." He retreats behind that bank of fog crowding his voice while I feel his mouth describing me.

Ah well?

"Leo!"

"It's too small for me, kiddo."

"What is?"

"You can't walk into that kitchen with me, don't you know? When you walk into that kitchen there should be garlands of flowers, salted bread, good wine, music."

"Now, wait—"

"What are they going to say about an aging drunk? Think about it."

"What do I care what they say?"

"Oh, you care, you care."

And then, he says, "One thing, kiddo, for me. Don't pretend it didn't happen."

A delicate surgery. A dead connection. I'm here in a polished room, he's somewhere rocking himself out of time with a bottle of Wild Turkey.

Outside, the night was cold and clear. I saw stars through the fretwork of pecan branches. The anger seeped away and I couldn't call it back, so I was alone with a tree trunk for support, thinking about strange old Hugo who thought he was king in a paradise he created on borrowed time, and Father, who thought he was inspired enough by Holy Orders to read the souls of men like Henry Brodenwort. And Leo. I didn't want to hide in a corner and throw a blanket over my head because he'd betrayed me. Leo hadn't betrayed me. It was worse. He told me the truth.

XIV

Without knowing it, I learned a new art. I became accomplished in seeming normal, timing the laugh, the nod, the "I see," in conversation, dressing and talking like the person they remembered, doing my duty daily, daily committing sacrilege at Communion. Myopic and heavy, standing on a dot of time, staring mindlessly at birds and trees because they couldn't harm me until something reminded me that they were doing their work while I stared, idle. So, even then, shame coiled in my stomach, my ears buzzed with static that made it hard to hear the simplest things, thought traveled to random fields, dangerous territory, to return with some small, wild creature killed in the hunt.

And silence from notable places. Leo retreated, finally, into shadow so deep there were moments when I believed I dreamed he happened.

I didn't notice the fever at first because it seemed normal until my bones ached, it hurt to brush my hair, and one morning, my stomach couldn't hold even water. I called Father to tell him I couldn't teach.

Josephine found me on the bathroom floor holding the toilet. She touched my forehead, ran water over a washcloth that she put in my hand and ran out. I was in bed when Camille came. She hardly spoke, just questions about how long I felt this way, did I have aspirin, had I eaten? Then quiet orders to lie on the sofa while she changed the bed, sit on the toilet top while she washed my face, found a clean nightgown and the bathrobe I'd never unpacked inside my trunk, bundled the dirty sheets and clothes, pulled the blankets up around me, asked where I kept the key, looked at me for a long time and left.

I drifted in and out of fever dreams. Someone was in the house. Camille with ginger ale and aspirin and an ice bag for my forehead. I heard cupboard doors open and close, running water, footsteps.

"Now the house is nice and clean," she said. "I've taken your notebook so I will know what to teach your classes. Do not worry."

I watched the world through window glass. My children climbing the steps before Mass, wild dogs prowling before noon, Harry Lee and his girlfriend holding hands after school, blackbirds swarming to call vespers before the bells rang.

One morning, I woke and stayed awake a long time. Camille came at lunch time with rice pudding and apple juice. I let her feed me with a spoon.

A little later, Gemma crossed the field toward town, made a U-turn and walked back toward my house. I sat up, too fast, stars in my eyes, swung my legs over the side of the bed, looked again to see her walking away from me, going to school. I took a walk around the little house without leaning on walls or furniture. Everything was in place. Clean clothes ironed or folded on top of the washer. Orange juice, ginger ale, cheese, bread in the refrigerator.

I fell asleep and woke to Camille watching me.

"I saw Gemma today," I told her. "She was coming to see me."

"No visitors," she said. "Not yet. Now, you will have a warm bath. I will stay nearby."

It was foamy with bubbles, warm, good. For a little while I couldn't feel my bones. And after, she gave me toast and ginger ale and I didn't feel sick.

The phone rang. She answered and talked a while.

I felt quiet and hopeful in a clean gown and fresh bed she must have remade while I was in the bath. I didn't care who was on the phone. She came in with a cluster of brick red chrysanthemums

in an ivory jug. Paula and Kay sent them. She took my tempera-
ture, straightened the blankets. I loved the way she walked
through the rooms, as though she were in church, silently,
thoughtfully, and while she watched me, I felt safe.

"Your mother called," she said. "She wanted to know how
you are. I told her you are getting better." She read the thermom-
eter. "Down to only a little over a hundred. Another week,
perhaps. And soon, you'll be able to eat more and heal faster."
I nodded.

She picked up her shawl, but put it down, pulled in a chair
from the kitchen and sat in the cramped space between my bed
and the wall.

"Do you miss your mother?" she asked.

"Yes, Sister."

"Of course. You come from a strong family. I watch things. I
see how you are with people."

Her hand is on my forehead as though to push back the pain
along with the hair that falls over my eyes. "We'll have some
tea," she says.

She brings it in on a tray I've never seen, pours milk into cups
from her convent, bends her heavy head to watch the amber and
white swirl, props my pillows and presses my hands around the
warm mug.

"Is she pleased?"

"Who, Sister?"

"Is your mother pleased that you have come here to do this
work?"

"No, I don't think so." I tried the tea, tasted cinnamon and
maybe, whiskey. "This is good. Thank you."

"But, she should be proud of you," she said suddenly.

"I only meant she didn't want me to leave."

"I see." She swallowed some tea carefully, slowly. "She holds
on to the things of this world too much. It will make her unhappy
in the end. 'This life is a mortal race. No one walks without
anxiety amid serpents and scorpions.' "

Saint Jerome's skull joined us.

"My own mother," she said, "made of me, her eldest daughter, a gift to God. It was the custom, but even if it weren't, she told me, 'for you it is an especially good thing. Next year, instead of high school, you will go to the sisters . . .' "

She would have been only thirteen, like Gemma. I tried to imagine her that young. Her cheekbones were low and muddied, so that even at thirteen when flesh is firm and forms itself to the line of bone beneath it, her face would have been lumpy, and worse, too large for her child's body. Even after baby fat melted, it would have revealed this frame of wide shoulders, a bulging rib cage, stocky legs. Was that what her mother meant, "especially for you?"

She said, "At first I was frightened. My mother saw. 'Do not be afraid,' she said. 'The nuns will guide you. It is a good life, a useful, peaceful life. It is decided.' I said, 'Yes, Mother,' and it was done."

"Forever?" I whispered, but she didn't hear me.

"When I was eighteen, I walked down a long aisle dressed like a bride. I saw my father weeping, I saw my mother's hands crossed over her heart. I said my vows to the priest with the beautiful face." She lingered. She was watching it happen. She murmured, " 'I went out from the home of my infancy. I forgot my father. I am reborn in Christ.' "

She looked up, out my window, her eyes like lamps searching for something, her face a portrait of ineffable suffering.

"Do not look for Gemma," she said. "Gemma is lost to us. She seems young and whole, but she is not. Give her up."

"Gemma is a child, a girl—?"

"She is old and wise in matters you can't know. You must let her go."

"Oh no, Sister. She can't help herself. We have to."

"She lives as we all do—by choice."

I was tired, too tired to fight, but I needed her to understand Gemma, to help me. I looked into her stony face and gave up. I didn't want to cry, but I couldn't help it.

She shook her head. "I am your mother, too," she said and

held my shoulders. "Shed your tears. Let them fall drop by drop forever on this world, but they will never touch the dry wick that is at its heart."

She pulled some letters from a deep pocket, covered herself with the shawl. She walked as though her feet were stones, her veil flipped like mimosa leaves in the wind. I lay very still on crisp sheets in a nightgown trimmed in eyelet for a long time, long enough for twilight to thicken to dark. I turned on my lamp to look at the letters. My mother's hand, Peggy's, Steve's. I opened his.

> *Claire!*
>
> *Where are my phone calls? My letters? I'm the one who hates to write, not you. You're supposed to keep up your end of this conversation, babe.*
>
> *I have news. We'll be at the Club three days after Christmas. Our party, I mean. We'll have pine, poinsettias and champagne. Is that good? My mother says she'll serve whatever you like, but she's done these parties for years, so I told her to go ahead—you'd love it if she took care of everything.*
>
> *Just a few more weeks and I'll have you in my arms . . .*

I put it down and closed my eyes. Facts. Steve dealt in facts. Dates, invitations, rings, promises made in public. I could see them, my family, at his country club, walking on plush carpets, murmuring, the men, about the "little things" they called "food." Stuffed mushrooms that should have been sliced and fried in olive oil with garlic and basil. Red bell peppers used as a garnish instead of diced in a sauce of tomatoes and black pepper. Uncle Patsy would look things over and whisper, "This is a fancy place." Aunt Nancy, after a glass of champagne, would remark, "My, don't these people drink a lot?" But she would be pleased; she thrived on romance at its start. She'd flirt with all the men in the room, a remarkably innocent and beautiful woman at fifty. Aunt Sylvia, who found the black drop in every joy, would cry in a corner until someone found her and told her to stop. My father would assume the smile he used on Sundays when he ushered Mass to respond to all the bright chatter he couldn't hear. My mother, suspicious of strangers, would remind me how long the path for a woman is afterwards. "A woman needs five men," she used to tell her sisters on the other side of my bedroom wall. "A lover, a provider, an intellectual, a laughing spirit, a father. If you're lucky, you get two out of five." Jeanne wouldn't be fooled, not by the champagne, the hovering waiters in white starched linen, not by the ring, which would be big, of course, but elegant, too, because I'd need to lift my hand for an inspection that would satisfy Steve's parents and their friends. She'd know this was all wrong for me.

I looked out my window and saw myself lying still, waiting for sleep. I woke in the dark, soaking wet, the deep ache inside my bones, chills, hot flashes, throwing off covers, pulling them to my chin, locked in that bedroom in a world as big as a nut. The letters fell on the floor when I ran to the bathroom, sick again. The fever rumbled through me, exploded in a cold sweat. I sat on the bathroom floor with a towel over my shoulders until it passed.

When I pulled myself up, I felt weak but calm. I changed into one of the nightgowns Camille left folded on the washer and slept through the matins bell. I looked at the clock when I woke. Ten. A mean, damp day, but my head was clear. And I was hungry.

The school door opened across the field. My children ran out as though they were playing follow-the-leader except for Harry and his girlfriend who held hands and watched. Gemma spearheaded the group, ran in crazy circles around the field until Camille appeared in the doorway. Just then, just as Paula nearly reached her, Gemma sprinted past my window on her way to town. Paula stopped, looking from where Gemma ran, to Father, who'd come to his back door. The other children were huddled together without their jackets making their way to Father when Bernard walked out.

A fire drill? But, why did Gemma run away? Paula, dead center, spun, faced Camille, shouted something to her, then ran to my house. I was in the archway pulling on my robe when she pounded.

"Where *were* you?" she said. Her face was flushed. She was crying.

"Here, Paula. I've been sick. What is it? What—"

"You should have *been* there!"

"Tell me, tell me what happened."

"Ask *her,* ask *her* what she did." She took her hand from her cheek. A welt slanted from the corner of her eye to her chin. "She's crazy, you know. Doesn't anybody *know* that?"

"Tell me what happened."

Inside the classroom, pulling down the map of Africa, Camille said how this, this country was a part of the world's malaise. She stared at the great golden triangle and said that there they could arbitrarily decide who should lead, and even a more simple thing, what to call a place. She let her pointer wander over the right side of the triangle and said that yesterday, she'd endured the disrespect of Paula Cobb, who'd stood, smirking, to tell her that there was no Northern Rhodesia anymore. It was called Zambia now. And the pointer had stiffened in her hand while she told Paula she'd known the change, repeated the old one by rote.

The wind and rain slashed through a few partly opened windows. Children in the row next to them embraced themselves, but no one asked permission to close them. Camille waited a moment, then satisfied, told Harry Lee to close them.

Her head listed. She was staring at the posters on the bulletin board in back. She looked sleepy, but sly. They waited, curious, excited. They'd seen this before.

She said, "Pass forward the homework, please."

They unlocked looseleaf sheets from notebooks, Camille grimly spotting the ones who didn't. "Now," she said, "let us see what you remember. Name the African states that border the Indian Ocean." Hands went up. Camille stared too long at some spot over their heads. Paula was frightened then. She waved her hand.

"What?" Camille demanded. "What do you want?"

Paula stood. "You asked for the African countries on the Indian Ocean. They are—"

"Sit down."

"But, you asked, Sister."

She gazed at Paula. "You must learn to stop showing off. You love to stand and be seen. Sit down. Brazen behavior is shameful in a young woman." She saw what she wanted across from Paula. "Gemma."

"Yes, S'ter?"

"Stand."

Gemma stood.

"Answer the question."

"I didn't hear it."

"I didn't hear it, *Sister.*"

"Sister."

"Why is that?"

Gemma rubbed her desktop.

"The question is to name the African states on the Indian Ocean."

"I don't know. Is one Nigeria?"

"Not nearly."

"Uganda? The Congo?" Gemma winked at Paula, but didn't read Paula's warning face.

"You didn't memorize these last night, did you?"

"No, but if you moved a little, I could read them off the map." Sister smiled. "Come to the front."

"Oh, come on, Sister. I'll stay in at lunch and do it."

"Come to the front."

"Okay, give me five minutes and I'll say them."

"Now."

Gemma took a step, but Paula's arm shot across the aisle to block her. "Don't go," Paula said.

Gemma hesitated, waited for Paula's next move.

Camille brandished the pointer. "Taking longer will only prolong the punishment. And now, your accomplice may join you."

Paula stood. "She's not and I'm not. It's not fair!"

"BE STILL! You may not speak out like that."

"I told my father. He said no one should get hit with a pointer because they forgot their work."

Camille screamed, "Stop it!"

"No, I won't stop! You wouldn't do this if Miss DeStefano was here!"

"I am not surprised that you defy me. You have been taught defiance. 'She shall be stripped and her hinder parts shall be bared in her own sight.' I predict that for such a girl."

"I don't care what you say about me. I don't care! Leave us alone!"

"You will be sorry that you made this scene."

The rest of the children stared at the triangle Paula, Gemma and Camille formed in the aisle near the windows. They were framed in silvered rain. Then Camille surprised them. They'd expected her scream, part whine, part howl. Instead, she used the pointer like someone clearing brush as she made her way to the bulletin board to rip off the posters. The only sound or movement in that room was the swish and flash of the pointer whipping air.

Camille struck Paula, whose hand flew to her cheek, her palm against the pain there, the pointer striking her knuckles on its return and glancing off Gemma's shoulder. Camille retreated a few steps for better purchase. She found the creases behind Gemma's knees, the unprotected arm above her elbow, her cheek, neck, her hand on its way to cover her eyes. The pointer whirred and slapped its way against flesh. Red lines crisscrossed Gemma's calves when she finally thought to run. Camille followed her to the front of the room into the corner between the map and the windows until Paula pulled the pointer from Camille's hand when she raised it on a backswing. Camille felt her empty hand, flexed it, grabbed Gemma's hair. Gemma finally found her tongue. "Get her off me! Get her *off* me!" she said while she crouched, pulling in her legs and hugging herself.

Camille pressed herself against the map and stared, her lips loose, her eyes vacant. She touched the leather girdle ringing her waist, felt for the beads beneath while she whispered Hail Marys and waited for something she couldn't remember.

Paula helped Gemma up and just as quickly, Gemma pushed open the door and ran.

"Drink a glass of water," I told Paula. "I'll be dressed in a minute."

She called into the bedroom where I was pushing my feet into a pair of jeans, "What are we going to do?"

"We're going to find Gemma."

XV

We were driving through the storm in a stolen car under a sky of buffalo skin, lightning its ribs and spine. I was speeding like a criminal fleeing a crime with a little girl hugging her knees beside me. We didn't talk because the wind and rain were too loud. Paula pointed to a ripped branch, its leaves rolling silver to green, black bark like a missile aimed at the headlights. The Chrysler took a bootleg turn, skidded over leaves and water, lumped over fields, back on the shining asphalt, crossing the barren stretch at Three Sands where nothing grew in salty soil, all the way to the Cimarron Turnpike and back.

Josephine hadn't hesitated when I told her to give me Father's keys. When I told Paula we'd stop at Jerry Ridgeway's first, she asked, "How did *you* know?" Jerry was watching cartoons between chores. "It's gonna be thick out there when I go for the cows," he said. He told us that Gemma had called him a little while back, told him she wanted him to pick her up on the highway, but he couldn't because his dad had the pickup and his mother, the car. He thought it was funny for her to call when she should have been in school, thought she sounded funny, too. But, Gemma had a mind of her own. Mr. Magoo was stepping safely over a yawning hole in the street and Jerry was giggling when we left.

In the car, Paula said, "Our spot. It's a secret. It's all I can think of." We drove along the Arkansas River churning with new water. Saplings bent into it like brooms sweeping the broken twigs the storm had flung. Oklahoma dust was glue in the downpour. It sucked a tennis shoe from my foot. The "spot" was a thicket at the river's edge, a stand of evergreens planted in a circle like a living tepee. Inside, it was only damp in a bed of old pine straw. We kept our heads down, shoulders hunched against the wild flail of pine branches. "She was here," Paula said. A Hershey bar, a roll of lifesavers, a lipstick. Paula knelt, opened it, looked up. "Hot coral," she said.

"I have to take you home, Paula."

"What'll you do?"

"I'll think of something."

"She told me she has to keep moving, Miss DeStefano, always has to go someplace else where no one knows her. I mean, it wasn't just Sister. She was going to anyway. She told me."

"Did she tell you why?"

"No. I figured it was 'cause of her father. He was always after her to be, you know, perfect or something."

So, I was in a select group of knowers. I felt the way my mother looked after Frank announced his engagement. What now? What next?

The Brodenworts were next. Ellen answered the back door, then stood in the entry like a barricade. "Oooh, it's you!" she said. "Right after Father called, I started in to call you. Look!" She pointed toward a counter cluttered with dishes, pans, tins, wadded up dishtowels, to a small cleared space where a pie sat. "See, it's Wednesday. I bake her a berry pie every Wednesday, and we have a snack at just seven, then she does her lessons while I clear up."

I knew this system. She'd tell me about snowy white sheets and pretty new clothes and fresh air and a good healthy routine as though it mattered. She would if I let her.

"May I come inside?"

"Oh, yes, yes, I'm sorry. She isn't with you?"

"I don't know where she is."

I followed her to the living room where she fussed around touching doilies, turning on lamps, straightening music sheets on an old upright. He was already there, sitting in a blue satin armchair, his legs spread to accommodate his stomach that dropped like a sack of grain between his thighs. He smiled a little scallop of a smile.

"Did she call here?" I asked him.

"No, she didn't," Ellen answered. "And it's just terrible out there. Look at you! You're soaking wet."

"I didn't think she would."

Henry said, "Now you got that right. I'd be the last person she'd call after she got herself in a fix like this here. She knows what I'd do about it."

Ellen asked if I wanted a cup of hot tea. He thought maybe I'd like a nice little drink to warm me up.

"That's not it," I said.

"Not tea? Not a drink?" Ellen asked at the door.

"That's not why she wouldn't call you, Henry."

His chin wobbled. I think because I called him Henry.

"Parents," he said, "parents always get a bad deal from their kids, 'specially if they're tryin to set 'em straight."

"No, Henry, that's not it either."

So now he looked directly at me because the script was definitely wrong. I glanced at the open door to his den.

"She was gettin' purty good on the piano. Her mother over there was teachin' her." Ellen nodded. "But you see, she wouldn't practice," he said. "Now she's run off for the same reason—wouldn't do her lessons."

"It was stupid to ask if she called here," I said.

Ellen whimpered, "I know, I know. They warned us, didn't they Henry? Once a runaway, always a runaway's what they told us at the start."

Henry rested his plump hands on the crown of his stomach. "I hear you been sick, still maybe got a touch of the fever?" he asked.

"Because," I said into those dead eyes, "she's running away from *you.*"

"Got to admit, she's a youngster that's real stubborn. Couldn't take criticism," he said. And in the sly, confiding tone of a little boy in trouble, added, "Ask my wife."

"Criticism? *That's* what she couldn't take?"

He sipped his drink.

"Thirteen, Henry. Gemma is thirteen years old, you bastard."

Ellen collapsed on the piano stool.

"What I'm going to do, Henry, is drive to the police station and tell the chief that Gemma is alone somewhere in this storm, that it's coming on night and she won't be home, she won't ever come 'home' because of what her 'father' does to her in that den. And I'll stick to him like glue until we find her."

Ellen was crying. "What's she saying? What's she talking about?" Her elbow hit the treble keys.

"And afterwards, Henry, I'll testify. I'll tell the court what I know, and I know everything. I'll get it published in the newspaper."

"What's she *mean?*" Ellen asked and covered her face. Sensible shoes, skirt and blouse, hair parted in the center, neat and straight, too big for the piano stool. I could have slapped her.

"I mean that you take care of a child who lives in your house. You watch out for her, Ellen. You pay attention."

"Henry was right," she gulped and swallowed. "He said you'd be stubborn—all you eyetalians are—eyetalians and Germans, they don't ever get along because—"

"Never mind, Ellie, never mind," her husband told her.

"Everything, Henry," I said. "In writing."

I bumped into the curb in front of the police station and hit my chin against the steering wheel on the bounce. The chief, Ned Frickett, sat at his desk. He stuck whatever he was reading into his top drawer when I began, before he held up a hand to stop me.

"Got the news already," he said.

"No you haven't. Only what happened at the school," I said. The hand went up again.

"Now, hold on. That Hoffert girl, that's her real name," he said, "she's a wild one. I warned the Brodenworts, warned 'em early on, only Henry, he was real high on doin' for a child now his own are gone. And that priest of yours *would* push it."

"That's history."

"Has a bearing, wouldn't you say, you bein' a teacher and all?"

"No, I wouldn't. There's more, chief. There's what happened to her at home."

"Hold on," he said. "Can't be dealin' in hearsay, now can we?"

"You aren't going to listen to me, are you? You already know, don't you?"

He examined the pen he was toying with.

"Don't you?" I shouted.

"I can hear you ma'am. So can everyone else in the jail." He smiled, a doctor to patient smile. "Now it's your turn to listen up. There's four roads outta town. East and west to farmland. North and south Ponca and Blackfoot. She's probably gone and picked herself up a ride on one of those—most likely from a stranger—in a car that could be anywheres by now."

"You aren't going to search?" I felt as crazy as his face suggested. I stopped to take a breath, but I needed to pull in more than air. I smelled the place, urine, disinfectant, disused furniture, mildew. I saw the desktop silty with dust, the two drunk Indians in the twin cells, one lying on a cot covered with an old army blanket, one shuffling and muttering because we woke him. Ned pushed a chair behind me.

"You all right, ma'am?"

Schifoso was my people's ingenious word that told of nausea, the refusal to eat or touch anything in a dirty place because their primitive fear promised that if they did, the dirt would spread in them. But, I had to swallow it back because I needed the chair.

"Heard you had the flu, ma'am. Now that'll make the joints ache, won't it?"

I looked into his good ole boy smile.

"You comfortable, ma'am? Okay, so you see, I was tellin' you, four roads, one patrol car, two prisoners and a town to keep in order. See my problem. This ain't no big city like you come from. She'll come back on her own if the goin' gets rough. Mark my words."

"She won't come back." All I had to do was get up, out of this greasy chair, and walk to the door. Only, all the stuff was out of me for a minute. I saw his mouth moving again.

". . . new here, and maybe you're carryin' on a little too serious for the situation. Course, I understand you're her teacher and all—"

"We both know she'll never come near this town again, not while Henry Brodenwort is alive and well here, no matter what happens to her."

"Might. Never can tell. You say you don't want history, but the girl's—"

"Her name is Gemma." I pushed against the arms of the chair, planted my feet on the floor and was up.

"Uh-huh. She's got herself a long sheet. Came from trouble, makes it wherever she goes, then runs off."

". . . some goddamn sleep around here," I heard the Indian mutter.

Ned's chair squeaked when he leaned back to watch me leave. "If she don't want to be found, ma'am, she sure won't be. She's real good at hidin'."

"She's had real good teachers."

And that was it. That was what I did for Gemma. Henry was safe in his satin armchair with his wife ministering to him while his pal sat in a dirty jail reading a dime novel. The wind slammed the jail door shut, the rain hit my face. On the slow drive home, the lights in every house beckoned to me, small white frame squares, edged in privet hedge, the people inside, warm and dry.

I drove into a noon of spotlights at the rectory. Father was watching for me. He struggled with an umbrella on his back porch while I opened the garage door. He fought his way like a swordsman, his skirts whipped up to ruffles, to get to me. The wind blew the umbrella up, divided it neatly into bat's wings. He pointed it at me the way my mother pointed a bread knife to punctuate a scolding. When we were both inside the garage, he shot off questions without waiting for answers like any angry parent. "Where were you? What in the world got into you? Do you know how many calls I've made?" and so on.

It was only then that I remembered how all of this started. "What about Sister?" I asked.

"It's taken care of. I called the Motherhouse. They're coming for her. She's going home for a rest."

Going home.

"You look terrible," he said. "I'll talk to you about this to-morrow. Get home and get yourself to bed. I can't have you getting pneumonia now. I need you."

On his way back to the house, he muttered that he'd had just about enough of women—independent women. Two were quite enough—three might tip the balance. Did anyone around here—anyone—remember who was ordained—*ordained*—to give the orders?

I was finally dry, wrapped in my robe with a towel around my head, in perfect timing with the storm. It stopped suddenly as though some great-palmed god stayed the wind, wet a finger to put out the lightning and cupped his hands to catch the rain.

I lay on top of the bed with the phone next to my pillow. In case. I meant to wait, but I fell asleep. The ringing was mixed up with the doorbell in my dream. Charlie Pepper and I were sitting on a big lawn in front of a marble estate, pink in sunset. There were other derelicts spotted around, drinking from bottles in paper bags, sleeping, shooting the breeze, when a car pulled up. Jimmy Durante got out, took a look at all of us and said, "Hey! This ain't no place for you. Come on in, have a sandwich or something." We followed him to the great doors. "Ya know," he said, "I never remember the key ta this place." He pushed the bell and I felt the vibration of my phone ringing. Quarters chimed down a pay phone slot.

She sounded out of breath, out of time. "Hi. I called to tell you I'm okay, okay?"

"Gemma? Gemma, I was looking for you."

"I figured. Leave it alone now, ya know? I know what I'm doin'. I'm on my way."

"Wait. You'll need things, uh, clothes and money. Let me bring them. I can get a car—"

"You don't get it. I travel light."

"Gemma, I won't tell anyone."

A pause.

"You won't mean to."

"Listen! Are you listening? If you let me bring you back, I *will* tell. I'll tell someone—the bishop, a judge—someone in authority who's out of town. I know, Gemma, I know there's no one here who'll listen."

She didn't answer. I heard distant laughter, cars swooshing to a stop.

"I'm your *teacher*. I have no reason to lie. They'll have to believe me."

"Ah, you don't know. You just don't know."

"You can strap me to your side, Gemma. I keep my promises."

"I only called to tell you I was okay. I gotta go now."

"Go? Go where?"

"My ride's leaving in a minute. We're all gassed up."

She must have brushed the receiver against her shoulder on its way back to the hook. I pressed mine against my ear. I remembered the last time I saw her at the bottom of the church steps after Sunday Mass. *His* fingers just touching her shoulder, her "mother" pushing back curls the wind blew into Gemma's eyes. The family. Now she was a voice traveling through wires, restricted to a time prescribed by a supply of quarters some stranger mysteriously counted.

"Miss DeStefano? You still there?"

"Yes, yes, I'm here."

"I got no time to call Paula. Will you?"

"What in the world am I supposed to tell her?"

"No, don't play around with me. Will you?"

"You know I will."

"See, I called you instead 'cause I wanted to let you off the hook. You get so *worried* about stuff. I gotta go now or I'll lose my ride."

Midnight. Gemma and I had met between eight and two every day for months, but we'd only spoken twice, twice at midnight.

The rest of the time we were walking around with bushel baskets pulled up around our middles. All of us. Except Camille who dropped hers, and she could be mad. Or Charlie Pepper, and he was a bum.

A silver Lincoln paused at the stop sign outside my front window. I saw Camille in profile in the back seat as the car glided like a shining barge down a narrow black stream. Going home.

The next morning, Father told me he called off school, but he wanted me to visit Sister Bernard to make plans for the children while Camille was away. His voice went flat when he told me the Brodenworts and Ned Frickett called him early, that the matter did not concern me any more, that he did not want the church dragged into a mess it had nothing to do with. That's how we sound with the bushel baskets in place.

I did what was left to do, my duty. Bernard had transformed the bare convent kitchen I'd seen in July into a gypsy circus. For her, no tablecloth with teapots and coffee mills. There were green hippos, purple giraffes, red monkeys and golden zebras peeking from behind chartreuse fronds in a rainbow jungle. She'd hung candy-striped valences over the windows, filled the counters with a good cook's tools, set pots of geraniums beneath one window, and herb pots under the other. I recognized the parsley and basil.

"Look at you, Claire, your cheeks are blooming. You must be better."

"Much better, thank you, Sister."

She was pleased to tell me she'd already made us coffee, the pot was warming over a low flame. She set out the mugs I remembered from Camille's visit, lined a soup dish with a red napkin and piled cookies into it.

"Oatmeal with raisins and nuts," she said. "Mother's favorite. She's a wonderful nurse, isn't she? She was so concerned about you last week. At home, the old sisters ask for her often. She gives them such comfort. It's a gift of God, you know, Claire. A talent she has."

She took a small platter with sliced strudel, cherries bursting from flaked shells, from the refrigerator. "But, you see, she pays a price. It takes so much out of her."

She poured coffee, basted a roast in the oven while I waited for her to continue, to tell me, explain to me what was eating at Camille's soul.

"Why do you call her Mother?" I asked.

"Because she's my superior in this convent. My Mother Superior. We call ourselves these names because we are a family in religion."

"She told me she was my mother, too."

"Of course." Behind her serene face, Bernard's soul sat quiet in certainties.

We settled the problem of teaching science and math quickly because neither one of us could do it. We would assign pages to the children and let them work the problems as well as they could. That made about as much sense as anything else that had happened.

"I'd like you to stay for supper," she said. "There is *such* a roast! But, you understand, I can't because Mother is not here."

How quietly and politely the rhythms of her universe marched on. All signs were intelligible to Bernard who was, as Camille said, young in religion, but at least ten years my senior. I wondered if it were innocence or wisdom.

She poured fresh coffee and asked shyly, "Will you be alone on Thanksgiving?"

Thanksgiving. Holidays were for the family. I had no plans for Thanksgiving.

She hurried on. "If we, if Mother and I were to be here, we would certainly have invited you. But, we'll be home at the convent this year so that Mother can be refreshed to continue her work. You understand."

One thing I understood. I had this longing to be at home at the table with my family speaking a language I understood. I needed a translator in Christopher Park.

XVI

Kay Cobb invited me for Thanksgiving Day. She had a supply of wines to last through Christmas. The reds were on the kitchen table, the whites in a glass tub as big as a bushel, their slender green necks rising from chunks of ice. She opened the oven. The turkey, wrapped in aluminum foil, glowed in the dark center. "I basted it with sauterne and wrapped it tight," Kay said. "What kind of wine do you need for your yams?"

"I think I only need butter and brown sugar," I said.

"No, I mean to drink while you work," Kay answered. "I think . . . chardonnay. Paula?"

"I got it, Mom."

"Doesn't it smell great?" T.J. asked. We were using the front burners together.

"What are you doing?" I asked him.

"Finishing touches. For my chili."

"See, the turkey's gonna taste boiled," Paula said. "And the dressing sort of like oatmeal you forgot to put the salt in."

"And sauterne," Kay smiled. "Doesn't matter. Anyone who's honest will admit turkey is boring. It's the aroma they love. Also, stuffing is actually a disgusting notion. And when you get right down to it, so's the damned holiday. I don't know where we get the goddamn nerve to celebrate it in Oklahoma."

"She means what we did to the Indians," Paula told me.

"Are doing. Present tense," Kay said.

T.J. breathed in. "Kay, this house is redolent, absolutely fragrant with promise. Take a look at Claire, huh? Looks like she could use a heap of food on those bones. You been eatin'?"

"She had the flu," Paula reminded him and put a crystal tulip glass of citron in my free hand. "Chardonnay," she said. She looked authentic, like a pilgrim in a green corduroy jumper and white blouse. We were twins in those blouses. You can hide the woman or the girl behind a lace collar and bib.

"You need to work out a rhythm," Kay said. "Sip and cook, sip and talk, sip and eat, and the whole day goes past like a running brook. You'll figure it out."

The Ridgeways arrived with Jerry and his brothers.

"Father won't be here until he really eats, usually at the Shawvers. Mrs. Shawver's the best cook in town," Paula said.

"He's not coming at all," I told her. That was one of the best reasons I had for being there.

"Nah, he always says that. I *told* you my mom practically boils the turkey. But, he always shows up later—for supper. Come on, I want to show you something."

She led me through the back bedroom, her parents', into what seemed, at first, a greenhouse. Kay's studio. "My dad built it for her," Paula said. "To keep her close to home, he said." Three walls of glass, track lighting running up four corners to a spoked network in the ceiling circling a skylight in the center as big as an old carriage wheel. I bumped into a big work table because I was looking up. The sharp smell of paint and turpentine stung.

I leaned against the table to look at Kay's canvases stacked against the low walls and found what I came to see in the first place. Gold. Buttercream fields bent in the wind toward a glowering sky. Another wheatfield suffused with light that scorched the sky as though the sun were beneath the earth. The granary, rising pure and white from asphalt and cinders, a spire. The bank of the Arkansas River, water-smeared and green in spring, with light playing off its rushing waters.

Paula went to a covered easel set up for work. "She ruined all your pictures," she said. "Did you see?"

I nodded. She meant Camille ripping my posters from the bulletin board.

"I told my mother, and I took your book with the picture of Emily Dickinson in front," Paula said. "My mom's real busy now. She's doing all this stuff for a bank in Tulsa. But, I told her to hurry up and finish this for today, so you could see, like your Christmas present or something."

She uncovered an oil portrait. I looked into the sherry eyes of Kay's Emily Dickinson, who did not resemble a white nun who lived a passionately chaste life. This face told of desire, the slow fire climbing her cheek as though she'd just heard: "He's coming. He's here!"

Paula went right to Kay's side when we got back to the kitchen. She slipped her arm around her mother's waist, which must have been unusual, because Kay said, "What?"

"The portrait, Kay," I said. "I don't know what to say."

"Oh, she showed you."

The ancients said the most you could know about something beautiful was that you were in its presence. And it called you back. Anything you say is only *about* it. Still, something, I had to try to say something. "It's beautiful, it's—"

"Don't gush," she answered. "It's not dry and I have to frame it, and I didn't have nearly enough time, but my daughter can be imperious as you probably know."

"But, I want to tell you what it means—"

"Hush now, Claire. Pay attention to the rhythms. Sip."

Mr. Ridgeway walked into the kitchen to smile at us and ask how things were coming along. He took some beers into the living room where the men were watching a football game. Martha Ridgeway inspected my yams for a little while before she asked if I didn't think maybe I ought to take the potatoes out of the pan while I boiled down the syrup.

Maybe. I must have missed that when I watched my mother. My fingers were numb so I didn't feel the burn from touching the skillet handle for a second. T.J. bandaged it and told me to get the hell out of harm's way and go set the table or something. Paula said we should set all twelve places in case anyone unexpected showed up.

"Fill her glass," Kay called.

While we laid out silver and plates, Paula said, "What about this Hemingway? I mean, he doesn't know *anything* about women. Did you ever read the stuff he makes them *say?* Is he supposed to be good or something?"

"That's the consensus."

"Yeah, well I'm not in on it. And another thing, *Moby Dick.* Herman writes like he thought it was his last chance to tell everything he knew!"

"So, you've been reading on your own?"

"Yeah. So? Am I right?"

"Did you read both books to the end?" I asked her.

"Sure I did."

"Then Herman and Hemingway would agree you have a right to your opinion. But I hope you won't shut the door on them altogether."

"You mean it? You do. Okay, I won't."

We sat at four. Kay said grace. It was mostly asking God to forgive us Anglo Saxons for betraying the Indians. She unwrapped the turkey, which was pale and spongy. But Paula was wrong about the stuffing. It was brick hard.

"Try any of the reds with dinner," Kay suggested. "Merlot, zinfandel, you know, for a little spice." She turned to T.J. "Like you pal, you're the spice in my feast. Actually," she told me and the Ridgeways, "you might like to pour the wine *over* the turkey. Looks like it'll absorb it."

Paula said it was time for the champagne, which was the only kind she liked. T.J. heard, and was up popping the cork of the first bottle.

Father Foley walked in an hour later, sat, began describing menus at "tables where I have eaten." T.J. winked. "Saved a little room for later, I hope." Father said he'd driven Josephine to her daughter's home in Ponca City where her daughter had greeted them with breakfast and a gift for her mother, a hand-beaded evening bag that Josephine had dangled from an elegant satin strap while she told her daughter it was just what she needed. Kay sighed. "God, what a blessing," she said. "I mean, Claire, would you want her at this table tasting your yams?" My yams were pulp. A baby would have no trouble swallowing them.

"What's she doing?" Father asked T.J. in reference to my wine glass, which had somehow been replaced with a fluted champagne glass.

"Drinking," T.J. answered. "Kay made her do it."

"I found the rhythm," I told Father. "Or it found me." I couldn't feel the backs of my hands or my kneecaps. And the day was unfolding as sweetly as a kaleidoscope spin.

"Seven A.M.—tomorrow," Father said. "If you're well enough to drink, you're well enough to get to Mass."

Jerry Ridgeway complimented me on the yams and asked, "So what have you heard from Gemma?"

Paula was beside me, refilling my glass and answering for me. "We don't want to talk about that today, Jerry."

"Yeah, well she was a nice kid."

"She's not dead," I said.

"Where there's life, there's hope," T.J. said.

"I'm gonna have another brew," Jerry said and we all walked over that little land mine safely. Just in time for me to see the front door open and Leo walk in. It was either Leo or his ghost in fawn pants and olive drab sweater.

"Hel-*lo!*" he said to me. "Look who's here."

"We've been here all day," Paula said. "Where've you been?"

"Just got back to town."

"Takin' the cure?" T.J. asked.

"Yup."

"Work?"

"So far. How about our ladies?"

"Mostly intelligible," T.J. said. "But then, it's only six o'clock."

"When you breakin' out the chili?" Leo asked him.

"Soon's they free up the plates."

Then Leo sat beside me. "Why Claire, your cheeks are in full bloom." He touched the lace at my throat. "I like this." Father put his coffee cup down and scratched his chin while he watched us. "Ah," Leo said, "you aren't speaking to me tonight, that right, Claire?" Then he bent his head so his ear was near my mouth. Father leaned forward.

"Claire just told me she's mad about the trip to the granary so she's definitely not speaking to me."

"She didn't tell *me* anything about any trip to the granary," Father said.

"Maybe she's not speaking to you, either," Leo suggested. "Went up in the elevator. Vertigo. She lost her balance. No, sweetie," he said to Paula's offer of champagne. "Ginger ale, today."

"That's what this is," she told him. "I'm not dumb! Were you drunk when you took Miss DeStefano up the elevator, Uncle Leo?"

"Nope. Sober as a you-know-what."

Kay put her hand on the back of my head and whispered, "Hang on, my dear. You can ride this out."

"Also," Leo was saying, "there's a rumor afoot about some strange alliance between her and Charlie Pepper. It gives me pause."

"Oh yeah?" Paula said. "Who's spreading that rumor?"

"Charlie is," Leo said. "He actually likes our Claire. He brings her catfish." Father pushed back from the table and cleared his throat like a sleepy lion. Leo picked up on his gaze. "When'd you last hear of Charlie Pepper taking a shine to anyone, Father? I mean, you have your finger on the pulse of this town."

I slapped the back of my butter knife against Leo's leg under the table which made him break into a grin and cover my leg with his hand. "Think your missionary's leadin' a double life, Father?"

I unwrapped my voice. "I'm helping Paula with the dishes," I said.

". . . what's going on here," Father's voice trailed to the kitchen while I still felt the warm spread of Leo's hand on my thigh. T.J. slipped his arm around my waist while I washed dishes at the sink.

"Now keep your eye peeled, Claire," he said. "This here's when we'll have real cause for thanksgiving. I'll be serving my chili in fifteen minutes."

Martha Ridgeway, who was drying, murmured, "He's a

handsome one, that Leo Fennery, but trouble, don't ya know. Broke a few hearts in this town."

Kay, who sat in a kitchen chair examining Martha's pumpkin pies, said, "Leo's crazy as a coot, which, of course, makes him sexy."

Paula said, "Uncle Leo is what I would call an exile."

"You would?" her mother said.

"Sure. See, he's really an Easterner at heart, he told me. He doesn't belong here. Want the rest of my theory?"

"This is new," Kay said. "She has formed a theory on pretty much everything that passes before her eyes these days. I blame you, Claire."

Martha asked, "How old are you now, Paula Rae?"

"Thirteen and three-fourths. Want my theory?"

"I want more champagne," I said.

"The thing is," Paula said while she refilled my glass, "he was just about to blow this town before you came."

"How do you know that?" Kay asked.

" 'Cause he *told* me. People actually *talk* to me, Mom." She had our attention. "See, that's how I know he's got a crush on you, Miss DeStefano. And, add to that, he hasn't been away for a cure for a really long time, right?"

"Right," Kay said and smiled at me.

"I have to go," I said.

"Of course you do," Kay answered.

I kissed them all good-bye, sweet faces in a wonderful blur, all except Leo and Father who growled, "Seven A.M. *sharp.*" I planted my feet on the porch, took one careful step down and felt Leo beside me, putting his arm around me.

"This is interesting," he said, keeping me balanced, "Claire as a mute. Usually, my dear, at unusual moments, you are relentlessly talking."

"Why would I talk to a man who walked away, left his dust in my face?"

"I think you move too fast for dust to settle on you."

I stared ahead. "I have seen enough sky, enough plain, enough flat for the rest of my natural life."

"The lady doesn't care for the view?"

I didn't answer.

" 'The wilderness and the waterless region will exult and the desert plain will be joyful and blossom as the saffron.' "

"What's that?"

"That's your Isaiah. And, then, too, that's you."

I tripped on broken cement. "I have this perfectly nice boy at home who absolutely adores me, is waiting for me, wants to marry me. Today, Leo, he'd marry me today if I let him."

"I figured something like that."

"So what do I want with you? You leave for weeks without a damned word. You reappear in a doorway. And what? I'm supposed to drop everything, give up everything and let you in? I don't think so. You do damage."

"Don't drop anything. Don't give up anything."

"Don't tell me what to do. Who was she? Who was that woman who made you stop in this godforsaken town and start drinking whiskey at noon?"

"She has gone clean out of my mind, kiddo."

"I think you're still looking for her."

"I think you're shying away from me."

"Wouldn't you? If you were me?"

He stopped my stumbling and wrapped his arms around me while we leaned against the telephone pole fifty feet from the streetlight in front of my little house. "No, I wouldn't, Claire."

I muttered into his shoulder where I was home safe, "Four weeks! And I saw you with Louise. I saw you."

"I know. Can't fool a sharp-eyed Eastern girl like you."

"What are you trying to do to me, Leo?"

"Trying to love you." He nudged me under the chin. "Look up here."

Stars trick you. Me, anyway. They call up this longing to fly to them. Fly away. "I can't believe it," I told him. "What I did with you. After years of—and then, I just said yes."

"I don't know, maybe that's what it means to be human, doing exactly what you thought you'd never do."

"What's that supposed to mean?"

"Welcome to the human race."

"And just what crowd have I been hanging around with for the last twenty years?"

"Relax Claire, it isn't that dramatic."

"You don't think so?"

"Uh-uh."

I stepped away from him, my spine against the pole. "Pretty soon you'll tell me you'll do anything for me. I bet you'll tell me that. You'll come to Cleveland and face them if I ask. But, if you came we'd never leave the station. All your baggage would keep us there. We'd be like refugees sorting and picking through all the stuff you brought so nothing would be lost. By then, the place would be deserted, no one to help us. And we could never manage alone. So, before you tell me that you love me and you'll do anything in the world for me, let me tell *you* something. I think it'd be better for a lover to stay home unless he decides he can leave and travel light."

"So, you aren't mute."

He and I walked to my back step under a quarter slice of moon.

"Are you pretty sure it was me you were talking about back there?" he asked.

"Not sure of anything."

He lit a cigarette for me, one for himself. "Can't give up everything, not all at once." He smiled, pushed my hair behind my ears, and left his open palm against my cheek. "I missed this face," he said.

"What are we going to do, Leo?"

"Meet me at the grill in the morning for breakfast? What do you think?"

"I think we're headed for big trouble."

"Of course we are."

"What time?"

"Right after the command performance at Mass. I'll be waiting for you. It's my turn, right kiddo?" He kissed me. "I'll have Annie's dense coffee waiting. You're going to have a hangover. Ever had one? No, I didn't think so. Your head'll throb, your eyes'll swell, your legs'll feel hollow. But, you can make it to town and the walk'll help. And after coffee and juice, we can walk off the rest of it together."

"Leo?"

"Mmm?"

"I'm the one with the baggage."

"Ah, you're not the only one."

"You, too?"

"Sure. You weren't in my plans. That last time, when I watched you going inside this house alone, you looked so small. I felt the fifteen years between us like a punch in the stomach. Saw you importing me to your mother's kitchen like a stray. I still do, but I'm back."

"The night at the red hotel? That night?"

"The very one. After that night, I couldn't turn my back with my usual ruthless vigor."

I let him leave, finally, went inside the neat little house, scrubbed and shining, made ready for guests, and sat on the sofa, legs akimbo. I hugged myself while the quiet seeped in. After a while, I stretched out, put a pillow under my head and drifted into a sweet, deep sleep, and if I dreamed a dream that night, I don't remember.

XVII

The month before Christmas felt like a kind of holiday because Camille was missing and Leo'd come back. Days began the same, the sun climbed the belfry, which seemed to make the bells ring and pigeons scatter. I'd run to Mass with my trench coat over my pajamas, take Communion with the saints, run back to eat an orange for my mother's sake and change for school. I didn't go out on the census anymore because I didn't think I had a mission anymore. Except to teach the children who were left. Gemma was lost. She'd danced like a will-o'-the-wisp into the dark where she couldn't be found. But, she'd left a mark on Paula who went cold on me.

Kay said it was the same at home. She'd come in and ask if there were any mail for her, if anyone called. When her mother told her no, she'd grab a book, throw herself on the sofa, turn on the television and stare at the ceiling until suppertime when she'd pick at her food and mumble.

"She thinks Gemma's coming back," Kay said. "I wonder how long this is going to last."

She was slouched at her desk, staring out the window when I called on her to answer a simple grammar question. "Can you tell us, Paula?"

She straightened, colored, cleared her throat and slumped back. "Sorry," she said. "I dunno."

The bell rang, but I kept them to read a mimeographed sheet Sister Bernard sent about the annual Christmas pageant.

Paula came to life. "I will *not* be the Blessed Virgin! I will *not* wear a veil and stare at some stupid doll while everyone else stands around in their bathrobes, and that's that!"

"Sister Bernard says you do it every year," I said. "And Father already put the announcement in Sunday's bulletin."

"So what?" Paula said.

"Yeah," Mike said. "So what?"

"Why can't we do something different?" Paula asked the rest of them, not me. I saw their faces, alert, when they caught her drift. Sister Camille was gone. Anything was possible.

"There's no time, Paula," I answered before they could. "We have two weeks, and first we'd need a new idea and then I'd have to write the script—"

"*I'll* think of the idea," she said. "And *I'll* write it."

"No, I don't think so," I said. I asked her to stay after the others left. "What's going on?" I asked her.

"What do you mean? Look, I gotta go."

"I mean why didn't you answer when I called on you? You were going to. You knew the answer. And then you stopped yourself."

"I don't know what you're talking about."

Pushing me into a corner where I'd have to strike back. Standing with a hand on her hip, head cocked to the side. Gemma's stance. Gemma's arrogance.

"You know what I'm talking about."

"Boy, Gemma was right. You won't leave anything alone. I didn't do my homework, okay? Once! And now it's a federal case." Her face was flaming. This path would take us nowhere.

"Do you really think you can write a Christmas play by tomorrow?"

"What?"

"That's not much time."

"I can do it."

"Okay, do it."

She dropped the stance. "You mean it?"

I nodded.

She looked back when she was outside, then ran up the street.

When I called Kay a little while later, she told me, "She's in her room with a jar of peanut butter, a box of crackers and rock and roll blaring. She says she's writing a play. She says it's just the beginning. She's decided to become a writer.''

''Did she say that?''

''She did. So, if you're going to change your mind, do it now before this goes too far.''

''I'm not going to change my mind.''

''Okay, tell you what,'' Kay said. ''Why don't you come over for supper tonight? It's safe. T.J.'s cooking. And why don't I call Leo, too?''

''Why don't you,'' I said.

''I'm doing Adam and Eve,'' Paula told us at supper. ''I s'pose I'll have to be Eve 'cause Gemma's not here. But, we need a real God. Someone with a deep voice, you know, and tall. I guess we need a grown-up.''

''Does God have a big part, Paula?'' Leo asked.

''Yeah, pretty big. After Eve and the snake. Want to do it, Uncle Leo?''

''Nah, I'm a behind-the-scenes-man myself.''

''Okay, I'll think of someone,'' she said while she watched her dad bite into a drumstick. ''Mike should be the snake. We can wrap him in aluminum foil so he shines.''

''You're already casting,'' I said. ''Is it nearly written?''

''Pretty much. Except for the ending. So, may I be excused? I have work to do.''

I noticed her plate was empty.

The next day, I sat with the rest of the class when Paula went up to the stage in the church basement to tell us about her play. ''It's one act,'' she said. ''We're in Eden with this tree in the middle. Adam and me are having a picnic and the snake comes and talks to us, and Adam pretends he doesn't hear and just keeps on eating, but, of course, he *does* hear and God's hiding behind the tree the whole time because this is the first exciting thing that's happened since He made the world so He doesn't want to miss anything. And all the rest of you guys are gonna be angels who're hanging around to see what happens.''

''Whattya mean hangin' around?'' Mike asked. ''Don't they *say* anything?''

"I don't know if angels talk," Paula said. "I know they sing."

"I'm not wearin' wings," Mike said.

"You don't have to, Mike," Paula told him. "You're the snake. You get to crawl."

"I'll wear wings," Harry Lee said.

"No, I want you to be Adam," Paula said.

"How come we're doing Adam and Eve, anyway?" Mike asked me. "This is supposed to be a *Christmas* play."

"Because," Paula said, "I think it's the real beginning of Christmas."

T.J., who was eventually cast as God, made the tree of the knowledge of good and evil from papier-mâché and chicken wire and set it up on the stage for Kay to paint. Kay wanted to create some fantastic new fruit to hang from it, but Paula insisted on a real apple. Mrs. Ridgeway came in to measure shoulders for angel gowns and remarked that it would be a blessed relief not to have to see the whole town's flannel bathrobes marching out, for once. "I can get us some ostrich feathers," she said. "They'll float on air. Now, won't that be pretty?"

Leo said the Tigres and Euphrates should flank the Garden. He built ramps that Kay painted into rivers. "The angels can stand on them," Leo said. "Angels can stand on water, can't they?" he asked me. "Were you ever a Catholic, an *any*thing?" I asked him. He was bent over a saw horse in T.J.'s garage and looked as good to me as Eve's apple.

After the first run-through, I told Paula that when God sent them out of the Garden, He was supposed to have the last word.

"Who said?" she asked. "I don't know who wrote this in the first place, but he left stuff out. I mean, when God says that it's gonna hurt to have children and then He says go out and have them, can you believe Eve wouldn't say something?"

"To *God,* Paula?"

"Well, they were all pals then, weren't they?"

"Maybe Adam should say something, too."

Harry looked up.

"Don't you wish?" Paula said. "The way I see it, Adam just lets stuff happen."

One of the angels asked, "Is Jesus going to get born at the end?"

Paula looked at the clipboard she'd taken to carrying. "I'll make a note. Maybe."

Within a week, Leo was setting up the Tigris and Euphrates on stage, Mrs. Ridgeway was fitting T.J.'s white robe, and Kay was humming while she painted the Garden of Eden on the flat behind the rivers. Father surprised us.

"Hello," he said while he took in the scene. "What're you all doing? What's this?"

"The set for the Christmas pageant," I said. "Isn't it nice?"

"I don't recognize it," he said. "Where's the stable? Where's the crib? What are those blue things?"

"Rivers," Leo said. "They meet at the Fertile Crescent."

"Uh-huh," Father said. "Need you for a minute, Claire." He did that sweeping turn so his cassock flared when he walked up the steps. My set designers, who refused to look at me, went back to their work.

I hugged myself against the wind outside the basement door.

"Do you know what you're doing down there?" he asked me.

"Yes, Father."

He started to say something, checked himself, shook his head while he looked at the ground. I shivered.

"You better had," he said finally and went in to lunch.

Paula met me at the grill for a coke late Saturday afternoon before dress rehearsal.

"My dad got the spotlight from the junior college and he's setting it up now. And my mom's mimeographing the programs at the library."

"I bought the makeup," I said and dumped it out on the table. "See if I have everything."

She sorted through eyebrow pencils, mascara, powder, stopped at a lipstick. "Look," she said, "Hot Coral."

Both of us were back in that copse of pine in the storm, searching.

"I wonder where she is, every day," Paula said. She wrapped

both hands around her glass, looked into it and then at me. "Why don't you ever talk about her, Miss DeStefano? I mean people spend more time talking about a wallet they lost, you know?

A question that bit through the crust. She didn't wait for an answer.

"I went over to see her mom and dad, well they aren't really her mom and dad. Did you know?"

I nodded. "What did they say?"

She frowned. "Mrs. Brodenwort never says anything. And all her dad wanted was to make sure I knew how good they were to take her in. Like she was some kind of charity case or something. Like she wasn't a person." She swept the makeup into the bag and stuffed it into a corner of the booth. "She was my best friend."

A woman in white pushed open the door to the back room in front of me, and stood there swaying. Melanie Bright, black leather purse on her wrist, looking vague, like someone who'd just missed a bus. She looked at me and slid into the seat beside me as though we'd planned to meet.

"H'lo there, young lady," she said to Paula who smiled at her. "Do you know this nice lady, too?"

"She's my teacher," Paula told her.

Melanie's smile was fortified with bourbon. "She come to see me, once," Melanie told her, "and she was real good to me. Made me some tea." Her eyes were brimming in watery rheum. The rusty braid that should have been coiled and pinned was hanging to her waist. She sat, a little girl in dimity, and, artless as a child, pried open her purse to show us the two one dollar bills "that nice Bobby Mudd just give me."

I ordered her a cup of hot tea while Paula promised her we'd walk her home when she finished.

By then, the low sun threw shadows into the street as though the houses were casting off hoods. Paula was quiet until we were near the church on the way back. "Did you see all those dolls on her bed?" she asked.

I nodded, hoping she wouldn't ask what those two one dollar bills were for.

But she only said, "It must be terrible to live all alone. I hope Gemma isn't."

Opening night. Backstage, we could hear people settling into the first rows. When their voices began to compete with the Christmas carol tape, I went out front to have a look. Harry Lee's mother took my arm and introduced me to the minister from The First Church of Christ and the four rows of church members who'd come to see Harry Lee play Adam. My convert was right behind them with his Baptist friends. Lily Smith, in a scarlet dress and beret that barely sat over hair teased into a brittle helmet, was seating her girlfriends. "Something to do on a Sunday night," she said. Even Josephine was there, in the first row next to Sister Bernard, all dressed up in a little blue suit with a string of pearls around her neck and her beaded handbag on her lap. Faces like pale balloons bobbing all the way to the back. I sent two angels without wings to go set up more folding chairs.

When I left Leo and the cast backstage, made-up and giddy, it was just five minutes to curtain, and Father was still at the bottom of the basement steps greeting strangers like a good host. I stood in the back.

When Leo changed the tape to Beethoven's Ninth, one of the angels snapped off the house lights on cue and both of them ran up the side aisle to get behind the curtain. The crowd settled down and suddenly, it was quiet.

Two angels, floating ostrich feathers, lifted their legs high in time to "Ode to Joy," and pulled back the curtain where more angels marched in place on the Tigris and Euphrates. Eve entered with a picnic basket and called to Adam, "Here's a place, right under this pretty tree." Harry Lee entered wrapped in green leaves sewn into a sort of leotard. Eve's was chartreuse. She spread a blanket under the tree and set out fried chicken and a chocolate cake while the red-headed serpent, wrapped in burlap studded with foil, slithered in on his stomach and propped his chin on his hand to eavesdrop. God, in a white graduation robe with silver moons and stars stuck on it, looked out from behind the tree.

The angels hovered.

Adam and Eve talked about the perfect weather, pretty flowers and nice animals that God made until the serpent crawled onto their blanket. Eve petted him and asked if he'd like a piece of cake. But he said he had this question to ask. When he finished, Eve looked up at the apple and said to Adam, "What do you think?" And Adam answered, "I'll leave it up to you, Eve." Eve plucked the apple, stood with it cupped in her hands while she mused, "What could be bad about something so beautiful?" God took a few steps from behind the tree, folded His hands in prayer while the serpent watched Eve and Adam kept on eating. People actually gasped when she took a bite. "It's good," she said. "Then let me have some, too," Adam said. After he'd bitten into it, the stage lights flicked on and off like lightning. Leo left only half of them on so the stage was darker after the Fall.

God swept center stage into the good light and cursed the serpent who chuckled before he crept out of Paradise. The angels were weeping; they wiped their eyes with the tips of their wings. When God spoke to Adam and Eve, Adam dropped his head, knelt, nodded yes, to his fate. But, Eve, who knelt at first, grew more erect as the list of punishments grew, her face aflame. Then God said, "Go out of this Garden, toil and work hard. And multiply. But you will bring forth your children in pain. Your final punishment will be that you will remember what you have lost." Eve rose up before His face, leaving Adam in the shadows, and said, "We'll go. We'll toil and multiply and cover the earth. But, remember that I said this, God. Someday, You'll want something from us, something only we can give You. This very thing, a child born in pain."

That's when Harry Lee's sister from the third grade, wearing a blue mantle over someone's First Communion dress, walked on stage with her baby brother, half as big as she was, straddling her body. His head was buried under her chin, his arms locked around her neck. When she hoisted him, he blinked in the lights and began to cry. Harry's little sister stopped on the spot and sat down on the stage in the corner to make him comfortable. The baby had seen his brother and was kicking out of his swaddling clothes and squirming to get free. Harry Lee scrambled up from his dark corner of Eden. He put his face on the baby's stomach and tickled with his nose while the baby gurgled and pulled his brother's pompadour into silky straws.

Eve motioned the angels to leave the rivers and stand behind the baby at the left corner to adore. The spotlight followed in a sort of sputter.

Then Eve finished, "And when you ask, God, my daughter, she'll do it for You." Just before the angels sang, "Adeste Fide-lis," we all heard the sweet, pure sound of a baby laughing.

XVIII

I walked up the aisle of the Santa Fe Texas Chief speeding north, through coach car doors, sucking air, releasing it, on my way to the club car. Anonymous for the first time in months. Bound for Cleveland. Strangers in the club car were friendly because it was, after all, a Christmas train, and once out of Oklahoma, a wet train. I ordered Scotch and opened my book to the passage I'd saved to read, Fred telling his Uncle Scrooge that Christmas was "the only time I know of in the long calendar of the year, when men and women seem by one consent to open their shut-up hearts freely, and to think of other people below them as if they really were fellow-passengers to the grave and not another race of creatures bound on other journeys."

I waited for it to put me back together the way it always had, but I was cheating. I had news for my mother and father: I'd fallen in love with a stranger. And Steve was waiting. The Dickens passage wasn't going to work on any of them. It was up to me to break clean, which was why I felt suspended, like the bridge spanning the Arkansas, between two countries, at the moment, native to neither.

A table of bridge was forming. I was invited by a couple in their dotage, I mean they doted on one another. Delia told me she stirred a raw egg into Sammy's oatmeal every morning, even on the train, because "I read it prevents heart attacks." My partner was a bald, Chicago businessman who was ruddy with martinis and sharp as a tack.

"Four no-trump," I say.

"Is she going into Blackwood?" Delia asks Sammy.

"Table talk," Chicago says. "Five hearts."

"Six spades," I answer.

"My God!" Delia says.

Chicago looks up from what have to be the three kings I don't have, reads my eyes, and drawls, "Seven spades. Your spades, honey."

He lays down a fit people dream of. But only two kings. I need one finesse to make the seven.

Two days before, Father had packed the Chrysler with my white suitcases and driven the forty miles to Ponca City while I sat in the back seat and he talked to me through the rear view mirror, an arrangement that suited church decorum and the nature of our relationship. We were to pay our respects to Sister Camille at her convent before he took me to the depot.

The bleak fields behind, we turned into the private drive that led over rolling grounds to the convent. Even in December after the fire of leaves was spent, there was a spare elegance in the planting, maple and pecan, dogwood and sycamore with peeling bark, the delicacy of their tangled branches slim and brave in a tearing wind. There was the stature of a stand of blue spruce planted in a circle, like Gemma's spot. Small bunches of evergreens, some low and dense, some tall, tapering like fingers, defined the outlines of the brick buildings they fronted. Holly and firethorn bore berries. The grass was bright, like grass under lights at a night baseball game. The sun, indirect and diffused, burned behind thin clouds. We passed a summer gazebo, glass replacing summer screens. A statue of Mary, formed in cement, arms outstretched, palms up, summoned from a niche in an outside wall. The sun rolled free of the curl of thick cloud racing against it just as the porter nun answered our ring and light spread like spilled honey into the entry.

Mother Superior, slender and tall, crosses polished tiles to meet us, tells us Sister Camille has had another small "lapse" and is in the infirmary. She and Father decide that I should go up to visit her alone while she takes Father to the dining room to serve him port and cookies.

I climb the marble stairs with my eyes on the hem of the silent porter nun, arrange a smile when I enter. Camille's room is white with a carved oak crucifix above her bed. Besides the cross, the only other thing in the room that is not white or chrome is the leather bound prayer book on the coverlet. The cover lifts itself from the gold leaved pages as though a wind were blowing in. When she sees me, her hand flutters, touches the book, holds it. It's strange to see her lying in bed. She looks like someone's grandmother with a white bonnet edged in a frill.

After I put her presents down, I ask, "How are you, Sister?" I stuff my hands into my pockets, my fingers fumbling for something to hold.

"Have you noticed," she answers, "that we have reversed positions? Now I am the one in the bed. It's a little trick God plays on us when we become arrogant."

"Do you need anything? A glass of water—"

"I have everything I need. Don't be anxious. Sit down. Visit with me before you have to go."

"Would you like to open your gifts first? I'll do it for you."

She waves her free hand that says, if you like.

I open the gloves first. These were special. My mother found them for me in Cleveland, and she paid for them. "These are kid, Sister, with a cashmere lining. For chilly days, the walk to Mass and school—"

"You chose them?"

"Yes, Sister."

"Yes. Beautiful. But, unnecessary." She touches the lining. "A gift from an untried heart."

I give her Josephine's fruitcake, a book of meditations from Father and three Irish linen handkerchieves that Kay sent in Paula's name, and bite my lip.

Sister holds the handkerchieves to her cheek, then slips them under the covers. "Give the rest to Mother," she instructs. "She'll know what to do."

I put things back into their boxes, look for a waste basket for the torn paper when I hear her say my name. It's a warning.

"I wonder what will happen to you. What you will be after Christmas."

"Two weeks, Sister. I'll only be home for two weeks," I say, trying to angle us toward the calendar, weather, news. I don't want to go where she's headed.

"But that's long enough for a seduction," she says.

Her eyes grow smokey and dark while she waits for me. I feel it again, the cold wedge of panic because somehow I believe she knows what she cannot possibly know—what Leo and I will do later.

"Listen now," she says, and I do while she tells me about her "lapse."

She was in a white nightgown without her headdress, her cropped hair, wiry, iron gray, standing in front of her sink and mirror. She held her washcloth while, with dreamlike care, she touched the taps, old brass turns with "hot" and "cold" etched in script across the flat of both. She traced h-o-t, turned it on, touched the stream of water, but didn't feel it burning. The cloth fell from her fingers. Her head tipped forward until her forehead hit the mirror and it was as if she'd fallen through to the other side when He came to her, showed Himself to her. Her eyes were heavy, but she held them open to see, to finally see Him. Later, they found her slumped sideways in the corner, the mirror cracked, a smear of blood on her forehead from the scratch.

"I've been waiting for you, to tell you," she says. "All of us are alone, every moment, until we find our Companion. Long years I've searched and waited. It took all of my life to make my heart pure. And then, He came to me. He'll stay with me now. From love. From His boundless love. They don't understand here. The doctor is arrogant. The priest is deaf. They make me mute. But, that is their sickness, not mine."

Her voice throbs with her vision, a heaven filled with thrilling wingbeats, eyes held in thrall, globes of pure light filling space, music vibrating in bone, music that makes the harmonies of earth a thin prelude.

I start to speak but she stops me.

"Hush now, listen. One must accept. One must say, yes. I tell you because I know you understand. Do you hear me, child? You are a gift made for God. You must be careful. You must become a good and pleasing gift."

The porter nun knocks, says it is time, and I'm released.

While Father drives to the depot, I can see Camille while she waits and watches. Her hands meander, her fingers languid with no task to set them to. She watches for a signal no clock will chime. She sets her spine with a wrench of will. She nods with her heartbeat. She whispers to herself, beside herself, "Do not divide me from what I love."

When Father braked the car, I woke from the daydream and looked around. His was the only car in the lot behind the station house. I got out and wandered over to the empty bench in front of the rails that shone like twin snails' tracks straight on for miles. Father set my suitcases beside me and told me to go inside and show my ticket to the stationmaster.

"Forty-five minutes 'til train time," he told us.

"I hate public good-byes," I told Father.

"Is that right?" He looked as though I'd offered him a festival supper.

"Oh yeah, I've always hated them."

"Give your parents my best, then. And get some rest while you can. You let me know when your train back arrives, and I'll send someone to fetch you."

We were facing that little problem we had, no touching. I patted his sleeve, he nodded and waved after he opened his door.

I felt eels in my stomach, felt the stationmaster's eyes on me, so I went outside. I had a pack of cigarettes in my pocket, one in my purse one in my overnight case. All opened. I lit one, inhaled and heard the whistling Chevrolet.

Leo was as deft as a scene changer. My bags were in his trunk, I was in the front seat, and we were headed for the red hotel before I finished that cigarette.

In the club car, Chicago says, "That's right, honey, all you needed was that diamond finesse. Drink?"

"Sure," I answer.

Delia and Sammy warn us about the effects of alcohol on the liver.

"Where'd you learn to play the game?" Chicago asks me.

Not the way I learned to play pinochle. The night I met Steve, he'd asked if I played, and I said, "Sure." Our first date was supposed to be a bridge game. I was ready a half hour early, so I called Peggy, who played bridge daily in the smoker at school.

"Peggy," I said, "how do you play bridge?"

"What?"

"Just give me the basics because I have to play with Steve and his friends tonight."

"You actually *told* him you know how to play?"

"How hard can it be? I can play pinochle."

A long pause.

"Y'know, Claire, you deserve everything that's gonna happen tonight."

Deserve everything that happens. Three days before Father packed the Chrysler, Leo had knocked at my door at midnight, stood just inside the doorway, his voice soft as though raising it might break something. "I have an idea," he'd said. "Don't answer now, just think about it. Christmas. Our own. At our own place. One whole night and morning. No, no. Don't say anything now. Tell me tomorrow." I felt the rush of damp wind when he opened the door to leave. I watched from my window while his car disappeared up Seventh Street, looked at the dark windows at the rectory and convent. And looked around my house, at my books, my letters, the cake box, the pictures stuck in the dresser mirror, familiar things that would have brought me back if I hadn't already said yes to Leo.

Slow, a slow study. It took a while for the news to reach my stomach, which always followed to suffer the panic my mind could buffer at first. I had to call home and find some reason for being twenty-four hours late. I assured Leo there was no problem, that I didn't need to answer to the two generations of adults who lived there. I knew my mother would light the candle for my safe trip and when it burned low enough, she'd tell my dad to get out the Nickle Plate schedule and call to confirm if my train were on time. They'd be at the terminal at least an hour before train time, waiting at the head of the marble steps I'd climb.

Chicago says, "Pass," with delight because he likes defense more than I do, but I understand when Delia bids four hearts and my pal punches out, "Double." Delia shoots back, "Redouble," and Sammy groans, "Did you think, Delia? Did you think?" I hold no hearts, but unless Delia is void in spades, I have two quick tricks and Chicago has to have two in hearts. I lead my spade ace and Chicago smiles.

At the red hotel, Leo stayed downstairs to order our supper from room service so I could make the call home. The lie outright.

"Mama?"

"Where *are* you? How can you call from a train?"

"I'm not on a train. I'm in Ponca City, but Father thinks I'm on the train." (Keep it as close to the truth as you can, and tell them what they want to hear. I learned that from Frank who could juggle three of these at once.)

"What are you talking about? Are you all right? Just a minute! It's your daughter," she told my dad, "and she's not on the train."

"There's someone here I have to see, and I couldn't tell Father. So, everything's the same, except one day later."

"What did you say?"

I had to repeat it.

"What do you have to do?"

"It's about a student."

"Which student?"

"The girl who ran away."

She told my father, "I don't know yet, but I *do* know that I can't talk to both of you at once!" Silence in the background. "She says it's about one of her students."

And to me, directly into the speaker, "Gemma? That student?" My mother had an incredible intuitive memory.

"Yes, Gemma. I need to talk to a judge about her and Father doesn't want me to do it, so I lied to him."

She didn't ask the judge's name, the reason for the meeting, where they found Gemma, how it happened that Ponca City and not Christopher Park was the jurisdiction, nothing that I'd memorized and had at the ready.

"Then that's different," she said and told my father who answered so that I could hear, "If it's her work, then she has to do it." My mother asked, "What does that mean for us?"

"Only that I'll be home on Tuesday instead of Monday. Same time, everything, okay?"

She was mentally putting away the food she'd prepared for tomorrow, rescheduling the next day, putting anticipation in a more remote place.

"I guess it'll have to be."

"I love you, Mama."

"I know you do. Here, talk to your father."

"Papa?"

"The tree's a beauty, hits the ceiling the way you like. There's not much room left in the living room."

"Then we'll give the tree the living room and we'll take Mama's kitchen."

"Be careful in Chicago."

I hung up the phone. Leo was behind me. He handed me a tiny porcelain Holstein, her body curved and generous. I put my thumb in the hollow of its midsection, the place where I'd leaned my head that day at Joey's. "So you don't forget me when you get back to the big city," Leo said.

"I don't have anything for you."

"Is *that* what you think?" he said.

After we ate, we stopped talking until early in the morning in the dark, while the train in Galveston was being washed outside, vacuumed inside. While we took a shower, and I giggled, my mouth full of water most of the time because I didn't know the etiquette and bumped into Leo or blocked the water until he asked me if I needed stage directions, the train was crossing the Brazos River. When we ordered breakfast and ate inside that room as big as the world I loved after Communion, the train crossed the Red River. We took a walk in a drizzle, and before we ran up the two flights of stairs, I noticed the man at the desk smile at us as though we were something new in the world. When the Santa Fe rumbled over the Washita, and the day was dimming, I began to talk, to hurry, and Leo seemed to understand I couldn't stop either.

We were driving to the depot while the train crossed the Cimarron. Leo carried my bags to the platform where the stationmaster, who did a double-take when he saw me, tagged them.

"Six minutes 'til train time," he said. I felt for the tiny Holstein in my pocket as though I were reaching for my mother's hand.

"Remember kiddo, remember what I said."

"What, Leo?"

"Don't pretend it didn't happen."

We heard the Santa Fe growl, felt the trembling beneath us before we saw the yellow and black bumblebee cars. It hissed to a stop.

Suddenly, a conductor was putting a little stool underneath the steps.

I had one foot up, one down, Leo's arm around my waist.

The conductor urged me forward. "We'll take good care of your young lady, sir," he said to Leo.

Leo whispered, "You call me after you chuck that guy. I'll be waiting."

And then, I was sitting in a coach car on the aisle, straining to see Leo who didn't look back.

"Three no-trump," Chicago says. "Game and rubber. C'mon, kid, let's have a nightcap."

We sip brandy while the Santa Fe Texas Chief rocks us over the Missouri.

XIX

Cleveland was clamped in an oyster shell. So we walked through twilit noons in the mist and drizzle from clouds that drooped from an opal sky to settle on treetops. It couldn't get cold enough to snow.

The first few days were full of jobs. In the mornings, my mother and I were inside grocery stores buying fresh cheeses and greens. Afternoons, we stopped at department stores downtown to make final choices. A young clerk at Halle's told me the Gino Paoli sweater I was considering for my father was, as far as he knew, only one of two the buyer had brought to Cleveland, but the hand tooled jewelry case he set atop the glass counter was a must for any man of taste. I chose the sweater because the wool was the same moss green as my father's eyes, and it was a good, thick knit that would keep him warm when he walked outside early on chilly spring mornings to think about what would push up from the mud that year. If I'd had money of my own and my mother weren't watching, I'd have had the other sweater sent to Leo. I picked the leather case for Steve. Merry Christmas and good-bye.

"Did Sister like the gloves?" my mother asked while the clerk wrapped the gifts and she paid for them.

"Loved them," I told her.

That night, I stayed downtown to meet Steve who had tickets for the ballet. I'd meet him at the 39 bus stop beside the library on Third and Superior. I ducked into the crowded shelter with a homecoming crowd of last minute shoppers staring into space, glassy-eyed, stuffed thigh to thigh, embracing shopping bags on their laps. Rain skipped under the shelter panels.

A man sat in dove gray near a corner flanked by women with furred breasts, heads covered in bright silk. The only space left free on the bench were the few inches on either side of him. He rocked, hugged himself, whimpering, "Oh-oh-ohm-oohm . . ." He wasn't dressed like a mantra chanter; he was dressed like a Bunce Brothers ad.

I bent in front of him the way you do to find something in a child's eye and asked him what was wrong. He told me he'd come downtown to have dinner at The Tavern, his first time there since his wife died. She died Halloween night. While he was eating, he missed her afresh because her face wasn't across from his at their Saturday night table. He couldn't eat anymore. So he drank until the oak panels blurred, then walked in the rain until he had to sit. Now, he wanted to go home, but he didn't know where he was.

I walked him up Superior, penny bright under street lamps. "Wait here," I told him while I propped him against the side entrance of the Hollendon Hotel. I ran down the garage parking ramp, caught the eye of the attendant and told him I needed a cab. "Around the corner," he said. "In front of the main entrance." There were a dozen lined up looking as though they were wearing wet yellow slickers. I helped him inside the first, used his wallet to give the address, fare and a Christmas tip. I told the driver he was my uncle and I'd appreciate some care. He nodded and tossed me a pillow he had up front. I tucked in Mr. Soltane who hadn't told me his name and he rode home to Shaker Heights, drunk and neat in sober gray.

Steve scolded me because he had to circle the block three times. After I told him about Mr. Soltane, he shook his head. "That was damned foolish. That guy could have been anybody. You're back in town, babe, use your head." He had the same tilt of head and weary tone as my father when he'd say, "What's gotten into you?" I was still simmering a half hour later while Steve watched me watch *The Nutcracker*. Probably waiting for his apology. I stared at the dancers returning from their leaps.

I bumped into my mother in the kitchen the next morning, but she was so glad to see me, she didn't kick me out.

"What's that?" I asked to open the conversation so she could ask me about last night.

"You know."

"I forget." Ask me, I thought, ask me about Steve.

"Baccala."

"Why are you soaking it?"

"Because it's dried, Claire. I have to put the water back in and soak out the salt."

Watching my mother with the mysterious wall of cod reminded me of the cow wrapped in plastic in the church basement and what Frank said was the difference between me and my great grandmother. She wouldn't have thought it remarkable to go into her backyard, wring a chicken's neck, pluck it and serve it for supper. But, if a fly flew into the kitchen, he'd said, I'd probably say we should give the fly the first floor and suggest we all go outside to have supper. "The stuff in Italian women is waning." He had a point.

Steve called. He wanted to go to Harvey's for drinks later. His tone told me he was still waiting for an apology. I told him I couldn't make it because I needed to help my mother, who heard me and lifted her eyebrows.

"He wants to know what he can bring for Christmas Eve," I said while she lifted pale slabs of refreshened fish from the sink.

"I make the dinner," she answered. She didn't like strangers around on Christmas Eve. She turned to have a look at me. "You go ahead and go out tonight if you want." She wasn't going to ask.

"I think I'll call Frank," I said, giving up.

"Whatever." She set a kettle on to boil. "Where's my red pepper?"

"I don't know. Should I look?"

I was dialing. She noticed. "Never mind. You'll just get in the way."

Frank and I had one of our clever chats. He made a few lofty jokes about the cretins in Cincinnati and I called him an elitist snob.

"So, Frank's not coming?" my father asked a few hours later.

"There's a Christmas special on in twenty minutes," my mother said, "and I'd appreciate it if the two of you would finish eating so I can get these dishes done and finally sit down. Perry Como's going to sing 'O Holy Night.' "

My mom and dad shared the sofa in front of the television. I sat on the floor between them. Every once in a while my dad would set his big hand on my head. Christmas. The chorus that opened the show sang carols that answered all the questions we wondered about but forgot to ask in ordinary time. I thought of one of those first men, a pagan. He was small, feral, watching the sun disappear until three days after the shortest day in black cold. He was crouched, watching, running then, running to the women, the children, this leader, to tell them the sun came back. We could sit in rooms where we made out checks for heat, boiled water for pasta, folded sheets, read the newspaper, and tonight, listen to Judy Garland, Nat King Cole and Perry Como sing yes, heaven was waiting. Jesus was waiting. We were safe clamped beneath the oyster sky, winter waiting now for the sun. We weren't afraid to hope.

Father sent an oversize card addressed to my family. He copied out a quote from Saint Paul that suggested the birth of Christ had been a lot of trouble for nothing if people refused to obey his priests. Camille's convent sent a reproduction of Botticelli's angels adoring the babe with a printed signature: SISTERS OF THE FELICIAN ORDER OF MARY. Paula sent a card with a tipsy Santa who looked like my grandfather. He was too laden with bags to get down the chimney. He leaned against it, drinking wine from a green bottle tied with a scarlet bow. She wished me a Merry Christmas with three exclamation points. She told me her mother was finished with her commission for the bank and the portrait of Emily was dry and framed, so when I got back we could all play pinochle together. Kay wrote along the margin: "Happy Days, Claire. A certain handsome man is wandering abroad— sober—looking for someone. Miracles everywhere!"

Kay's message made me feel fragile, and in that condition I treated everyone very carefully so I wouldn't break. Leo had this way of slipping into my life, fully dressed and ready for action, just when I was free floating, pretending as he asked me not to, that nothing had happened. There were moments when I was afraid I'd never see Leo again because I'd let him see too much.

On Christmas Eve morning my dad and I set out twelve box-wood wreaths at Lakeview Cemetery behind the rose granite stones that my mother's father had cut before he died. I scraped off moss and wiped ice crystals from his stone and wondered how he had felt with his hammer and chisel cutting the gothic letters of his own name.

My dad and I worked together without talking. People called him taciturn. They thought his silence was a warning, that he wore his temper like his everyday work clothes, easy and at the ready. But, it was in the silence working together that my father and I spoke. I asked him once on the way back from setting out the Christmas wreaths what kind of work he did in those green twills. "I'm in construction," he'd answered. "And when will you be finished?" I asked. He shook his head.

When we got home, my mother told me to hurry and change, that people came early. Then she handed me the card that arrived while Papa and I were gone. I took it to my bedroom. A square of cream vellum engraved in the center with two holly leaves sharing one bright berry. Leo wrote underneath: " 'Claire' is native to the French. She is pure light."

Steve was prompt.

"So, here's your young man," Uncle Patsy said.

When Aunt Sylvia's husband, Joe, overtook my dad as host, my mother excused herself to fry the smelts.

"Here, Steve," Uncle Joe said. "You don't have a glass. Claire, your friend doesn't have a glass. Wait a minute, maybe you don't want this wine. Want a shot instead?"

Steve was following a plan. He was acquiescent. "Why thank you," the Scotch-drinker said, "I'd prefer wine."

"So, can you make real money in your work? You're an engineer, is that right?" Uncle Joe asked.

"Yes sir, it's possible. I can look to make—"

"Enough to travel?" Uncle Patsy wanted to know. "C'mere Ginnie, tell them about our trip to the old country. Stayed a month. What the hell, I said, Business is good. If you can't enjoy yourself a little after all the years you put in, what good is it? Tell him, Ginnie."

Aunt Ginnie frowned. "It was a nice vacation, I s'pose. Only I told my husband I wouldn't go unless I could have a private bathroom in every hotel."

"First class all the way."

"Do you speak Italian?" Steve asked. He drank the wine in gulps.

"Sure, only they speak in funny dialects over there," my uncle said. "I couldn't understand them. But, the food was wonderful."

Aunt Sylvia joined us. "I could never get used to eating so late," she said. "My stomach . . . I have a very delicate stomach."

Uncle Joe said, "You got to use a lot of money to travel like that, and then, afterwards, what do you have to show for it? Snapshots?"

Uncle Patsy smiled. "A little more, Joe."

"Ah! You're a romantic. Memories go up in smoke. Investments last."

"I invested," Uncle Patsy said and glanced toward his sons. "I got a little grocery business over forty years, Steve, and it finally paid off. I let my boys do most of the work now. It belongs to them anyway."

"And that's another thing," Uncle Joe began and I steered Steve away toward the kids near the Christmas tree. Aunt Nancy was dipping her finger in an oil and vinegar sauce and offering it to Jeannie's baby. He refused. She tried a bit of black olive that he tried to swallow whole.

My mother called that the smelts were nearly ready and sent Jeannie and me to set up two card tables in the livingroom. We carried in the chairs and tables stored in phantom Frank's closet.

"All right," Jeannie said. "Let's have it. Something's going on with you."

"I can't talk about it now."

"So I'm right. There's some guy?"

"Yeah, but not now."

"Did you meet him in the middle of September?"

"How did you know?"

"Your letters changed."

"No kidding?"

"Steve doesn't know, right?"

"Right. And he's got a ring. He could whip it out any time."

"You have to tell him."

"I want to tell him."

"You've been home for three days."

"I'm waiting for the right moment," I said.

"There's no right moment, Claire. None. Ever."

She set a chair in place while she thought it over. "Do you love this other guy?" she asked.

I nodded.

"Thunderbolts?"

"Uh-huh," I admitted.

She put an arm around me. "Finally! Don't worry. We'll figure something out. But, take that look off your face. It's like a sign or something. We can't spoil the family's Christmas Eve. You're safe for tonight."

"Claire! Jeannie!" My mother saw an entire table set without linen napkins. I headed for my room where she kept them in my bottom dresser drawer. Aunt Sylvia and Steve were standing in the doorway.

"Claire's room," she was saying. "My sister, Mary, crocheted that bedspread, and that desk belonged to my father, God rest his soul. Claire's a sloppy girl, but she's young and someday, I think, she'll take good care of her things."

"Excuse me," I said and brushed past them into my room made perfect for company. "Napkins," I said to Aunt Sylvia who smiled through her tears. Steve's face was flushed. He looked too big for my parents' hallway.

Jeannie put Steve next to her at the table and me down the line. But, he interrupted the plan. He was up, smiling at my cousin next to me, asking if he could trade places. We are a courteous people, especially to guests in our homes.

Uncle Patsy brushed the top of my head and winked at Steve before he sat down.

"This is a lovely party," Steve said to everyone, then whispered to me, "I cannot believe you fit all these people into this tiny house."

"What do you think of the wine? Tell the truth," Uncle Patsy said.

"Wonderful," Steve answered.

"Ohio concord. My sons and I make it every year."

"And every year you drink too much," my father said.

"It's good to see you at this table again," Uncle Patsy told me.

"And *eat* something," Aunt Nancy said. "You got thin."

Steve whispered, "I've got a room for us—downtown—soon as we get out of here."

Just then, my mother announced, "I have the bowls warming in the oven, Claire. It'll turn to paste if I let it stand, and I didn't do all this work to serve glue."

Aunt Sylvia wound through the two rooms and left bowls of flaked baccala with olive oil and red pepper, platters of sliced navel oranges with black pepper, and relish dishes with olives and celery behind. Aunt Nancy tucked her grandson into a makeshift high chair while my dad sliced the bread, the loaf held to his chest, slicing towards his heart. He dropped the heel, picked it up and kissed it. "The staff of life," he said. If Frank had been home, he'd have drained the pasta, but as it was, Uncle Patsy did it.

"Where's your brother tonight?" he asked me while he shook the colander.

"Who knows?" I said. "When does he tell you anything? I miss him tonight."

"Something wrong?"

"We have to get this on the table, Uncle. My mother'll kill us."

When everything was ready and on the table, my mother sat. "Well, has Claire told you about her adventures in the West, Steve?" She passed him the smelts. "Try some."

He fumbled with his napkin. Maybe he thought they were

minnows. He cut one in half, bit a small piece of that and said, "Mild. It has a mild flavor."

My dad grinned. "You hate it," he said. "Drink something and rinse the taste out of your mouth." He emptied Steve's plate and filled it with pasta. He was very generous with my mother's sauce. Uncle Patsy put a fresh bottle of wine in front of Steve, who looked at his plate and then at me for deliverance. He put the first forkful to his mouth and smiled with relief.

"Lovely," he told my mother. Later he asked for more, added a shake of pepper seeds, and sprinkled cheese, like snow, over it all. Underneath the tablecloth, he found my knee when he could take time from his plate. His glass was always full.

After dinner, I said, "Your eyes are glazed."

"Can we go now?" He asked. "I mean, we *did* dinner. Who'd notice?"

The women, except for Jeannie who was putting her baby to bed, were gathering around the sink to do dishes. My uncles were folding the card tables and chairs, and my dad was sweeping crumbs from the living room rug. Who'd notice?

"Everyone," I told him.

"What about the Hollendon? I told you, I have a room for us tonight. When *can* we leave?"

"I am not leaving. It's nearly time for Mass."

"Christ Claire," he said. "How long are we going to play this game?"

The things we say to one another. There it was in my hands. The opening. I could have settled the question of Steve right there and then. Instead, I said, "You're drunk."

"I am not drunk. I know exactly what I'm saying and what we'll do when we're alone. How long am I supposed to wait?"

I stepped back so I could give him a more level look.

"Go home, Steve. Or go to that room at the Hollendon by yourself. That's who you're talking to anyway."

"What the hell—" he started, but my dad interrupted.

"Excuse me," he said. "Can I talk to you?"

"Sure," I answered, "Steve has to leave. He was just saying good-bye."

My dad took me as far as the door to the furnace room and said as softly as he could, "Call your brother and tell him to call here. Surprise your mother."

"Ah, Papa . . ."

"Take the phone into the utility room. No one'll notice."

"But Papa . . ."

He was finished talking. I heard the echo of my mother's last words on the subject that afternoon while we polished furniture: "And I don't care if I *never* hear from him. Don't you *dare* let him know we even talked about him, do you hear me, Claire?"

They were neither of them easy people to lie to. Which one tonight? That dumb Frank could have dialed our number, I thought, and heard myself begin to think like my mother. I took the phone into the utility room and called collect. Susan answered. We exchanged Merry Christmases warily. I waited as I was supposed to for her to ask if I'd like to speak to Frank.

"Frank! Merry Christmas!"

"Hi," a bleak, remote voice.

"I called because, you know, everyone's here tonight. And maybe you'd like to call and surprise them."

"I have people in right now." (The cretins?) "I was going to call tomorrow."

So why not call both times, I thought. "Sure," I said, "only you know, Christmas Eve is special for—"

"For Mama?" he asked. "Is that it? Is it a contest?"

"Never mind," I said. "Happy New Year."

I put the phone back while my father watched.

"And?" his cocked head asked.

"I don't know," my shrug answered.

The phone didn't ring.

Steve made the rounds and finished, after thanking my mother and father, by glaring at me. When the door closed behind him, Jeannie held up her thumb and index finger touching in a circle.

Aunt Sylvia reminded us it was almost time for midnight Mass, no more coffee or cookies. We had to fast for Communion. She read the whole church law from her Sunday bulletin every Christmas as though our transgressions would go on her record. Afterwards, she took my arm. "Why did your young man leave?" I hugged her. "His family, Aunt, he wanted to be with his family."

"How sweet . . . how good," she murmured.

Old Father Sebastian was the celebrant. His face was an olive wash and withered like a shrinking pear. He looked lost in his holiday robes, and tired. He was up late. We sat at perfect attention in the first rows, we DeStefanos, and at Communion we stood before this little priest with our mouths open like babies waiting for food.

I went right to bed after Mass. I heard my mother on the other side of the wall. "Some cocoa?" My dad said yes.

"I don't think she's happy with that Steve," my mother said and my dad growled some response.

"She'll never tell us," my mother said.

I sat up.

"You don't suppose she'll go through with it just so she won't upset anyone?"

My father didn't answer.

"We did something wrong," my mother said. "They're both like that."

"She speaks up," my father said.

"Don't let that fool you. She only does that here. With us."

"Talk to her," my dad said.

"She won't give me an opening."

"That never stopped you before."

"She's unhappy. Something's happened. Something's changed and she doesn't know what to do."

"Talk to her."

"I don't know. I don't know," my mother said.

I thought they were finished because they were quiet for so long. Then my father said, "Don't worry. She can take care of herself."

XX

"Do me a favor," my mother said a few days after Christmas. "Don't talk about Steve to your father."

"Why not?"

"Because I don't think he likes him. He doesn't trust a man who says lovely. That's what he told me, anyway."

"Lovely?"

"He called my pasta lovely. Your father noticed that."

"What about you?"

"Finish your breakfast. If you're going to Peggy's wedding— and that *party*—you need a dress." It was an order. "Jeanne's going with you to pick it out." She put a blank check in front of my cereal bowl.

"What for?" I nodded to the boxes of new clothes underneath the Christmas tree.

"A *good* dress," she said.

Jeanne and I went to a small shop my mother reserved for occasions of pride: her son's graduation from medical school, her granddaughter's baptism, Jeanne's wedding. She thought Mrs. Anderson's party belonged in the same company. So far, I was the only one who knew I wasn't going to that party. Jeanne pulled a dress from the group a svelte woman brought out for me. "This one," she said. It was a silk the color of Santa Rosa plums, and it wrapped perfectly around my waist. It was so light that it fluttered in a whisper of air. When I saw myself tripled on the mirrored platform, I was surprised.

"I look—"

"Elegant," Jeanne said. "See what the right dress can do?"

"But I don't need it. I'm not going to that engagement party."

"Take it back with you. It's the only thing you own that isn't a sack. He'll love it."

"Leo?"

"Wear it for him. Now, what are you going to tell Steve?"

"Why don't you tell me what to tell him?"

"Nope. Not my field. What about the truth?"

She had a point.

My mother was pleased. "Put your coat on in the bedroom before you leave. I don't want your father to see you looking like that."

A dress. A day given over to a dress that cost too much. I could translate it into hours my father spent working in ditches, and if I thought longer, to my mother's scant closet. My volunteer work was costing my parents a lot of money. It was a gift that shouldn't be wasted, I thought, while I did everything I could think of to make my face and hair beautiful before Peggy's wedding.

Peggy, in white velvet, walked up a long aisle, said her vows to Lou while the priest listened. She knelt, left a sheaf of roses at the Blessed Virgin's altar and turned to face us in perfect timing with the organ's peal. I smiled at them when they passed me, looking for signs of change. But, it was a puff of smoke, this ceremony, a secret. I missed the exchange. I took my eyes off the magician's hands.

Afterwards, we drank champagne and ate lobster puffs and drank more champagne in the ancient paneled room of the Wade Park Manor. We were dressed in Christmas red, emerald green, peacock blue. My friends applauded the plum silk. Waiters in white starched cotton carried trays of champagne bubbling in slender coils. We were like a moving painting within those dark, mellow walls. We absorbed the light. We all drank too much. I'd glance at Peggy and Lou now and then like a spy, but the secret was safe with them. Steve looked perfect in this room, bending to pick up a tart, offering me a bite, his arm around my waist, squiring me from group to group. "Aren't five months enough?" he asked. "You don't have to go back. You didn't sign a contract." When I didn't answer, he indulged me.

Leo would have been preposterous here. They wouldn't have been able to classify him.

I listened to Ella Fitzgerald on the ride home. When we parked in front of my house, knee to knee, elbow to elbow in Steve's Austin Healy, I knew the wedding was finally over. Lou and Peggy were in a plane on their way to New York and the Waldorf, but Steve and I were back where we began, only without the grape hyacinth and dappled moonlight. I was out of time, too. The engagement party was two days off.

The street was glazed with ice, bare branches were steel blue under the streetlight. Steve took my hand and slipped on the ring. The stone was a marquis. The setting was old, heavy. It slipped sideways, between my fingers. I held my hand away from myself and it flashed.

"I know something about you," Steve said.

What did he know. That I wanted this ring off my finger?

"I knew you didn't want me to give you this in front of other people. Am I right?"

"It's beautiful," I began.

"It's a perfect stone, Claire, no flaws. Like you. The setting's my grandmother's." Then gently, "Are you sure?"

My God, I thought, he knows I'm not sure.

"There wouldn't be anything wrong if you weren't, you know," he said.

"Yes, I do, I do know. That's right."

He nodded with me. "There might be if you'd signed a contract with that priest," he went on, "but you didn't. You've already done more than most people would dream of doing, and I bet no one's thanked you for it. You weren't meant for that kind of life. And you don't owe anyone, anything. One phone call, Claire, five minutes, and you're home free. In a month, two, we'll have a wedding like this one. My mother will arrange the whole thing. And then, Paris first, after that, it's up to you."

I shivered.

He turned on the motor and heater and waited, smiling, beautiful. I took three deep breaths before I pulled it off.

"I can't keep this," I said.

His smile didn't change.

I opened his hand and put the ring into his palm and babbled, "It's beautiful—it really is—but since I left here—I mean—since I began to teach—things changed—I don't know—things happened. I'm just not ready for this."

"You're just a little scared. It's all right." He put the ring back into my hand and closed my fingers over it. "Keep it overnight, babe. Show it to your parents in the morning. I'll come by early, and you'll see, everything will be fine."

"No, Steve, no, everything will not be fine."

"Sure it will."

No spring breeze, no sun and water to put me back together, no friends in the crowd to help and panic bubbling from the deeps.

"Steve, listen—"

"I'm listening."

He was.

"I can't marry you."

He shifted. His smile thinned. "All right, all right, forget what I said. Go back and finish the year if you think you have to."

"That's not it. That's not the reason."

He began to unbutton my coat. "I love you in that dress. You're so pretty . . ."

I pushed his hands away. I said, "I'm not in love with you."

"What you're not is relaxed. Hush now, just hush. Go inside and get some sleep. That's all you need, a little sleep. The champagne and this, it's too much at once."

I backed against the door, cornered. "You don't want me to repeat that, do you?"

It seemed I waited a long time for an answer and it came as a question in a voice I'd never heard. "Is there someone else?"

"Of course not." A reflex. But what business was it of his? What right did he have to ask that? Who did he think he was?

"Who is it? Someone in that farm town? A *farmer?*"

I returned the ring once more and rubbed out the nicks in my palm from clutching it. "I would never be happy with you, Steve."

"That's it? I'm supposed to take that with no argument?"

"This isn't an argument. It's just the way things are."

"You don't have the first idea how things are. You go off somewhere like a goddamn romantic with this glint in your eye, and you come back to tell me—for reasons unknown—that you aren't in love with me anymore."

"I was never in love with you."

"What the hell did you think you were doing, then? Do you remember what you wrote to me? What were those phone calls about? Do you remember those phone calls at two in the morning?"

That was me, too. "I remember," I told him. "I'm sorry."

"Sorry? You're sorry?"

"Yes, I'm sorry. But, that's all. You can't shove yourself in front of someone and say, 'Love me!' It doesn't work that way. I know. I tried. Are you supposed to have to try?"

"So, there *is* another guy? I wonder what he's offering."

No confession with Father Sebastian had been as painful as this. My dress was damp from sweating inside my winter coat, and there was the familiar pricking underneath my arms. But, I hung on because I was past the worst.

". . . in some fairy tale," he was saying. "Walking around in a bubble—"

"Stop that!"

"You know, my mother warned me. Marriage is a practical matter and she told me you aren't a practical woman. She knew what she was talking about. She made it work with my father. He'd have been a solitary old drunk without her. And look at him!"

Befuddled nightly after too many martinis, picking his way to bed after murky bridge games with his son and wife and me. We, politely ignoring his slurring and stumbling.

"You'll be back, babe," he said. "You'll be calling my number when you're lonely. But, I'm not promising anything."

It was over. He finished with a threat. I pushed down my door handle. I thought maybe you never know anyone, really know them, until you tell them, no. I was on the top step of the porch when I heard him gun the motor and felt something like delight, the first pleasant sensation from this broken engagement. Then, wild with relief once I was inside, I opened the refrigerator and took out a bowl of olives, whispering to myself, "It's over! I did it! I did it!" I looked at myself in the living room mirror. She looked right back, the pretty girl in the plum silk. Funny, how that made me feel strong and clear so I knew that the only thing left to do before sleeping in peace was to call Leo.

Five rings. A sort of shuffling pick-up.

"H'lo?" I heard. I missed the "hel-*lo* there" that was mine.

"Leo?"

"Claire? Is that you?"

"Yes. I know, I know it's three in the morning, but I have something wonderful, just wonderful to tell you."

And it was somewhere in the middle of the telling that I heard the cough, the catarrh cough of a heavy smoker, the treble note that unmistakably identified it as a woman's cough.

I put the receiver back onto its cradle. I hung my new dress in my closet, folded my slip, and found an old pair of ski pajamas in my bottom drawer under my mother's linens. Barefoot, I walked across the hall to my mother's room, which was Frank's old bedroom and wondered, fleeting thought, why my mother and father slept in separate bedrooms. She kept little red pills, like M&Ms, in an envelope marked FOR NERVES in the top drawer of Frank's old bureau. I took one while I watched her for signs of waking, but she slept on. In the kitchen, I took the pill and methodically rinsed out the empty olive dish remembering my mother's warning to Frank and me before company came: "Two olives each and that's all!" Tonight though, like a squint-eyed child, I'd eaten them all.

I picked my way to my bedroom like Mr. Anderson, weirdly sober, in a haze. I sat at my desk for a moment to see from my window what had been my world for twenty years, and it looked different. There was a reason. It finally got cold enough to snow.

XXI

The next morning I woke in the dark, bright with the moon glancing off snow. I came awake slowly, drifting into consciousness, trying to remember how I ended up on top of the covers wrapped in my robe. Rinsing the olive bowl at the sink was the last thing I could call up. I felt something unfinished, like the bent corner of a page that can't be smoothed out until the book is opened and that page read, but it was a blur until my bare feet touched the cold floor. And I remembered. I heard my window shiver in a blast of wind, the click of a bare rose bush hitting it.

While I pulled on wool socks and old jeans lined in flannel, I tried to remember a day in my life when I was up and dressed before my dad stoked the furnace and shoveled in the first coal of the day, and couldn't. I found my old skating jacket near the snow shovel in the utility room and went outside to clear the driveway, but the porch was filled with a drift of sugary snow capped with frozen crystals. I didn't want to touch it. I caught snowflakes on my tongue, squinted up to see them settling on my hair. But, it was so cold, I had to move, finally. I broke into the pretty drift with the edge of the shovel and worked down the steps while the moon sank and the sun rose, sending gold and coral streams rushing over the perfect snow.

The kitchen windows flared with sudden yellow light.

My mother opened the door a crack and yelled, "Get in here! It's *zero* out there!" I stamped snow off my boots and saw her in early light wrapped in a crimson robe, her hair loose, falling in auburn waves to her shoulders. She was beautiful right then. She turned her back after I shut the door, busy at the stove toasting bread and heating milk for cocoa. My throat ached and I couldn't swallow it back.

"What's this?" she said. "What *is* this?" while she took me by the shoulders and pushed me into a chair. She turned off the burner and sat facing me.

"Stop crying, Claire. You've just been out in the freezing cold and you'll chap your face."

But I couldn't stop, so she brought me tissues and waited a little while.

"All right now, that's enough. Something's very wrong here and I want to know what it is. Did that Steve do something to hurt you?"

I managed to tell her between blowing my nose and sucking in shuddering breaths that Steve had given me a ring and I had given it right back.

"I had a feeling about him. Now, is that what you really wanted to do?"

I nodded.

"You're not sorry this morning?"

"Oh, no."

She put her hand at the back of my neck to feel for a fever. "All right then, all right. Then you can stop crying. Remember, everything passes, even the good things. But I think there's something else. Ever since you got back, I've had the feeling that something happened in that town that you didn't tell me about. Is there something else? Tell me the truth."

It was what I'd asked Leo the last time we were together. "Is there a chance for us. Do you think so? Tell me the truth." And he'd said, "How can I tell you the truth if I think it might help you to think twice? When I want to tell you only the things that will convince you it's perfect for you to love me."

"Yes." I answered my mother before I could stop myself. "Something happened."

The *Cleveland Plain Dealer* whacked against the door, the paperboy's ski cap passing like a scarlet fish in the lowest door panes just as my dad walked into the kitchen dressed in his green twills. He took one look at my mother bending over me and made a wide path around us to the furnace where he pulled out clinkers and shoveled in coal with smooth, fluid strokes. I stuffed used Kleenex into my pockets while my mother stared me down. "You'd think the enemy had landed," she muttered. Papa brought the newspaper in and handed me the funnies. "Aren't you two up a little early?" he asked.

"Right. I wanted to shovel out the driveway for you," I said evenly.

"Claire," my mother said, "what were you going to tell me?"

I shrugged, nothing. She threw up her hands and went back to making cocoa.

"I'll be right back," I said. "Have to wash my face."

I heard my dad ask, "What's wrong with her?"

My mother lapsed into the Italian she used when she wanted to keep something from Frank and me. *"Essa piange.* Leave her alone."

"But why?"

"I still don't know. You walked in too soon."

In a little while the kitchen was warm. My mother was serving us and murmuring to herself. She took the Sunday sauce with spareribs for me from the refrigerator while my dad looked over the sports page and I pretended to read the comics. "We'll just have this tonight even if it isn't Sunday," she said.

"What, Mary?"

"I said we'll have pasta tonight instead of Sunday," she answered.

"No kidding?" he said, putting down the newspaper. "So then, let's decide," he said, beginning the ritual of choosing the pasta. He opened a cupboard and took down a few boxes. "These?"

My mother glanced at the box. "She doesn't like stovepipes, Andy, and she's only home for another week."

"Then how about the linguine? You like linguine, don't you, Claire?" he asked, teasing.

"Sure, Dad."

"You do not," my mother said. "Say what you mean, for

once." And to my father, "She likes cappellini and you know it."

"But we just had them on Christmas Eve," my dad said. "Claire won't mind if we have the . . ."

"What?" my mother demanded. She didn't like nonsense when one of her children showed up wounded. She was scrubbing the clean stove furiously. "Have the *what?*"

When my dad didn't answer, I looked at him. My mother stopped scrubbing and looked, too. He was leaning against the counter with a silly grin on his face. He looked a little drunk.

"What is the *matter* with you? Tell us what you want, will you please," my mother said.

My father spoke. It was the sound of animals.

When he stopped, he looked at us as though he'd answered.

My mother was beside him. I stared, frozen. She took the box from his hands, the compromise box which we knew was spaghetti because it always was. "Spaghetti, Andy. Say spa-ghet-ti."

He looked at the box, at her, and tried again. Gibberish. He looked as though he were chewing taffy. My mother repeated that word over and over. Papa lifted an arm so slowly, it seemed to float. More guttural sounds broke from his mouth. His eyes were open, unblinking, as if he were a reluctant audience to this scene. I put a kitchen chair behind him, and Mama helped him into it. His mouth was still working.

"Call an ambulance," she told me.

The next time we saw him, his green twills were on a hanger against the white curtain in the emergency room cubicle. An adolescent neurosurgeon was bending over him.

"What happened to my father?" I asked.

"A small stroke," the boy answered. He wore an oversize silver-and-turquoise belt buckle like a trophy. He kept talking, explaining in latinate phrases, but I didn't hear him. My mother, at the bed, holding my father's hand, didn't even pretend to listen.

I broke into his monologue. "I want you to call my brother," I told him. "He's an internist in Cincinnati. I'll give you his number. You call him and you tell him everything."

I wiped my father's face which was red and damp with perspiration. He pulled back from my touch.

We stayed with him until they assigned him a private room on the seventh floor overlooking a roiled Lake Erie. He tried to make words all that morning, but stopped trying toward afternoon. He set his mouth and his eyes against us. He watched the lake do its work. At first dark, they asked us to leave.

When I kissed him good-bye, he seemed to come awake. He said something that ended with "key." "Key?" I asked. "We have our keys."

He shook his head, no, an angry, whatisthematterwithyou, no. "Key—key—kkkhee—" He looked at his hand so I would, too, and clenched his fist over and over.

"Keep?" I asked.

He nodded. Then, "Mmm—mmm—mmmph—" and looked at my mother.

"Mama?" I said.

Yes. And with more effort, straining, he tried, "Kuh—kuh—kkk—" He swallowed, pushed his lips together like a Mussolini mask and hummed, "Ummm—ummmm."

"Kuh—um," I repeated like Harry Lee, as lost as he must have been. Papa put his hands together over and over, and it came to me that he was shaking his own hand. "Company, Papa?"

He let out a strained breath, dismissed me with a wave of his hand and closed his eyes. I was to keep my mother company.

The parking lot was nearly empty. New snow, falling and drifting at the lake edge, filled tire tracks and footprints, so our tracks to my dad's car, an enormous white Mercury that he and Mama nicknamed Queen Mary, broke the crust and puddled where my mother stopped to check her purse for her house keys and wallet a couple of times. Midway, she slipped her hand in mine.

My dad bought a model with push button drive because it was new, I guess. It was certainly new to me. I stared at the small panel of typewriter keys glowing to the left of the steering wheel without really seeing them. I pushed drive instead of reverse, then stalled in neutral and jerked backwards. My mother stared ahead at the boiling lake, forgetting to light the cigarette she held in a gloved hand, forgetting to scold me for skidding. She wore rubber boots that snapped at the ankle and the snaps were undone. Snow filled the opening. Something told me not to brush it away.

We could hear the phone ringing while she fumbled with the house key on the dark porch. It stopped and started immediately once we were inside. She forgot to switch on the lights. She walked right past the ringing phone. I lifted the receiver carefully and said, "Yes?"

A stranger asked if I were Mrs. DeStefano. "Yes," I answered. The woman identified herself as the neurosurgeon's nurse. She sounded old enough to be his mother. I watched my mother return the house keys to her purse, zip it, open it, reach inside for the keys, tuck them back. I gritted my teeth. She still wore her coat and snow from her boots was melting on the living room carpet. The woman, the nurse, was telling me that the doctor had contacted Dr. DeStefano. It took me a second to place him as Frank. She said that Dr. DeStefano had been "fully apprised of the current situation." I thanked her and told her we'd see her in the morning.

"Just a moment," she said. A moment. I waited. My mother had wandered to the sofa and then down the hallway. "It would appear that your husband has suffered another episode."

"Episode?" I asked to stop her.

"Yes, one that has rendered him unconscious for now."

"Unconscious," I repeated.

"For now," she said.

I whispered, "He's in a coma?"

"Yes," she answered. "We're giving him every possible assistance. There's no immediate danger. Of course, there's no way of telling right now how long this situation will continue."

"Is he going to die?" I asked the nurse, but I hadn't spoken.

"Are you there?" she asked.

"Yes," I said.

"Your son suggests that you wait to hear from him before anything else. He will call tonight. There is absolutely nothing you can do at the hospital. Mrs. DeStefano?"

"Yes."

"Do you understand?"

"Thank you," I said and hung up.

I was shivering in my coat. The monolithic furnace wasn't blowing. I read VIKING STOKER scripted inside an oval on the door Papa opened with a gloved hand when he shoveled in the coal. I touched it with a wet finger, like testing an iron. It was cool. I opened it. Pale gold embers glowed inside. I picked up his coal shovel, a slick short-handled, cupped spade, pulled open the low door of the coal bin behind me. I slid the shovel inside the way I'd seen him do it, brought it out on a low swing, arcing up, and spilled the coal. I picked it up and threw it inside. I watched a little flame, a candle flare, rise and die. When I stopped imitating his swift, sure strokes, I got most of the coal inside and wondered how much was enough. I stopped shoveling when I saw a crust of flame, sapphire licked with gold, burn steadily. I waited for the buzzing growl that signaled blowers starting. It happened. Miracles everywhere. I was black and silty when I came out and washed up, just like my father, at the kitchen sink. Coal dust didn't belong in our bathroom.

Then Frank called.

My mother listened to him for a long time, her face unaltered by whatever she heard. She motioned to me with her index and third finger touching that she wanted her cigarettes. The Chesterfields were on the coffee table where Papa left them. I carried them like a relic to the kitchen with his matches and the ashtray that held his dead stub from the morning. My mother smoked, holding that cigarette like a wand, winking smoke away from the corner of her eye. She stabbed it into the ashtray at the end without ever saying much of anything to Frank. "Here's your sister," she said and handed me the phone. "Tell her." She left the room.

"Does she know?" Frank asked, breathless.

"What?"

"Does she know Papa's in a coma?"

"I didn't tell her."

"Thank God. I was hoping to get through before they called her."

"They called. They thought I was her. They told me."

"Okay, good so far," he said. "What you do is make her eat something."

"She doesn't even know the house is cold and dark. How am I supposed to—"

"Okay, if she won't eat, give her some orange juice and make her go to bed. She needs sleep more than anything."

"Frank?"

"What?"

"Is he going to die?"

"Of course not."

"How do you know?"

"Cut that out. She'll hear you."

"She didn't even hear *you*. She's not listening to anything."

"It isn't tragedy yet, Claire."

"Say that in this kitchen, buddy."

"All right, take it easy," he said.

We let a little long distance time pass.

"What's she going to say when she finds out we kept this from her?"

"We both know," he said. "But I'll be home as soon as I can clear my calendar. I'll tell her it was my idea. Okay?"

I told him it was okay because I couldn't imagine myself telling her the truth.

"You, too," he was saying. "You get some sleep."

He talked like it was a piece of fruit you could pick off a tree.

"And try to keep the family at bay," he finished.

I found my mother sitting on the edge of my dad's bed in the dark. I turned on the light. "You can take off your coat now," I told her. "The house is warming up." I knelt to pull off her boots. She pulled her foot back.

"Warm up the car," she said. "We have to go back. I have this feeling."

"Mama, no. It's late. And Frank says—"

"What in the world does Frank know? Frank lives on the other side of the world."

She opened a drawer and found a scarf. She tied it over her hair. "Do we have enough gas in the tank?" she asked.

We heard car tires crunching snow outside, then the flare of headlights in the bedroom window. I answered the door to Uncle Patsy just as the phone rang again. It was Aunt Nancy, who said she was on her way, but not before she told me she wondered just what was going on in my mind that I didn't call and tell her what happened. She had to hear from a neighbor that my mother and I were leaving the hospital at suppertime.

It was all so strange because until she said that, I thought it must be midnight, an odd hour for my aunts and uncle to be up. I looked at the clock. It was only six-thirty.

"Make some coffee, dear," Aunt Sylvia said a half hour later. "Put out the nice bone china cups to cheer up your mother." I made the coffee and filled the cups and put out my mother's holiday butter ring. And they sat in their places and talked it over, gave orders, touched my shoulder. A thrill of panic made me shiver. I knew things they didn't. I knew they couldn't help at all. My mother sat with them and belonged with them. No one was with my father. And no one knew where he had traveled alone tonight. They asked me questions and for a while I answered carefully. Only, they didn't want answers. Uncle Patsy wanted a blueprint. Aunt Nancy wanted a happy ending. My pockets were empty. "Call Frank," I said.

They left by nine. My mother and I looked at one another. There was more night than we needed.

I poured a glass of orange juice for her and brought her two of the little red pills from her envelope. I couldn't believe she didn't protest either. Or my help putting her to bed. I remembered her hand holding mine in the parking lot.

I watched her fall asleep. For a while, she lay too still, and then, a polite turn, a courtesy to the mattress. Her hair loosened and fell over the arch of a high cheekbone, her eyes shut to light and images, mouth in repose.

I put away the Sunday sauce before I swallowed one of her little red pills and thought just before the swift rush of euphoria dropped me into slow eddies of sleep, I'd have to tell Frank to bring us more of them.

XXII

The next morning, I stalled in my bedroom as long as I could. My mother called for me to hurry.

"We can't see him until eleven," I called back.

"There's plenty to do before we leave. And I want to be there early."

We'll be there soon enough, I thought, while Uncle Patsy, who'd come at dawn, forced the old furnace to rumble into action.

We were at the hospital before ten and passed the nurses' station unnoticed. The door to my father's room was open. He lay in state except for the tubes attached to him. My mother knelt to wake him. When she understood that he wasn't responding the way he should, her voice rose in a ragged scream. The floor nurse took her out all the while telling her that my father could hear her and understand everything we said. My mother actually believed her.

"Why wasn't I informed?" she asked, the formal woman.

"But you were. By the night staff. I have a note on my chart." I held my breath.

"I received no such call. Do you think I could have been told such a thing and stayed away? I'd have slept on your couch!"

The nurse apologized while I hung back. They agreed there had been a mistake, someone's mistake.

"Where is that *doctor?*" my mother asked. "I want to have a little talk with *him.*"

The nurse promised to notify her as soon as he started rounds. That satisfied her, and I was safe for the moment unless she decided to track down the night nurse who called. My mother could be relentless. Right now, she pulled up a chair to the head of my dad's bed next to his good ear and spoke to him.

". . . and she's getting the hang of the car now, Andy," she was telling him, "only you'd have clenched your teeth that first day. The snow, oh, you should have seen the snow on the boulevard. We made the first tracks this morning. Frank'll be here soon, you know. Did I tell you? Tonight if the snow isn't too bad. I lit the candle. And don't worry about the furnace because Patsy's starting it up mornings. Our famous children are too intellectual for that kind of thing. I don't even want to mention the mess Claire made when she tried doing it. And, anyway, I think it's time we got a gas furnace like everyone else in America, don't you? I guess I'll let Claire tell you about the Browns. I read something about Paul Brown and Jim Brown fighting about something. I didn't pay much attention . . ."

The nurse whispered close to her ear that the doctor was in the hospital, so my mother said, "I'm going to the cafeteria to have a cigarette and a cup of coffee. Claire's here and I'll be right back."

I bent to kiss him and he seemed to slip away from me. It was missing, the tobacco and ripe sawdust and damp earth I smelled when I kissed him hello after work. They'd shaved him and washed him and now he smelled like hospital soap. I sat in Mama's chair and started with my cue about the Browns which led me nowhere. I listened to him breathing. I talked about the fields in Christopher Park, the hawk I saw carrying a baby bird that escaped, and waited for him to interrupt. My father didn't have conversations, he couldn't hear them. He'd speak and leave. This was new. If he'd only listen for a minute, I used to think. He was listening now. What could I tell him?

"I love you, Papa."

I remembered the last thing we did together, he and I, painting the living room just before I left town. "Remember that, Papa?" I asked. We had to move all the furniture first. "Let's start with the sofa," he'd said. "Tip it to the right, to the *right,* at a slant, that's what *tip* means. No, no, don't sit down. Mary, she's sitting on the floor laughing. What's the matter with her?" And my mother said, *"Help* your father, Claire." My father stood in the middle of the living room, holding up his end, asking, "Are you finished now? Your mother wants this room painted today some time." I tried. I focused on the directions he gave in that patient tone as though he were talking to someone who was very sick. "Okay, good enough, through the arch, the same thing! Tip it. Shim it a little. Now we're steamboating! Now walk these legs sideways so we don't scratch the walls. *Side*ways! Up a little more—can't you *see?* Wait now, stop, you're pushing me into the stove. Let it down. I'll carry the weight . . ."

By the time we left, my mother's eyes were shadowed in fatigue. On the drive home in the early dark, she slipped away like Papa did, both of them meditating, awake and asleep. I watched the neon glow of the rising moon cap the marquee of the Shore Theater, the couples bent against the wind buying tickets. It looked so simple. Buy a ticket, see a movie, have a hamburger afterwards and talk it over.

By the time I'd picked up the morning newspaper and unlocked the back door, my mother was almost as remote as my father. I stood under the kitchen light while she drifted through, touching the oilcloth, the radio in the living room. Leo and I should have walked hand in hand through this kitchen door. My mother and father should have nodded yes when we did. Yes, that's the man for her. But, my father quit before it could happen. And my mother sat on the sofa like a guest in her own home, searching corners for escape, sat like Camille, swimming in time with only numbered hours to divide the day into reasons.

The phone rang.

"Frank's on the way," I told her. "He stopped downtown to call. He'll be here in a half hour."

"Make sure there's something for him to eat," she said without looking up. "And change the bed in there."

I changed the sheets on Frank's bed where I was allowed to work but not visit and wondered if the silent thing that swallowed my parents would get Frank, too.

Frank arrived with Susan instead of my niece, who was the

only one who might have saved us a little. Susan was bristling with tension. While we were alone in the kitchen, she told me she didn't want to leave my niece with a sitter, but it seemed more important to come. I should understand. No one should go unprotected into this family warren.

"And will you please tell me, Claire, why your mother insists on making coffee in that pitiful little drip pot over and over instead of using the big one?"

"I don't know. I guess because it's what she always does."

"Well, it's ridiculous. Why don't you tell her to get that big pot out of the cupboard and do it right?"

I didn't like the look on Susan's pretty face. "Because I don't tell my mother what to do," I said.

"That's the damn trouble with this family," she said just as Frank and my mother came into the kitchen.

"It was terrible when it happened," my mother said. "But not as terrible as this sleeping."

"Coma," Susan said.

"They didn't even tell me," my mother said, letting Susan dangle in the wind. "He could have died last night and they didn't even tell me. I should have been with him."

"They told Claire," Frank said.

Oh great, Frank, I thought, just great.

"What is he talking about, young lady?"

Frank said, "I told Claire not to tell you last night."

"Is that right?" my mother said.

"Because I knew you needed to sleep and there was really nothing you could do."

"And when did that happen?" she asked us.

"Now, Mother," Frank began in his doctor voice.

"Did you two know that I was going to have him moved to another hospital? I didn't want him in that one where they thought they knew better than me what I should know. But, I see the problem's closer to home."

"Let it go, Mama," Frank said.

"When did it happen?" she repeated. "Or has it been going on for a long time and I haven't noticed?"

"What are you talking about?" Susan asked.

"My children. My children who seem to know what's best for me all of a sudden. My children who left home to seek their fortunes, and then come back to tell me what to do. Do I have that right?"

"Mama, don't," I said. "We were just trying to save you a little."

Her skin was taut over those high cheekbones, pale, with two spots of high color scooping out the curve beneath. I'd never seen her this angry.

"And you," she said to me, "Why don't you go finish what you started somewhere else and I'll do the same right here."

She was up, out of the kitchen. She went to my father's bedroom and shut the door against us.

The next morning we pretended nothing had happened. After we ate and the dishes were done, we went to the hospital. Frank went in first, alone. He was in there fifteen minutes. When he came out, my mother asked him a hundred questions.

"There's no change," he kept saying.

Frank didn't know anything, either.

Father Sebastian glided in, touched my mother's shoulder and told her, "I'll just have a moment with Andy." She nodded. He got a smile.

"Just exactly what's he doing in there alone?" I asked her.

She waved her hand.

"Is he giving my father Extreme Unction? Is he?"

Father was out in a minute. A duty call. He stopped long enough to remind my mother, who was leaning against Frank's shoulder, that the source of her strength was the grace of God. Who could take this little old man seriously when he couldn't see what was right before his eyes?

That night, while we ate swiss steak that my mother had somehow managed to put together, we felt the weight of my father's stroke drop on us. It seemed to take on a life of its own that drained ours.

Susan said, "This needs salt, Mary."

Frank passed the salt.

Susan said, "Is there something to drink? I could use a drink."

I got up to open a bottle of Uncle Patsy's Ohio Concord and rinse out a wine glass. In a fleet image, I saw Kay's Thanksgiving. Centuries ago.

Frank said, "This bread's too hard."

My family fixed on little things: this cheese is too salty, this peach is too ripe, until you had to ask yourself if they knew the difference between the trivial and the serious. "Dip it in the gravy," I told him.

My mother got up to do the dishes in silence with a set to her spine that told us to leave her alone. Susan took the bottle and her glass into the living room where she turned on the television. Frank went down the hall to his room. I dressed for the cold and shoveled snow from the walk before my aunts and uncle came for that evening's visit.

The snow was wet and heavy. My niece and I could have built a wonderful snowman. I shoveled hard and fast, Father Sebastian's platitudes to the right, the child-doctor's speculations to the left. My mouth was dry and my nose was running. I stopped to catch my breath and blow my nose, angry that I'd ever behaved as though a priest or a doctor could interpret my life, could somehow make sense of it all. The errant wind flung fresh snow into my face. In the end, all anyone would be able to tell us was that he died.

When I went inside, Susan was laughing at something she watched. The bottle on the coffee table was almost empty. My mother was setting out the cups and saucers.

"It's snowing again," I said in case she felt like talking. She nodded. "My clothes are all wet. I'm going to change."

"Go ahead. I don't need you here."

I heard a funny sound outside Frank's door. Like a cold engine refusing to start. He was probably playing with some old toy in there, avoiding us. Maybe the crystal radio he made that beeped and squawked while he tried to get Japan and Germany during the war, and my mother, who hated the noise, had pointed out there was a perfectly good Philco in the living room.

Breaking the rule of a lifetime, I opened his door without knocking. He didn't see me. He was sitting at his old desk, his back to me, one hand rubbing the desktop, the other fisted against his mouth. He was rocking a little. I'd never seen Frank cry.

"Frank?" I whispered.

He didn't hear me.

"Frank."

He froze. I took the few steps that marked the difference between standing in his doorway and standing inside his room. I waited for him to tell me to get out, but he didn't. So I sat on a corner of his bed.

"Listen," I said, but I had no idea what he should listen to. "It's going to be all right."

"What makes you say that?" he asked. I'd never noticed how much he looked like Papa.

"Because there's something iron in him. This isn't the way Papa should die."

Frank shifted and straightened, cleared his throat. "Did you ever ask him for a hot dog?"

Funny, I knew exactly what he meant. "At the games?"

"Yeah."

"No, did you?"

"Uh-uh," he said.

"Did you want one?"

"Every time. You, too?"

"Sure."

"Why didn't we ask?" Frank said.

"I don't know."

"Does he still call the plays?"

"Yeah. And reviews the mistakes right after. But, he misses Otto Graham and Motley and everyone. And there's that trouble with Paul Brown and Jim Brown, now."

"The glory years," Frank said. "They're over. Had to happen. He'd have done it, though, you know."

"Who?"

"Papa. All we had to do was ask. It just never occurred to him that we wanted a hot dog."

"Are you all right?" I asked.

"Sure."

And he was all through that night's visit from the family. No one died, but once again, we were living in high drama while we pretended to be intent on details, coffee pots and gas furnaces and bone china cups. We couldn't help one another much because that's how we set the stage.

I heard voices on the other side of the wall late that night and for a moment I thought I was dreaming.

"Exactly how long are you planning for us to stay here?" Susan asked Frank.

"I dunno."

"You know perfectly well this could go on for weeks."

No answer.

"Where did Claire get that wine?"

"In the cupboard, over the stove."

"Oh, that's just wonderful," she said. "A hot, dry place." Some shuffling, a cupboard door slamming, the chink of glass hitting glass. "And while we're on the subject, have you noticed what's happening to your sister? They've got her bound and gagged. She'll never get out of here alive."

"What do you want?"

"Tell her she could leave tonight and never look back. And never feel guilty for one thing. And I don't want to hang around here for the deathwatch one minute more than I have to. We have a daughter, a life. The minute you walk through this door, I lose you, goddamn it!"

"Enough!" he said, just like my father. And there was a small space of quiet.

"It's my father," he began before his voice crumbled.

I heard Susan making soothing sounds and I knew they'd leave soon.

They stayed another day. Before they left, Frank gave me a bottle of the little red pills, a hundred of them. "Be careful with these," he said. "She could get dependent."

I wasn't sure a hundred would be enough. "Can you write us a prescription if she needs more?"

"She won't need more."

"But if she does?"

"I suppose," he said, his thoughts somewhere else.

He left money, too, just in case. And a separate check for a gas furnace.

"What are you going to do?" he asked me. "Are you going back?"

"We'll see," I answered.

XXIII

For three weeks HAPPY NEW YEAR flashed in pinpoint lights from a window across the street. My mother rose earlier and earlier to turn up the thermostat of the new gas furnace.

One morning I heard her before dawn and couldn't fall asleep again. I went to the kitchen where she was already busy at the sink. The scent of apples filled the rooms. I stayed in the shadow of the living room and watched her. She was working at an angle peeling green apples for a pie. The crusts were already rolled out. She began peeling at the stem and spiraled to the bottom. Perfect circles fell from her knife. Frank used to hold them above his head and eat his way to the top. There was something funny about her shoulders; they were out of rhythm with her work, doing something on their own. She had to turn a little to find the butter, and in the overhead light, I saw her face was shining, wet. She pulled back from the counter to wipe her eyes with her sleeve, but no sound escaped her. She held the pie aloft on one hand while she cut pastry from the sides with a butter knife, set it down and fluted the edges without looking at her fingers, snuffing in air, letting it out in ragged gasps. Then she stopped. She stared at it. Her shoulders heaved and I heard a terrible sigh.

She stood there within my reach. I took a step, then the rest all the way to her side.

"Let me put it in the oven for you," I said. She cleared her throat, straightened her shoulders.

"What? 350 degrees?" I asked.

"425."

While I was still bent, closing the oven door, I said, "You

should have warned me when I was five that you have to break new ground every day."

"And would you have believed me when you were five?"

We looked at one another.

"It's a terrible struggle, isn't it?" she said.

"What is?"

"This 'loving' someone."

Every morning at eight, Aunt Nancy would call. "Fine, I'm fine today," my mother would tell her. "I'm changing the beds," which she did every three days. "No reason not to with this new washer and dryer," she said. I was the one who'd complained about the old Easy Spindryer dancing across the kitchen floor, about Monday's damp sheets hanging in the kitchen so I needed to practically crawl through to get to the living room. This morning race to clean and sort everything for the automatic twins before we left for the hospital was worse, as crazed as the rest of the day while we waited for my father to wake or sink deeper.

Aunt Sylvia would arrive just before we left. The first day she carried a brown paper sack. She told us she had everything she needed to make a meatloaf that would bake in our oven so we could have a nice hot supper when we got home and she'd have enough to take home for her and Uncle Joe. No matter what happened, we would eat good food and sleep on clean sheets.

The nurses on the seventh floor allowed us to see my dad earlier and earlier, and I had less and less to say. I hated the sound of my own voice. My father looked stern and angry in the wilderness of a terrible dream. We took turns talking to him, touching his face, holding his hands, making up a life that sounded perfect, one ready for him to reenter.

We were home by three. The drift of afternoon. Aunt Sylvia left before sunset, time enough for my mother to cry, but hardly time to recover by supper. Days when she was dry-eyed were even worse. I'd stare out the window at his wild dogwood transplanted from the woods, his rhododendron, hear his whisper to it when he planted it, "There, you're home," soaking it, feeding it, sealing its fate beneath a window where, in May, it spread cerise blooms bigger than his hand.

I hated being in rooms in winter. I'd walk outside most afternoons on scraps of crusty snow, grass blackened by frost poking through ice crystals and remember my game in summer, barefoot and little, running on his lawn, the thick pad springing under my feet. I'd lie face down, watch the grass become a rain forest, ants, giant predators, hear the call of a macaw in the jay, see sunlight splintered between bars of grass, my nose filled with the scent of earth.

At dusk, HAPPY NEW YEAR blinking in my eyes, I'd go inside for the night. I watched my mother get up from the sofa as though she were arthritic, go to the sink to wash one leaf of lettuce at a time under achingly cold water, break them into a bowl, set it in the ice box to crisp, forget to cover it, forget to eat it.

Night. All the dark hours. Figures and light jumping from the television screen, but her eyes skewed off. "You know, Mama," I'd say, "there are worse things. I've met people who've never loved anybody, never had children. A man who lives alone in a shack with beer and the Radio Church of the Air for company, and this woman, who must be seventy, she makes two dollars a trick in the back room of a diner, I mean, that's how she makes a living. She has, maybe, fifty, sixty dolls piled on her bed. She makes them by hand even when she's drunk and she sends them to her granddaughter in New Orleans, only she can never see her granddaughter because her son won't allow it. And a crazy old man, who hates his mother because she made him stay home to take care of her, who spends most of his life looking for U.F.O.'s. And Camille, she was *thirteen* when her mother sent her to the convent and something went wrong inside her and now she's lost in this world. And another child, Gemma—" I stopped.

I couldn't talk about Gemma. My mother thought I'd saved her the day before I came home. The day before I came home. I counted them. Thirty days ago and Leo was marching through my mother's house whether I liked it or not.

I looked up to see if she noticed that I'd broken off. It didn't matter. She wasn't listening. I couldn't mark the hour or the day she stopped, but now, sometimes, I wanted to slap her awake. We sat in stupid silence most nights, dulled in the too-much heat of the new gas furnace, my eyes watering, my nose stuffy, my mother petrifying. I'd daydream my way to bedtime, sitting in Myra Russel's living room, Kay's studio, my classroom, up the grain elevator, in Cals, Adele's where I had to stop because there the memory grew dangerous. I'd look up and see that maybe ten minutes had passed.

One phone call, five minutes, just as Steve had said, and my work in Christopher Park was covered. "Don't you worry about a thing," Father Foley had said. "You take care of things at home, see to your mother. Sister is back. We'll hold the fort."

The fort. What was she doing to my children with no one watching? I wondered until it was time to take a pill and go to sleep.

"Mail for you, dear," Aunt Sylvia said one dim afternoon. I saw Leo's hand on the envelope. My mother and aunt were watching so I tossed it on the coffee table.

"Why don't those people leave you alone?" my mother said.

"I'll open it later," I said. I felt the blood racing to my face, prickling under my arms.

"That's good," my aunt said, "because you need to sit down and eat right away. Our cousins are coming for a visit, and soon. I made you a nice stew."

I was putting the dishes away when they knocked, our West Side cousins who crossed the Cuyahoga to keep us company. I took their coats and scooped up my letter on the way to my bedroom. Alone, in a strange moment, I wondered if I wanted to know what was inside. I pulled open the flap, unfolded the sheet.

> *My Love,*
>
> *did you ever hear the story about the lady at the cocktail party who corners the only psychiatrist in the room and asks, "Why is it after I've played with the children all day, fixed a nice supper, cleaned the house and made myself look pretty, that at six o'clock the children begin to whine,*

fight with one another, and my husband walks in muttering about traffic and ignores me and my beautiful dinner?" The psychiatrist looks sympathetic and says, "Well, the reason for that is expectation. The children want you and supper and their father, and he's faced a day paying attention to details that are probably roundly boring and he's just getting rid of all that when he walks in, and you're disappointed because all your good efforts to create the perfect evening are futile. And, then, of course, there's the real reason." "The real reason," the housewife says. "What's the real reason?" And the psychiatrist answers, "We're all afraid of the dark."

Which is to tell you, Claire, that I do not remember our entering a mutual pact to stop talking to one another. In fact, I'm under the impression that Italian-American women can do almost anything beautifully except *stop talking. Don't leave me in the dark, kiddo. Come back, come back and talk to me. I'll hear anything you have to tell me.*

Leo

My mother called, "Claire? What are you doing in there? Come out and be with us."

I folded Leo's letter and got up, only I couldn't leave it behind. I slipped it inside my waistband and pulled my sweater over the top.

"Here she is!" Cousin Nick said. "Pretty as a picture."

"How good to have her home with you," Ange said. "It's good to have a daughter. And me with three sons."

I sat on the floor near my mother, and Ange, plump and neat in a starched cotton housedress, wings of jet hair pulled back from a face round as a plate, tawny eyes set deep. Her brother Ross, drinking a beer, sat in my dad's chair, and Nick, restless, bit his nails until it was his turn to say something.

Ange, a widow, told my mother that only two days before her husband died, she'd made him a beautiful soup, used the sweet ribs to make a hash, and he'd died, *died* before he tasted either.

Ross said, "It's all in the will of God, all in His plan. It doesn't do any good to fight it. Life goes on." Then he told Mama, again, how he had to carry a dead wife home from Florida. He went out early that morning to get her a cup of coffee because she couldn't start a day without a cup of fresh brewed coffee and when he got back—.

Ange's patient whine, the men's bass punctuating lulled me. I pressed the place where the letter rested and thought it was good to have them here. As dark as their talk was, they said, See? We lasted. We made it.

Ange put her hand on the crown of my head, and it startled me. "Ah, she was just a little girl then, wasn't she? And she could have been made an orphan, that's what I told my husband."

"She was ten," my mother said.

"And Andy could have got himself killed. We all said so."

Nick said, "Basta! These women need their sleep."

We all hugged one another when they left.

"What was Ange talking about?" I asked my mother. "When could my father have been killed?"

"When he started the union at the shop." She was flushed and alive after the visit. She lit a cigarette and relaxed after the first puff.

"My dad started a union?"

"In the winter of forty-nine." It sounded like a slogan. "Of course, it wasn't his idea. It was the men's. They picked your father to speak for them. Remember Joe Clark and Bill?"

They were the other men who wore green twills and fixed the John Deere and Caterpillar tractors that C.J. Floyd sold all over the midwest.

"That winter they decided to strike because they didn't get good wages. They came here and told your father they ought to be paid right and have a pension."

"What did my dad say?"

"He didn't say much. He listened. Then he talked to C.J."

"What happened?"

"Your father said C.J. got beet red, then calmed down and offered your father more money and a bigger bonus than the other men. To stop."

"So what happened?"

"Claire! You know your father. What do you think happened? He told C.J. to pay attention. But he didn't. The funny thing is your father didn't believe in unions, not for himself. He like being independent. Anyway, when they went on strike, things got dangerous. No one could prove it, but we all knew C.J. hired thugs to break up the picket line. Remember the wicker basket? You helped me fill it."

I did remember. Midnight picnics. My mother fit everything into that basket, spaghetti and meatballs, roast pork and potatoes, pumpkin pie. I'd fold the silverware into the napkins and Papa would show up in the dark just before I went to bed to pick it up and kiss my mother on the mouth, something I noticed, and leave for the picket line to feed his men.

In the end, C.J. capitulated.

"So, your dad started the local and the men got paid union wages and got union benefits. C.J. made a speech—no more hockey tickets, no more Christmas bonuses, no more summer picnics at his farm. He said if he had to hire spies, he didn't have to entertain them. So, your dad went right out and bought his own hockey tickets because we liked going. And, you know, it wasn't six years later he quit C.J. so he could take his pension in cash for Frank's medical school. To this day he feels guilty about you."

"Why?"

"Because you had to go to college in town."

"I wanted to."

"No you didn't. You wanted to go to Northwestern."

"It didn't matter."

"It matters to him. He kept the letter, the one that said you were accepted. Oh," she said, catching a yawn, "I'm sleepy."

"Go to bed, Mama. I'll clear the things in the kitchen."

Afterwards, I went into his bedroom, opened the top drawer of his chest, the back corner of the liner paper bumped up. That was where he kept his important papers. A sacred heart medal, a Father's Day card from Frank when he was maybe five and still printing, a sepia photo of his mother wrapped in a white apron and hair kerchief, a letter folded in business thirds with a Northwestern heading that said I was accepted into their university.

I think that was the first night in a long string of them that my mother and I fell asleep without a red pill. Hope is a strange guest. It puts you back among the living.

XXIV

It's ten o'clock, Friday morning, the last one in January. My mother opens the venetian blinds in my dad's room. I cover the back of his hand with mine to be sure he's warm enough and blink in the bright light of a clear day, the pools in the melting lake a mirror for the sun. I pull up a chair for my mother, who's hanging her coat in the locker. I see a shadow, a flicker, I think, some light moving across my father's face.

"Mama?"

"Just a minute."

She's putting her gloves into her purse, zipping it, unzipping it to check for her wallet and keys. I look back just in time to see my father's eyelids ripple, I think.

"Will you leave that purse alone, Mama, and come here please?"

She's beside me.

"Watch his face," I tell her.

His eyelids flutter and his lips twitch like someone who feels a fly on his mouth while he's napping.

My mother leans against me. I put my arm around her. Who knows how long we stand there and stare at the field of his face while the clicking business sounds, voices, sotto voce, at the nurses' station outside filter in? My father opens his eyes. My mother bends to him.

"Andy? Andy, are you awake?"

He turns his head to her voice like a new baby, searching for something he hears but doesn't see.

He sees her. His eyes focus, shift, see me. We are looking at one another.

"Mary," he says in a voice hardly his, a voice cracked with disuse.

"Mary." His tongue is thick, it's in his way.

My mother, who has somehow gathered within herself all the grace Father Sebastian promised, holds his face in the palms of her hands. "Yes, yes, it's Mary. I'm right here." He closes his eyes and I'm afraid. But he opens them right away. "And Claire's here, right here. Show your father," she tells me.

He nods yes.

He blinks, furrows his brow.

"Is it too bright?" I ask.

He nods.

I fix the blinds and remember that this is a hospital and something has happened that they ought to know about. I go to tell the nurse at the station who has been all pepper and vinegar, but now she hugs me, puts in a call to the doctor and enters my dad's room in front of me.

"You aren't going to believe me right now, Andy, but you're going to be powerfully hungry pretty soon."

Mama and I look at her. We didn't know she called him Andy. He's giving her his usher smile, and I exhale a deep breath. My mother pours dimes and nickles into my hands and sends me to make the calls. I make only two, one to Frank who exhales the same way I did, and one to my aunt Nancy who promises to do the rest, then run upstairs to find him still awake, struggling, against the rules, to sit up.

My father woke to the world like a diver surfacing from the deeps that first week in February that was like early April. Flies buzzed outside the storm door that Uncle Patsy replaced with a screen. Snowdrops pushed up from our rainsoaked lawn, and early daffodils and tulips showed green heads. Breezes off the lake held the scent of water and fish.

My mother and aunt Nancy had new business in that kitchen

after Papa woke. My mother was at the stove furiously putting together a sauce while my aunt sat at the table sipping coffee, biting into an apricot danish. They talked about the day's business.

"After I finish this sauce, we'll change his bed," my mother said.

Aunt Sylvia walked in with a florist's box. "I bought him a camellia. I'll float it for him in a glass bowl."

"We'll hang his sheets to dry in the sun today," my mother said.

"I brought my scissors," Aunt Nancy said. "I'll trim his mustache."

They didn't notice me until Aunt Nancy said, "Sit down in this chair, sit down this minute, Claire. You look like a ragamuffin. I'm going to trim your hair."

My mother watched, bemused. My head felt lighter and lighter, like a rising balloon. I reached up to touch my head, but my aunt tapped my fingers with the flat of her scissors. I felt something tickling my forehead, the famous bangs she thought were fashionable. My mother swept long, lazy curls into a dust pan and dumped them.

"Done," Aunt Nancy said.

"You were right," Mama said.

"It's my business to be right about hair," Aunt Nancy said.

I looked into the mirror they handed me. I saw Joan of Arc, my eyes and mouth set in painful relief. I ran my fingers through it and felt air before I should have. I shook my head and nothing fell forward on my cheeks the way it should have.

"You go get yourself a nice pair of earrings," Aunt Nancy said. "They'll show up real nice now."

We all trooped to my dad's room an hour later.

"Why didn't you just shave off the rest?" he asked when he saw me.

I kissed him. He looked amused. He did. He looked as though he were watching Jimmy Durante. One eyelid drooped. He was a rake.

Early spring was a tease. The night before Papa was released from his seventh floor room, the sky, high in its dome, looked as though someone spilled waves of heavy cream into dense coffee. A translucent green light mysteriously brightened dusk. The moon, beyond the reeling treetops, disappeared behind snow clouds rolling like tumbled breasts. I went outside to cover the screendoor with plastic.

I leaned against the door out there when I was finished and looked up. I felt happy and grateful with no one to thank. Above the tops of bare branches, two clouds, as immense and murky as blue whales seen through water, swam to one another and met, as if for a kiss, then rolled apart to let moonlight suddenly stream between them. The wind shredded them into fingered streams and the snow began. I went inside to watch.

My father returned in disguise. At least, I didn't recognize him. I waited for the celebration to begin. When he caught me looking at him, he'd say, "Don't you have something to do? Go help your mother." I didn't have anything to do. My mother didn't need my help. I was "lurking" as Frank used to say, waiting to be dismissed. I thought if I got in their way, they might notice and suggest I do something useful like go back and finish my work. I was wrong.

My father touched the new furnace, frowned, turned his back on it. He told my mother he didn't want her to wash clothes when he was in the kitchen. He'd say things like, "I'm going to tear out that coal bin," and discover after ten minutes that his strength gave out. He prowled through the rooms looking for mistakes. He was terse with my aunts and uncles. There were no conversations on the other side of the wall at night.

One afternoon, when he and I found ourselves alone in the kitchen, he said, "Call your brother. Tell him I want to see him."

I shook my head, no. A slow anger, simmering for that interminable week of homecoming, answered for me.

"What do you mean no?" he asked.

"If you want to talk to Frank," I said, "you should call him yourself, I think."

"You think? When did you start thinking for me?"

That night, he addressed me through my mother.

I borrowed the Queen Mary the next morning and drove over to Jeannie's. She was sorting heaps of laundry.

"Hey!" she said when I walked in.

We worked through the sheets and diapers and baby clothes while we talked and the baby made caves and nests in the piles. At first, we talked about the miracle, my dad as Sleeping Beauty, while she set up the ironing board and I held the baby and fed him green beans and peaches from little jars. He looked like Sweet Pea in his nightgown. As soon as he finished, he squirmed to get down and crawl, but the piles were all gone, all of it folded in wicker baskets. He sat beside one of them and lifted a few of his undershirts from the top. Jeannie said, "Oh, let him. He loves it."

She made us tuna sandwiches and coffee, sat down, and said, "Okay, let's have it. What's going on?"

I finally told her that Leo was in bed with a woman when I'd called.

"Have you heard from him since then?" she asked.

"He sent a letter."

"So, what did he tell you?"

"He wants me to come back."

"And? Do you want to go back?"

"I don't want to talk about it."

"Oh yes you do."

Chris came home from work and told us to go out and have some fun. "I'll take care of him," he said, lifting the baby. "Go on, the streets are salted down, but dress warm."

We drove to our old neighborhood where we were children together and parked in front of a travel bureau that used to be a drugstore. "Remember Sunday mornings?" Jeanne asked. We'd go up to the tiny, skeletal pharmacist who'd take our dime for the Sunday paper that we delivered home. Sometimes he gave us each a packet of Sen Sen which we hated because it tasted like perfume, but it was something to experiment with.

And the grocery store with two counters and the man in the

white apron who reached into shelves behind him to fill the list our mothers wrote in pencil. Sometimes, he used a hooked stick that worked like a mechanical hand to pinch Mother's Oats from the top shelf. It was a hat shop now.

Fossy Drugs was still there, a dusty place where you could steal year-old gum and cough drops from the front because Mr. Fossy was a bookie and didn't really care.

And then, we turned the corner and stood in front of the white frame house where we'd begun. It looked warped, its sides bulging like overripe thighs, and we talked about lying on the maroon rug in front of the radio, filling our war bond sheets in triplicate while we listened to Lowell Thomas talk about Tibet and say, "Good night until tomorrow," which meant bedtime for us. Sometimes, we'd actually go to bed, but more often we'd crawl down the back stairs to the kitchen and eavesdrop or eat.

"Let's get out of here," Jeannie said, and we both knew we were heading for the lake. We could hear it pound like a heartbeat before we could see it. We walked into the wind on the deserted beach in a haze of wind-whipped snow, past sandy ice bubbles, bleached plastic pails abandoned by children in summer, smooth, curved bricks heaved up by the waves, neglected wind socks shredding in wintry blasts. We followed the curving shoreline formed when waves washed to shore and were stopped in ice. Then we sat in the crevice of an old rock formation where the wind couldn't reach us. We were shivering.

"Listen," she said. The water pounded in and sighed on its return. She walked toward it, hunched down and brought some periwinkle shells back. "There have to be more," she said. We hunted and there were, but she threw back as many as she kept.

"Wait," I said.

"You don't want this," she said. "It's cracked. And part of this one's missing." Then she laughed.

"What?" I asked, but I was laughing, too. She threw her arm around me and we ran back to the rocks.

"They could be a thousand years old," she said when she could, "and we're throwing them back because they're not perfect."

"That's how I feel, a thousand years old."

"Well you're not! Look, they're not the same as us."

"Who?"

"Guys. They're clumsy, I don't know, different. They can't help it. They're born that way. You should know. There's been a regular procession of them walking through your house for the last five years."

"But, I never thought about that."

"Well trust me, they're different. All of them. That would include your brother and your father."

"Are you explaining Leo and that woman or something?"

"It's in their nature, Claire. I told you, they can't help it. We do it, too. We flirt. It makes us feel alive. You know you flirt, Claire."

I thought about that.

"Pick your time and make your move. You have to find out about this guy or you'll always wonder." She dropped a handful of periwinkles in my hand and closed my fingers over them. "Maybe they'll tell you a thousand-year-old secret."

We had to leave. Finally, you have to go home. Dusk was gathering. The Northern Lights swelled on the horizon like luminous hills rising from the water. A plum haze, like smoke, drifted around them.

Tire tracks crisscrossed the street in front of my house. Cars were parked at the curb as though we were having a party inside. Uncle Patsy pulled me inside when I opened the door.

"Here she is!" he said to everyone. It was just like Christmas Eve. "Do we have a surprise for you!" he told me.

"Say Happy Birthday first," my mother said and they all wished it to me.

"It's not my birthday, not yet," I said.

"Let her take off her coat," Aunt Nancy said. "And just where do you think you've been all day without a word? You had your mother worried sick."

"I went to see Jeannie," I said.

"Oh, then that's different."

"Frank called while you were gone," my mother said. "He talked to your father."

"Good," I said with my eyes on a pile of envelopes on the table with my name on them. I reached for them, but my dad said, "You can read those later. Keep your coat on." He was zipping his jacket. "Come on outside with me," he said. "I've got something to show you." My mother smiled, a sister on either side of her.

My dad held my elbow and steered me to the curb where he pointed to a small white car easy to miss in the snowbanked street.

"They call it a Falcon, something new. Now, I don't like Fords much myself, but your Uncle Pat knew the man who was selling this. It's only got 20,000 miles on it, just broken in, and it's running smooth. I like a bigger car, but the gas this one uses is next to nothing." He was brushing snow from the windshield, opening the driver's door.

"Go on, get inside, see how it feels," he said. "You should be able to see over the hood. Can you see over the hood?"

I sat and looked. "Yeah," I said.

"Good, good." The streetlight backlit him as he slid in on the passenger side. He handed me a key in a leather holder. "Start it up."

It coughed and shuddered, stopped a few times, and my dad told me to pump the gas pedal, that it was too damned cold for a small car, that oil got heavy and solid in a freeze and needed time to warm up. The Falcon chugged into a quivering neutral.

"It's yours," he said. "From your mother and me."

I didn't know what to say. I felt as though the little Falcon were in gear driving me somewhere I didn't want to go. Then I saw the bright, expectant look on my dad's face. "It's wonderful, Papa, thank you," I said.

They were waiting for us inside.

"Well?" Uncle Patsy said, almost shy.

"Isn't it something?" I said.

"A car gives you independence," my uncle told me.

"I think it takes a little bit more than a car," his wife said.

I thanked them, told them I'd already eaten supper with Jeannie who would cover any story I told, and said I was going to take a hot bath because I was freezing. My mother told me to hurry because maybe we'd play pinochle in a little while.

"And I want my partner bright and alert," my dad said.

I took my robe and my letters into the bathroom where I ran the water and read what Father, Kay and Paula told me about the day the tornado came to Christopher Park.

XXV

It arrived on a warm wind sweetened with the scent of water. Cottonwoods whipped like wet eels. It sailed in as slow and deliberate as Camille's Lincoln. Pop, pop, pop, drops spitting on leaves, a fist of rain and then globes of water drove through leaves like nails. A pride of lions roared in the wheatfields.

The calm, unblinking eye of the storm spun silent in the center of the wild stew, the eye of a killer whale, round, wide, simple, and around it, madness. Blind and open, it coursed, etching a path in relief, whipping shards and sticks into missiles that pierced stone and shattered glass. Quiet, sure, wide-eyed. Inevitable, inescapable. Love your fate.

It lifted a tree maybe ninety years putting down roots, carried it tipped, like a broom upside down, across the center of town, that, itself, seemed like a saucer spinning aslant. It carried that tree sweeping the floor of town in a mess of dirt and cinders until the granary slammed into it. The tree broke the wall, stuck there like a stalk of celery, the scene a little drunk and silly, until Tom's cabin countersunk it and the grain spilled into the street.

It rolled in from the west behind the grill, the backroom a pile of cracker crumbs. Melanie Bright in starched eyelet embraced the debris. They found her there with her eyes open, yellow braid intact.

It lifted Ned Frickett's red pickup in the jail parking lot and tore the grill from the front while people across the street watched it become a boomerang pinned in the center of the hardware store, saw grains of brick and plaster sift through lath and splintered two-by-fours to settle on it.

Lily Smith was in the drugstore clutching a bottle of witch hazel with instructions for reducing the puffs, blue as skimmed milk, beneath her eyes. A thin, startling stream of blood leaked from a shining scalp beneath scant black hair. "They'll never bury me in this town," she'd said.

It dropped on Hugo Thode and sucked up his estate, carried it with him and his old Indian where no one could sort it all out. It scoured the land beneath leaving a rich, brown crater in its wake.

People would tell how fast it traveled, how wide the path, but no one was sure because it destroyed the instruments set to measure it. They went over to the Ridgeways to see what had been the farm and walked on the three flags of sandstone that led to a cement block perimeter surrounded by ripped sod. The Ridgeways would never find their house. They were living in the cyclone cellar.

The cabins and shacks on the west end of town where the man called for his angel to save him were sheared. There were no cyclone cellars in the shacks. But not one doll on Melanie Bright's bed was jostled.

What happens when wind and water fly out of control? People saw Camille run into the schoolyard and dance. The wind and water were her music. As though she wanted to be torn like the trees, to hurl herself into heaven, safe from the world, finally. Bernard clung to the doorpost and watched. And when it was over, Camille sank to the ground and shook her heavy head.

The rain and hail soaked the grain in Main Street. It sprouted and died in rot. Main Street smelled like a musty attic where someone spilled whiskey. The tires in front of the auto store were found in the middle of the football field ten miles away.

People with concussions and cuts went to the armory where pansies, untouched, were blooming in the neat bed fronting it. Two saplings, planted in the fall, were budding leaves. Ned Frickett's wife bandaged survivors in white gauze. They shuffled around inside the great room, bewildered, talking to themselves, blood seeping from snowy cotton.

Mrs. Frickett ordered Melanie Bright's dolls brought to the

armory for the children. She sent my students to the library to bring books. Harry Lee was her best and fastest messenger. Louise drove in from Cals and set up a place to take care of the babies. Helen couldn't keep up with the calls. Sometimes, she refused and let the board buzz. The telegraph boy made money in tips to last a month.

It struck at three, after morning chores, after school. When Leo was safe with Joey McWilliams on the farm, when Father was in his study, safe in the embrace of all those books he never read, while Henry Brodenwort took an afternoon nap in his den and Myra Russel visited an old friend on Hawk Road, when Kay and Paula were cleaning kitchen cupboards on Eleventh Street east of town. From their window they could see an oil drill twist like a bent paper clip and hear the wild scream of peahens pierce the roaring wind.

No stray dogs prowled the streets that night. Lights were on in all the houses and churches and stores that were unharmed. They were shelters for the homeless. The police station was filled with cots and bedrolls. Ned Frickett asked Myra Russel to serve up the food she brought for the people there and watched while she dished up soup and stew into the cups and dishes he'd scavenged. Someone heard him say that if the whole world went hungry, and he had to ask just one person to divvy up the food, he'd want it to be an Oklahoma farm wife.

Some farmers on the far western outskirts, who came out of cellars to see nothing, made their way to town. They were restless, pent up in the crowded shelters, walking in and out of doors in the rain, their minds crowded with pictures of ruin. "Get inside and stay dry," they were told. One of them, who'd driven cattle when he was a boy before he married and settled into farming said, "Need windows. Ask a cowboy about windows."

No one saw or heard from Charlie Pepper. No word.

Some died before I could get to them.

Melanie Bright. I'd only bothered with that one visit, just that once in her kitchen with her neighbor who hissed through bad false teeth while she scolded Melanie and watched with crimped lips while she showed me the dolls piled on the narrow bed, who made her a stern cup of tea that Melanie altered with a pint bottle in her pocket. It was all so hopeless, I'd thought. Leave it alone, I'd thought.

Lily Smith tried to tell me she was desperate, that she needed me. I saw the effort in the dyed eyebrows and hair, the bowed mouth drawn in lipstick. I should take her to Cals sometime, I'd thought, let her talk, maybe let someone find her and flirt with her there. But she was full of whines and aches. She was sour milk. I stayed clear.

Fifteen minutes. In fifteen minutes, Christopher Park, that had survived droughts and grasshoppers, a bust oil boom and the Depression was laid waste by weather. Sitting right next to the Dust Bowl at the heart of three rivers, it survived for over thirty years. Farmers planted, wives cooked, sons bought new acres, married, signed for loans on combines shrouded for a year like praying mantises waiting for a feed. In fifteen minutes, less time that it took for Henry Brodenwort to invade Gemma, for Melanie Bright to earn two dollars, for the little red pill I swallowed at night to take effect, in fifteen minutes a whirlwind wrecked things, killed people and dissolved itself.

XXVI

When Father Foley made his routine duty call early the next morning, he didn't bother to ask for me. He spoke with my mother who told me he said not to worry about anything except taking good care of things at home. "He's so concerned about your father and me, that dear man," she said.

"Papa's fine," I answered. She lifted her chin, sighed briefly. "Well, isn't he?" I asked.

"Finish your toast."

"Didn't Father tell you about the tornado?"

"He certainly did. Can you imagine? If you'd been there?"

"People I knew were there. They died," I told her.

But she wasn't going to have that conversation. "Imagine!" she said. "A thing like that, and I even told Father, not a mention of it in our paper."

"News travels slow from the other side of the Mississippi."

She glanced at me, but turned back to the stove when I met her eyes. "How do you know about it?" she asked.

I poured myself more coffee. "The letters that came for me yesterday. Why? Weren't you going to mention it?"

"There's been enough bad news around here lately."

"I see. Are you planning to censor the news, now?"

"You know what your trouble is, young lady? You've been hanging around this house too much. Go out with your friends. It's Saturday night."

"My friends go out in couples. I'm not a couple anymore."

"Then get yourself back in circulation."

"I bet you're going to tell me how to do that."

"I hear that tone of voice, but I know a few things about this life you and your brother don't, for all your books. And by the way, my librarian told me it would be a good idea for you to apply for a teaching job at the high school right now before everyone else does in April."

"Is that right?" I was as sweet as a quince.

My dad, dressed in work clothes, interrupted. "I'm going to rip out the coal bin today," he told us. "Claire, you give me a hand. You aren't doing anything, are you?"

"Ask Mama. It's Saturday. I'm supposed to dust my room and change my bed."

My mother glared, but my dad didn't notice.

"Never mind that," he said. "Come in here. Hand me that crowbar." And fifteen minutes later, "Take this pile and stack it beside the car, near the trunk. I'll drive it to the dump later."

"You are not allowed to drive yet," my mother said, busy making yet another supper that would tempt him. "Claire can do it."

I carried the sticks and lath outside thinking that I'd stopped eating. I'd stopped talking much. When I was little, they'd taken me to a doctor for that. Now they didn't seem to notice.

"I'm going to build your mother a pantry in here," he told me. "I'll get the wood tomorrow. You keep her busy so she doesn't notice I took the car." The criminal in him was returning.

Later that day, three of his men came to visit, shy in our house, refusing all refreshment. Papa told them he'd be back on the job in two weeks, but promised he'd stop by sooner to answer questions that were troubling them. "They're digging under a chemical plant," he told us after they left. "They're scared they'll cut the disposal lines and poison the water system. Delicate work." He was excited.

"That's none of your business," my mother said. "Don't you dare go there and pick up a shovel."

My father laughed. "We don't use shovels. We use the big equipment."

"Whatever," she said. "You promise me now." She handed

me a list for the grocery store. "Be careful. It's icy. And hurry back. I need the tomatoes for the salad."

When I passed the high school on the way home, I thought that this was where they wanted me, close to home.

What if I keep driving west, I wondered. Turned left on the boulevard and headed southwest. Just kept driving until . . .

I drove home with the groceries. My bedroom door was open. My father was in there.

"What's this?" he asked.

A snow crystal with a skinny skier bent-kneed speeding down a steep slope. Jeannie's Christmas present. It was sitting on the little platform he'd built on dowels on the top shelf of the bookcase he'd made me from a sketch I'd drawn on a notepad. The little platform was his own design. It was about as big as one of his handkerchieves.

"I made the shelf for this," he said and found the plaster-of-paris Virgin my mother had given me on the day of my First Communion, hidden behind bottles and jars on my dresser. He set it on the little stage.

"My goodness, no," I told him.

"Yes, that's what I made it for."

"No, not in my room," I insisted and returned Mary to her place behind lotions and tints.

"Don't tell *me!*" He plunged his hand back there to retrieve and reseat her. This time I watched because I knew he wanted me to. He stood beside her for a moment like a sentinel. He set his jaw.

I picked up Mary by the neck and stuck her on a corner of the dresser. My father was amazed. He didn't move for a second. A new sound was in the room. I felt the vibration of his muttering anger when he passed me with the Blessed Mother in both hands. He put her on the pedestal. The dowels creaked.

"Leave it there! That's where I want it, dammit!" He slammed the door behind him so hard it bounced open.

I knelt in front of the bookcase and watched the door. Maybe I needed a lock. I lay Mary on her side, felt the slick of fifteen years of fingertouch, saw the chips in her plaster, the pink cast of her tunic, her face as white as a fish belly. "What was all that about?" I whispered.

I didn't feel my hands trembling until I put the statue into my bottom drawer next to my Shirley Temple doll. I waited until I could breathe and speak without a quaver before I went into the kitchen.

"I'm going out for a while," I said. My father avoided my eyes.

"You aren't going anywhere," my mother said. "In the first place, I'm getting supper ready, and for another thing, there's a storm brewing out there and I don't want you driving that toy car in a blizzard."

I swallowed the stone in my throat.

"Did you hear your mother?" my father said. "Now take off those boots and behave."

The plates were set like jewels on the table. My mother's bone china cup was ready at her place for her strong coffee. A pot of chili simmered on the stove. The bridge lamp on the wall was lit instead of the overhead light so the edges of porcelain and chrome were softened. My mother was filling a bowl, lined with a napkin, with oyster crackers. My father refolded the sports section at his place at the table.

"I'm not hungry," I said carefully.

"You just sit down and eat something," my mother said. "Let's not make a story out of this."

Things were breaking in me slowly, wild things. I watched the red bubbles rise and burst inside the pot on the stove. A hypnotic rhythm, the music for the scene.

"Am I a prisoner here?" I said, low and dangerous.

My mother said, "Wait now—"

"Or do I just have to obey orders and then you'll let me out, like a trustee?"

"What are you talking about?" my mother asked, salvaging, saving.

"I'm wrong. You want me up on a shelf, don't you?"

"What's gotten into her?" my father asked my mother.

"Put me where you can see me, dust me off like an ornament

and trot me out for company. Do I have it right?"

"Claire! You stop it this minute!" my mother said.

"And every once in a while, buy me something to distract me. The car. A car's a great idea. Gives a person a sense of freedom. And then, when the ride's over, right back up there on the shelf."

"You have no right to say such things to me," my mother said. "What happened? What happened here?"

I wanted to stop. I told myself, shut up, shut up. But I couldn't. My tongue was as wicked as Camille's pointer. I heard myself saying things that seemed to come from someone else, things I didn't know I'd say. Things about Frank and his nifty entrances and exits, like a ballet dancer, leaping on my back. About them, clutching so hard they were breaking it. Until my mother couldn't bear it. It all seemed so slow, slow. First she put down the bowl of crackers and went to him and he put his arm around her.

"She can't talk to me this way," she told him. She was crying.

My father was out of place. He didn't know what to do, so he shouted, "You close your mouth. Right now! And take that look off your face!"

"*She* can speak for herself, can't she?" I said because I felt sorry for my dad, sorry that he had to live with her all these years. It was all her fault. *She* was the one who directed our lives. It was her we all tried to please. I wanted to tell him I understood that when he walked up to me. But, what he did was lift his hand, that big, calloused hand that shoveled and dug and built, and hit me across the side of my head. My head hit the wall.

I shivered in my father's cold gaze measuring me like a two-by-four that needed to be cut to size. My mother's eyes were brilliant in artificial light and they accused me of treason.

I ran past them while they stood staring.

I drove the Falcon over rutted snow and skidded on ice patches until I turned into the church parking lot. I left the motor running while I stared out the window at the fresh snowfall. The car puttered like an old man's cough. I felt like someone who'd been doing handsprings while the audience drowsed.

The little car shuddered in a blast of wind. I thought what had been harmless once, like the daily gossip that transported mornings, the duty that kept homes swept and dusted, the art of absorption in choosing food, and the very table where we sat to eat it were dangerous. I looked at the Gothic press of the church where I'd learned plainchant and dreaming and a myth of perfect love. Where I'd sung in the snug little choirloft at Easter and Christmas, counted tax stamps and won prizes. If I stayed, memories like that would be played out against a backdrop of clean sheets and good suppers on a kitchen floor tiled in eggshell.

I sat in the back row of the Shore Theater behind all the Saturday night couples with heads and shoulders touching until I was sure they'd be in bed. The house was dark at midnight. I entered like a cat burglar. Packing didn't take long because most of my things were still in the suitcase. I ran my hand over the plum silk, but it belonged here, not in Christopher Park. I had money. I'd saved it in a bath powder box because until now there was nothing to use it for. I counted a hundred and ninety dollars, a fortune. I held onto Leo's Holstein and Jeannie's periwinkles, love's silly signs, before I tied them at either end of a handkerchief and put it in my pocket. Suddenly, I was finished and I knew it.

An arcane fear, like a wolf roaring out of a cave, rushed into me. I couldn't take a breath. I saw their faces, my beautiful, proud mother, my strong father, and felt time reeling backwards melting them to children, my children. I felt as though I should hold them and change their fate. I opened my eyes and time returned like a record spinning to a stop on a turntable. I pulled back my curtain a little and saw a yellow bus, lighted inside, crawl up the street before I gagged and ran to the bathroom, knelt in front of the toilet and vomited. The chill of the tiles made me shiver. After I rinsed my mouth, I was overcome again. There was no food in me, only spasms wringing from my stomach to my throat. I needed water to help me swallow. After I palmed some into my mouth, I pulled a towel from the rack and buried my face in white terrycloth, stuffing everything back, but I was dizzy with my eyes closed. When I opened them, a little tomato dish from Tijuana, something my father chose for my mother where she kept combs and bobby pins, was in front of me. I saw my father's tomatoes the summer the vines grew two feet past the stakes and I was about two feet tall picking tomatoes as big as grapefruit. And Frank, sitting in the shade of the jungle they formed, biting into one, letting the juice run from his mouth while I concentrated on eating a perfect circle around mine. My mother had time to take a snapshot, one I'd stuck in the mirror at the little house. I blinked, swallowed air, coughed against my raw throat.

"My love," Leo had written.

"Stop this! Stop it!" I whispered to myself. "Let it go." Detachment, the nuns had taught me, detachment. Detach a plant from its soil. See the roots dangle. That's where detachment takes you.

Back in the gloom of my bedroom, I was amazed they hadn't wakened to the storm I made. I pulled back my curtains all the way to moonlight that was a radiance, a glow. But I longed to see the sun break in. I longed to see my mother and father smiling me on, to see Leo lit from within the way he was the morning he brought me the fruit. And I wondered if that was how it would always be with me, desiring everything that met my eyes.

I scratched words on paper:

Mama and Papa,
  I love you both. I'll call tonight.

I carried my suitcase, walked on the balls of my feet, then outside to the Falcon where I forgot which way to turn the ignition key and then turned on the windshield wipers instead of the headlights. I was jumping inside. Leo had tapped his forehead, telling me, "First, you have to believe it's possible. Up here." The motor kicked in.

I focused on facts. The gas stations would be open for morning traffic in a few hours, and I'd stop at one to buy gas and a map, draw a crooked line from Cleveland to Christopher Park, stop for the night in a city big enough to have a motel, call home. My mother would answer, arch, sniffing the air, her flat edged tone telling me she was unwilling to come into the clearing until it was safe. Then Frank. Funny, I knew what Frank would say the same way I knew he was talking about hot dogs at the Browns' games. Frank would tell me to take care of myself and he'd handle things at home. Then, I'd cross rivers and pass the time of day with men who pumped gas, look for notes from fellow travelers in the Gideon Bibles in orange and green plastic motel rooms, drive through hours of Missouri meadows and hills feeling as ordinary and free as the grass. I'd turn off on the back road west of town where Paula and I had followed a blind trail after Gemma, where the wind would bring me the ripe smell of cow dung and new green and stubby spokes of millet and wheat pushed up like a bush haircut. And that other landscape that lay in Morse Code, dot-dash-dash-dot, the path of the tornado etched in relief in pale February sun. I'd stop to read the brass plate that told of Dell, the wonder horse, who'd run with full packs and a man on his back across three rivers and hot plains at forty miles an hour on the day of the land rush, another pretty creation myth. The closer I got to Highway 35, the more I'd feel like that small, feral man running back to his companions to tell them that the sun returned.

Maybe I'd stop out of town at the grocery store near Cals and buy apples, finally make that deep dish apple pie, sit with it on the front step while it cooled, maybe dip a finger into the syrup, a honeyblush sticking to waxed paper, and taste cinnamon, butter and tart green apples while I waited for Leo who told me he loved me. I didn't know a thing about loving just one other person. A man. The sea of God's creation was easy.

The bravest thing I did that night, leaving Cleveland, was to keep my foot pressed on the accelerator. But, all the while, deep, deeper than the static in my head or the buzzing in my stomach, beneath all that I was moving like the rivers I'd cross, bubbling over rocks and sand, following the swell of the current to a meeting with the sea.

What did the moon see? A white dot of a car pinging up a snow frosted boulevard, the girl inside, Joan of Arc in silhouette, her cigarette smoke curling out the cracked window in a long, lazy spiral to the moon, the blue moon.